Jonas Langfo
Ailis Temple

SNOWFALL AND THE DUKE

The Silver Dukes
Book 4

by

Meara Platt

© Copyright 2025 by Myra Platt
Text by Meara Platt
Cover by Dar Albert

Dragonblade Publishing, Inc. is an imprint of Kathryn Le Veque Novels, Inc.
P.O. Box 23
Moreno Valley, CA 92556
ceo@dragonbladepublishing.com

Produced in the United States of America

First Edition June 2025
Print Edition

Reproduction of any kind except where it pertains to short quotes in relation to advertising or promotion is strictly prohibited.

All Rights Reserved.

The characters and events portrayed in this book are fictitious. Any similarity to real persons, living or dead, is purely coincidental and not intended by the author.

ARE YOU SIGNED UP FOR DRAGONBLADE'S BLOG?

You'll get the latest news and information on exclusive giveaways, exclusive excerpts, coming releases, sales, free books, cover reveals and more.

Check out our complete list of authors, too!

No spam, no junk. That's a promise!

Sign Up Here

www.dragonbladepublishing.com

Dearest Reader;

Thank you for your support of a small press. At Dragonblade Publishing, we strive to bring you the highest quality Historical Romance from some of the best authors in the business. Without your support, there is no 'us', so we sincerely hope you adore these stories and find some new favorite authors along the way.

Happy Reading!

CEO, Dragonblade Publishing

Additional Dragonblade books by Author Meara Platt

The Silver Dukes Series
Cherish and the Duke
Moonlight and the Duke
Two Nights with the Duke
Snowfall and the Duke
Starlight and the Duke
Crash Landing on the Duke

The Moonstone Landing Series
Moonstone Landing (Novella)
Moonstone Angel (Novella)
The Moonstone Duke
The Moonstone Marquess
The Moonstone Major
The Moonstone Governess
The Moonstone Hero
The Moonstone Pirate

The Book of Love Series
The Look of Love
The Touch of Love
The Taste of Love
The Song of Love
The Scent of Love
The Kiss of Love
The Chance of Love
The Gift of Love
The Heart of Love
The Hope of Love (Novella)

The Promise of Love
The Wonder of Love
The Journey of Love
The Dream of Love (Novella)
The Treasure of Love
The Dance of Love
The Miracle of Love
The Remembrance of Love (Novella)

Dark Gardens Series
Garden of Shadows
Garden of Light
Garden of Dragons
Garden of Destiny
Garden of Angels

The Farthingale Series
If You Wished For Me (Novella)

The Lyon's Den Series
Kiss of the Lyon
The Lyon's Surprise
Lyon in the Rough

Pirates of Britannia Series
Pearls of Fire

De Wolfe Pack: The Series
Nobody's Angel
Kiss an Angel
Bhrodi's Angel

Also from Meara Platt
Aislin
All I Want for Christmas
Once Upon a Haunted Cave

Chapter One

Langford Hall
Yorkshire, England
December 1817

"Grimes, tell her to go away."

Ailis Temple heard the Duke of Ramsdale's deeply resonant grumbling as she stood behind his butler, who had told her to wait in the visitor's parlor while he informed the duke of her presence.

Ailis was through waiting for the surly duke to be *at home* for her. Did he not owe her more courtesy considering how bitterly cold it was on this winter's day? Not to mention there was a snowstorm about to converge on their quiet village, and she needed to get back to the vicarage before the snow began to fall in earnest. "I have no intention of going away, Your Grace."

Your Graceless was the more apt term for this oaf of a man.

"Ah, Miss Temple. I am in no humor for your visit today," he said, frowning as he set aside some correspondence he had been reading that seemed to have displeased him. He rose from his chair and came around his massive desk that was piled high with more correspondence, invitations, and documents, to greet her with noticeable reluctance.

"This is the third time I have called upon you this week. Each time, you have turned me away. But I cannot allow it this time, for you are never in good humor," she remarked, trying not to shiver. The shiver had nothing to do with him but with the cold that had settled into her bones, a result of spending too much time outdoors on this raw day.

Fortunately, the duke had a lovely fire blazing in the hearth. She wanted to edge toward it, but his big body blocked her way as he stood beside her.

He stared down at her.

She smiled back at him. "I can see you are busy, so let us get straight to the point."

He sighed and nodded to Grimes. "Bring tea for Miss Temple. Her nose is an alarming shade of pink and in danger of falling off."

"It is nothing of the sort," Ailis muttered, touching the tip of it.

He then had the temerity to grin as he reached out to tuck a stray curl behind her ear. "Her ears are also pink and in danger of falling off."

Ugh.

This man was such a churl.

Of course, he was an impossibly handsome churl, and ladies could not look upon his dark eyes and dark hair that held a dash of silver at the temples without falling into a swoon. Fortunately, she was impervious to his charms…or lack thereof.

She was also undaunted by his impressive height and brawn.

"Have a seat beside the fire, Miss Temple," he said once his butler had gone off to attend to the task of ordering her tea. "The dangerous chill outside is no jest. What is it your uncle wants from me now? And why does he not have the courage to ask me himself?"

"As you well know," she said, settling in the comfortable leather chair he had offered and enjoying the warmth of the blaze upon her cheeks, "Vicar Temple has pressing duties about the parish and relies on me to handle the church's financial matters."

His snort was dismissive as he sank into the chair beside her. Despite its ample breadth, his broad shoulders were almost too large for the chair. "He thinks your pleasing smile and emerald eyes will soften a man and encourage him to open up his coffers. What is the dire need this time? Leaking roof? Crumbling stones?"

"Meals and other essentials for the poorest in the village," she said, clenching her fists in frustration. "You do remember the widows and orphans, the sick and disabled, who reside in this parish. A parish that rests within your demesne. Or are you too busy to think of anyone other than yourself?"

He chuckled heartily. "By heaven, you are as frosty as today's weather."

Sighing, she apologized. "I do not mean to sound waspish, but you sorely frustrate me. How do I get through to you? How do I convince you of the importance of caring for others when you seem to disdain everyone?"

He was spared a response when Grimes returned with a tea cart laden with cakes as well as a teapot and cups.

This surprised Ailis, for she did not expect to be treated as courteously as he might treat a guest of rank. Obviously, Grimes had misunderstood the duke's request. Yet the duke did not appear to be angry or the least put out.

Instead, he regarded her thoughtfully. "Grimes, hold on. Take Miss Temple's cloak and gloves. Her hat and scarf, too."

Did this mean he would allow her to stay and discuss the contributions he would make? Would he also agree to participate in the St. Augustine's Christmas charity ball? It wasn't really a ball so much as an all-day festival with games, baked goods, gifts for the children, and musical entertainments.

"Thank you, Grimes," she said, smiling up at the elderly retainer who had always been kind to her.

"Always a pleasure, Miss Temple," he said, taking her cloak and other items.

She hoped she had not made a mistake in handing them over. It would not take her long to complete her business and then be on her way.

However, the cup of tea and ginger cake were most welcome. She had been making her rounds to the needy all morning long. As a delicious heat seeped into her bones, she had to admit that the day's activities had left her cold and tired.

The afternoon sunlight had failed to chase the chill from the air.

The duke said nothing as she drank her tea and took a bite of the ginger cake.

"All right, Miss Temple of Virtue," he said once she appeared to have warmed up, "tell me what is on your mind."

Temple of Virtue, indeed.

Did he always have to be so rude?

The first thing on her mind was that she wanted to hit him over the head with the teapot. He seemed to take particular delight in riling her. What was so wrong with remaining respectable while holding out for a love marriage? And *not* liberally giving out her favors in the meanwhile? Not that she was likely to marry now that she was just shy of thirty years old and considered firmly on the shelf.

Worse, she had never been kissed.

He knew it, for rakish beasts like him seemed to sense these things. This was why he mockingly referred to her as Miss Temple of Virtue. Fortunately, he saved his mockery for whenever they were alone.

She appreciated that small regard, but he was still an unpleasant curmudgeon and a completely arrogant oaf. It did not matter that he was handsome and seemed to grow handsomer with each passing year. Other women might find him irresistible when he graced them with one of his devastating smiles.

She certainly did not.

"That spine of yours will crack if it stiffens any further," he remarked, finding her indignation most amusing.

He resembled a dark-maned lion toying with a helpless mouse before eating it. Big. Powerful. Daunting.

She did not like to think of herself as a helpless mouse. In truth, she was not easily daunted.

"I find it hard to feel at ease around you, Your Grace. Why do you purposely rile me at every turn? What have I ever done to you? If you do not wish to help out those to whom you owe a duty, then just say so and I will be on my way. Frankly, I have had enough of your high-handed manner. I refuse to get down on my knees and beg you for crumbs."

"Down on your knees?" He was giving her that intensely smoldering look again, that "beast amusing itself with its prey" regard that made her want to reach for the teapot again and crack it over his head. "Much as I would enjoy having you in that position before me…"

Why did he make this pious gesture sound dirty?

He cleared his throat. "Here is what I propose…"

Ugh.

He was going to bargain with her now? Why could he not simply give her the money and allow her to be on her way? "This has all been a waste of time," she muttered, getting to her feet and glancing out the window. "The snow is falling harder. I do not have time to knock heads with you. Pray, do not exert yourself by seeing me out."

He rose too, looming quite large beside her even though she was not a short woman. "I have not dismissed you, Ailis."

She glanced up, startled he was using her given name. It sounded soft upon his lips.

"I really must go, but thank you for the tea, Your Grace. I shall rule you off the charity ball committee, put you down as having offered *nothing* for the needy, and will never trouble you again. Enjoy your cold and lonely holidays."

He burst out laughing and gently grabbed her hand. "Sit down. Gad, you are impudent. I won't keep you long, for I realize the weather is turning dangerous. Despite my ogrish reputation, I do not ever wish you to come to harm."

"That is remarkably thoughtful of you. Quite out of character."

She frowned at him. "Why not show similar care to those in the village who truly need it?"

"Perhaps I ought to be more tolerant," he admitted. "But everyone always seeks to take from me."

"As I am doing now?"

"At least your cause is selfless. I get fed up with all who come to me with their hands outstretched merely for their personal gain. Do you realize how many requests I receive daily? I would be impoverished if I said yes to all of them. I seem to be particularly hounded at this time of year. The takers are out in force right now. And to make matters worse, there is a betting book now on me going around the *ton*, as though I required even more attention."

A blush ran up Ailis's cheeks as she realized how awful she must have sounded. "Oh, I see your point. I should have come to you offering something in return for your beneficence. It never occurred to me that a man with all your bounty would be in need of anything. And I am sincerely sorry you are now the talk of the *ton*. I know how private a person you are and how distressing opening up your life to one and all must be. Your Grace, is there something I can provide for you? Just ask. You shall have it, if it is in my power to give it."

A devastatingly attractive smile spread across his lips, and it was to be noted that he still had gentle hold of her hand. "Now that you mention it, in fact there is."

She waited a moment for him to explain.

"Um," she said when he remained silently studying her. Was she supposed to guess what was on his mind? "Your Grace? What may I give you?"

"How much are you hoping to raise at your charity ball?"

"One thousand pounds," she replied. "This is what we project is needed to supply food and clothing for those who are worst off throughout the winter and into the spring."

"That much?" he asked, obviously surprised.

"There are many families in dire poverty, a circumstance of the war ending and so many soldiers returning to find no work. I should think your estate manager would have reported this to you. But as I said, I am not seeking the full amount from you. There are other gentlemen of means in the area that I have yet to visit. I hope they will contribute. I am not asking for the entire sum from you."

He released her hand and folded his arms over his chest. "Forget the others. You shall have it all from me…on one condition."

She gasped in delight. "You would donate the entire amount?"

"Yes, but on one condition," he repeated, taking a surprising interest in her lips as she graced him with a smile. "In exchange, I would like you to give me ten kisses."

The smile froze on her lips. "What?"

"You heard me, Miss Temple of Virtue. You will receive one hundred pounds for every kiss. Care to start now? I shall write out the first bank draft for you this instant. It is completely up to you."

"You are taking the *ton*'s betting situation out on me, aren't you? What wagers have been placed on you?"

"It is none of your business nor any of your concern."

"I beg to differ. Why else would you make such a perverse offer to me? Ten kisses."

"Do you want your thousand pounds or not?"

"It isn't fair."

"It may be so, but this is what you have walked into. You should have run away when I told Grimes I was not *at home* to you. Do we have an agreement?"

Her heart fluttered. "You are *buying* my kisses?"

"Think of it as a barter arrangement."

The man was arrogant and a fool.

She had never kissed anyone before, as he well knew.

Was this why he set forth this demand? Did he think she would refuse him? After all, he considered her insufferably priggish and must have thought himself quite clever devising this scheme as a means to beg off donating to the church by placing the blame on her. Well, he would be shocked to learn that his Miss Temple of Virtue was going to take him up on the challenge.

Let him be mad at the world and behave like an oaf. She was getting his thousand pounds for the church coffers.

She tipped her head up and met his gaze. "I accept."

His eyes darkened. "What?"

"I have just accepted you. Why are you so shocked?"

He cleared his throat. "Ailis, you have never been kissed before."

"A fact that seems to have provided you with endless amusement over the years. And now I shall spoil your fun and be kissed." If he wanted the worst kisses ever received in his entire life, then who was she to dissuade him from this bad bargain?

She stifled a grin at the look of surprise on his face. "Reneging, Your Grace?"

"No." He tucked a finger under her chin. "Just hoping you know what you are getting into."

"You bargained for my kisses. One hundred pounds per kiss. I hope *you* know what you have just gotten yourself into." She glanced out the window, now worried, as the snow began to fall too rapidly for her liking. "Write that first bank draft, kiss me quickly, and allow me to be on my way."

He looked horrified.

He was obviously realizing how inappropriate a bargain it was, and perhaps feeling some remorse for offering it.

Too bad. She wanted those donations for the needy.

It wasn't as though she was giving him her body, merely her lips, which she intended to keep firmly pinched as his own pressed down on hers.

"Blessed saints," he muttered, returning to his desk and withdrawing a ledger from an upper drawer. He wrote out a draft and signed it with authority. "Here, just take it."

She checked to see that it was properly written out, then smiled and tucked it into her reticule. "All right," she said, her voice unexpectedly wobbling. "You may now have your kiss for this one hundred pounds."

She had not expected to feel quite so distressed. It wasn't from fear of him or the kiss. It was mostly the fear that she might *like* it.

She closed her eyes, appalled to realize her heart was hammering with anticipation. Why? And why from him? He was a grumpy ogre. Yes, he was also impossibly handsome, especially with that tinge of silver in his hair. But still…

She felt his warm breath against her cheek.

"Ailis, I'm sorry," he said with an agonized groan, and gave her a short, whisper-soft kiss on the lips. "Go, love. That wasn't fair of me. Consider the wager off."

Her eyes flew open and met the dark heat of his. "But you said one hundred pounds per kiss. I will not release you from the bargain."

"So you think I owe you nine more?" He raked a hand through his hair. "Go home, Ailis. I am many things, but not a debaucher of innocents."

"I was hardly in danger of being debauched by you. Was that the kiss? I hardly felt it. In fact, it was rather tepid, in my opinion."

His mouth gaped open. "Tepid?"

She nodded. "Eminently forgettable."

His jaw tightened. "Forgettable?"

"Eminently." She shook her head and sighed. "Rather weak, if you ask me."

He emitted a low growl. "Weak?"

"Yes, Your Grace. In fact, it was most disappointing."

"*Disappointing?*" Growling again, he drew her into his arms.

Goodness, he was nicely muscled. Her eyes widened as those hard bands encircled her in his embrace.

She had never been held romantically before.

"Close your eyes, Ailis," he said in a husky murmur that held a trace of irritation and determination.

Oh, this man was not used to women criticizing his kisses. He looked so deliciously out of sorts.

But should she not be the one irritated? What sort of first kiss was that? Barely a touch. Completely disappointing.

His voice was commanding and his eyes were blazing as he said, "Ailis, close them."

"All right," she grumbled, allowing her lids to flutter closed. Had she overdone it? "What next? I hope you—"

He crushed his lips to hers with an unexpectedly possessive heat and did not ease up until she was limp and melting against him. Somehow, her arms had worked their way upward to wrap around his neck.

She might have moaned softly, too.

"How was that?" he muttered, knowing he had completely set her insides on fire and was feeling quite arrogant and smug about it.

She looked up at him and smiled. *"That* was kiss number two. You owe me another hundred pounds. Pay up, Your Grace."

Chapter Two

Jonas Langford, the eighth Duke of Ramsdale, stared out the window of his study, his brow furrowed in concern as he watched Ailis Temple ride her old mare back to the vicarage in what had quickly turned into a rather severe blizzard. A fierce wind was blowing and snow whipped all around her, causing her dark cloak to twist and billow around her slender body. Her horse appeared unsteady, no doubt because of the patches of ice forming along the drive as the temperature began to drop precipitously.

"Grimes, have my curricle readied. I think I had better escort Miss Temple home."

He had barely gotten the words out before her mare skidded on one of those icy patches and sent Ailis tumbling onto the snow. "Grimes! She's hurt."

He raced out of the house, cursing himself for delaying her when he knew the conditions were turning bad and she needed to get home. But he had come to enjoy her company and the utter lack of deference shown for his status when voicing her opinions, which were always honest and well reasoned.

No one else ever dared speak to him so forthrightly.

There were other things he liked about the vicar's niece, but those attributes did not bear mentioning at the moment.

"Come with me," he barked at two footmen standing by the front door.

"Your Grace?" the senior said, momentarily confused by Jonas's purpose when he threw open the door and a blast of frigid air and snowflakes came swirling into the house.

"Miss Temple has fallen off her horse," he shouted, already running down the drive as fast as he dared. A chill seeped into his bones, for he had run out neglecting to don a hat, cloak, or scarf.

The footmen followed him out with all speed.

The wind howled and heavy snow blinded Jonas as he hurried to Ailis's side. "Don't move," he cautioned, his heart twisting into knots when she tried to sit up and couldn't. She sank back onto the snow and cried out in pain.

He had seen her land hard on her shoulder when taking the fall and realized by the odd position of her body that she must have dislocated it. This was the sort of injury he had learned to repair during his years of military service. Men often fell off horses in the heat of battle, and he had become quite adept at putting bones back in place. Basic medical knowledge was one of the necessities for survival if one hoped to make it through the war alive.

"Whittier, grab her belongings. Hanford, take her mare to the stable."

"Aye, Your Grace," each man said in turn.

Fortunately, Ailis's mount appeared not to be injured. Hanford quickly took control of the skittish horse and used soothing words to ease her out of her fright. The young footman was good with horses and easily handled the gentle beast.

Whittier, the more seasoned footman, grabbed Ailis's reticule and the baskets she had used to carry food to the needy. Jonas noted the baskets were empty, everything already given out, since she must have intended Langford Hall to be her last stop.

"Ailis, do not struggle," he said, trying to calm her while she appeared to be as skittish as her mare.

"My shoulder…"

Gad, she sounded in a lot of pain.

A vapor of cold air circled around them as he released a heavy breath. "I know. I fear it is dislocated, but I'll take care of it as soon as I have you back home. Rest your head against my chest. Don't struggle, Ailis. You are safe. I have you."

She said nothing as he lifted her in his arms.

Jonas did not know if she was merely resting quietly or had passed out. It did not matter, for he had to get her indoors fast.

Grimes and the Langford Hall housekeeper, Mrs. Fitch, were standing by the front door, both wringing their hands, as he strode in with Ailis in his arms. "Grimes, send one of the grooms to the vicarage to let Vicar Temple know what happened and assure him she will be in my care until this blizzard passes. In fact, send young Leo Curtis. His mother's house is near the vicarage. Let him stay with his family until the worst of the storm is over. Send him right now while there's still daylight left."

"Aye, m'lord."

He now turned to his trusted housekeeper. "Miss Temple needs a bed. Give her my best."

He had a dozen bedchambers in his house that were unused and would be finer than any she had ever slept in.

"Your Grace, I think she will enjoy the East Room," Mrs. Fitch said, scampering up the stairs behind him. She was referring to the guest chamber with flowers and butterflies on the wallpaper, a room so feminine and cheerful, it gave him a headache. "But I'll need a few minutes to get it ready."

"Fine, I'll put her in my bed in the meanwhile."

His housekeeper gasped. "Your Grace! It is indecent!"

"Do not lecture me, Mrs. Fitch. Is it decent to leave Miss Temple writhing in pain? Send one of the maids to serve as her chaperone. And do not send me someone squeamish. I need to set her shoulder back in its socket, and that is going to hurt like blazes."

"Oh, poor Miss Temple," she said, and scrambled off to carry out his orders.

Jonas carried Ailis into his bedchamber. An odd feeling came over him as he placed her gently on his bed. "Don't fall back, Ailis. Can you remain sitting up? Just for a little while longer."

"I'll try."

"I'll be quick, love. Then you can rest against the pillows." He propped them one atop the other before proceeding to remove her hat, scarf, cloak, and gloves, and then he knelt to remove her boots. He dared not take anything else off her without someone on his staff to chaperone. But when Ailis began to heave as though about to cast up her accounts, he slid the chamber pot out from under his bed and instructed her to aim there if she felt anything coming forth.

He waited a moment for her nausea to pass, but dared not hold off any longer. "Ailis, I need to get at your shoulder. I have to loosen your gown, love."

Why was he now referring to her by that endearment?

She stared up at him. The bejeweled green of her eyes met the dark brown of his.

By heaven, she had the prettiest eyes.

But that was to be pondered another time. "Your gown has to come off, Ailis. At least down to your waist. Well, it is best that you simply take it off, because it is damp from your fall into the snow and you'll catch a chill if you leave it on."

Besides, she wouldn't be going anywhere for days yet.

"All right," she said, each word holding an abundance of agony, so that he knew he had to work fast to undo the laces and tapes. There weren't too many in the way. Ailis's gowns were practical and most were the sort easily laced by herself.

He knew she did not have a lady's maid and probably counted upon the vicarage housekeeper—Leo's mother, Mrs. Curtis—to assist her into the one or two finer gowns in her possession.

"Your Grace," a gravelly, feminine voice called from the doorway. "Mrs. Fitch sent me up here to assist you."

He glanced at the middle-aged woman who had been in service to his family for ages. "Come in, Martha. You'll be serving as Miss Temple's chaperone. Help me get this gown off her."

"Your Grace!"

"Save your protestations for later," he said with a growl. "I am interested in her shoulder, not her body. Miss Temple has to be in excruciating pain. Be as gentle as possible. I'll hold her while you slip it off."

Despite having declared no interest in Ailis's body, he found it hard to ignore its surprising splendor. Heat shot through him as he wrapped an arm about her waist. She was soft and nicely shaped, full in all the right places and trim in others.

In truth, she was more beautiful than he had ever realized.

But the implications of this revelation, now extending to her eyes and her sweet body, was to be considered another time. "Miss Temple, I'm so sorry. This is going to hurt." *Hurt you terribly.* She would soon find out just how much, unfortunately.

He took her arm, holding it gently by the wrist while he began to raise and rotate it ever so carefully. With his other hand, he carefully guided the protruding bone back into its ball socket.

She cried out, for he had to repeat the slow rotation three times before her shoulder was securely back in place. It was an ordeal for Ailis, but she managed it as bravely as any soldier he had ever tended.

She could not hold back her tears, however. They streamed down her pale cheeks in a steady flow.

"The worst is over, Miss Temple," he said, addressing her with proper formality because they were not alone. "I've got it back in place now."

"Oh, thank heaven," Martha whispered.

Mrs. Fitch, having joined them while he was rotating Ailis's arm and witnessing the pain it caused her, also muttered words of praise. "The poor lamb. Her bed will be made up shortly, Your Grace."

He nodded as he took Ailis back in his arms and motioned for Martha to draw aside the covers. "Meanwhile, I'll keep her here. She'll be most comfortable with her back resting against the pillows, but she needs one more placed under her arm."

"She also needs a robe," Mrs. Fitch said, for Ailis only had on a linen chemise. It was a sturdy garment, appropriate for winter, but still a mere undergarment and showed too much of her skin for propriety.

"No, I need to put her arm in a sling first. Martha, get me another pillow and hurry back here. Mrs. Fitch, I'll need a sturdy cloth to form the sling. If you are shocked by the indecency, then get her a shawl to wrap around her shoulders for now. She is not to raise her arm or move it at all for the rest of the day. Probably not for several more days."

He glanced at Ailis as she now lay in his bed with her eyes closed and her golden curls in delicate disarray. He wanted to take the clips out of her hair, since she would be more comfortable without them, but decided to let the ladies take care of this once she was properly settled in the guest bedchamber.

He brushed a few curls off her brow. "Ailis," he said with quiet authority now that they were alone, "do you think you might have hit your head?"

He hadn't seen any bruises or lumps forming on her forehead, but that did not mean she had escaped such injuries.

Her eyes flickered open and he caught the full impact of their lovely emerald hue. "No, I don't think so. My left shoulder took all the brunt. My head did hit the ground, but it fell upon a snowy pile and the ground was soft beneath it."

He let out a breath. "And your hip? Any pain there?"

"I don't know. All I feel is the fire in my shoulder."

Every word spoken seemed to be an effort for her, so he did not wish to keep prying about her condition.

But was it not vital to check her thoroughly on the chance she had done more damage to herself?

"I need to ascertain whether there are any other breaks. I shall be as careful as possible, but…" He cleared his throat. "I have to run my hands along your body."

Ailis gasped. "You cannot! It isn't proper."

Martha had returned with an armful of pillows in time to hear their exchange, and protested the same. "Your Grace!"

His expression turned dark as thunder, for he was so tired of these stupid rules of propriety established by strangers who had nothing better to do than look for reasons to be scandalized. "She might have broken a rib, or her hip, or wrist. What if you have fractured a neck bone or your spine, Miss Temple? These are serious. I need to have a look at you."

Ailis had her eyes closed again and was silently crying.

His maid averted her gaze, but she had to know he was right. "What do you need me to do, Your Grace?"

"Stay here and act as chaperone while I examine her. I must check her bones. There is no way possible to avoid this. And you do not breathe a word to anyone. I shall have your promise now."

Martha gave him an earnest nod and promised.

He would demand the same of Mrs. Fitch when she returned. Both had been in the employ of the Langford family for decades, and he knew they could be trusted.

"Good, because I will not have Miss Temple disgraced when she has done nothing wrong. To utter a word would ruin her, and how is this fair after all the good she has done for everyone in Broadmoor?"

This was the thriving market town near the North Sea and within his demesne, where Ailis resided with her vicar uncle. The town was quite close-knit and people were still referred to as strangers after having lived there for twenty years. But not Ailis. Despite having arrived a mere six years ago, she was already considered the heart of this town. If someone took ill, Ailis was there to help them through it. If there was a family in need, Ailis was immediately on the task.

She was a righteous do-gooder but without the priggish attitude that often came with those of towering virtue. He had come to think of her as his Miss Temple of Virtue because of her exquisite kindness and the entrancing warmth of her beauty.

She always thought he was mocking her whenever he called her that, which he did sparingly and only when they would not be overheard by others. However, quite the opposite was true.

He held her in the greatest admiration. She was that rare mix of beauty and fire. Hence the appellation—Miss Temple of Virtue—that he'd shortened to merely Temple at times.

After releasing a breath, he started with an inspection of her head, and decided to remove the pins in order to better feel along her scalp. Waves of golden tresses spilled onto her shoulders as those pins came out.

Dear heaven.

So lovely.

He carefully brushed aside those that fell upon her injured shoulder before placing his fingers in that surprisingly silky mane to probe for bruising.

"Did that hurt?" he asked when he saw her wince.

"A little," she admitted.

"You might have a slight concussion." He turned to Martha. "We're not going to move Miss Temple out of my bed. I'll take the chamber Mrs. Fitch was preparing for her."

"Your Grace! But it—"

"Enough, Martha. This bed will do best for her. She'll need supervision for the next few days and nights. It is easiest to care for her here." He proceeded to run his hands along her neck and then her back, taking care to be very gentle with her spine. He did not suspect a neck or spinal injury, for he had seen her moving her fingers when he took off her gloves, and then moving her toes when he had taken off her boots.

The next part of her body he wished to check was her hip, but that would prove tricky because he needed to lift her chemise to get at it. How could he accomplish this without being obvious?

"Martha, grab one of my handkerchiefs from the top drawer of my bureau and moisten it. And I have some cologne in my dressing room. Fetch it quickly."

While Martha occupied herself with the chores he'd given her, Jonas took a quick look at Ailis's hip. Her eyes shot open the moment his hand touched her skin, but he warned her to stay quiet. A bruise had formed on her hip, but it appeared to be otherwise all right.

He lowered her chemise back in place, and then gave her cheek a gentle caress. "Temple, I'll take a closer look at your wrist next. You might have sprained it when bracing yourself for the fall."

She said nothing, merely looked humiliated.

Her cheeks were aflame, for they both knew he had seen more than her hip. But it couldn't be helped. "Any doctor would have done the same," he said quietly so as not to be overheard by Martha.

Ailis closed her eyes and attempted to turn her head away, then cried out when that slight movement proved painful.

He sighed, for there was nothing he could say to make the situation better. He had seen too much of her and she knew it. He attempted to soften her embarrassment anyway. "I learned a lot about battlefield wounds while fighting Napoleon in Spain. I'm probably more adept than most doctors here in Yorkshire."

"Still...you *saw* me," she said in a whisper. "We are no longer on equal footing."

"We never were. I am a duke. No one other than the royal family can claim a higher rank." He glanced around to make certain Martha was not listening in. "Not even our kisses will make us equal, much as

I enjoyed the experience."

She sniffled.

"Do not start crying again, Temple."

"That's Miss Temple to you."

"Temple," he insisted, irritated by how easily she got under his skin lately. It was the abridged version of Miss Temple of Virtue, and safest to use when others were too close by. Only he and Ailis were privy to its full meaning. He supposed it was not kind of him to call her that, but he never meant it as an insult. He liked that she held to her principles and yet was not a holier-than-thou sort of spinster with a puckered, prune-like face and a disapproving air.

She was always quick to put him in his place whenever he deserved it, which he often did because she had a way of rattling his complacency with her soft, sweet face and bright smile.

He also liked that she was sharp-witted enough to best him.

And now, there was another thing he liked about her…that insanely gorgeous body she had kept hidden under her serviceable and eminently practical gowns.

He took the moistened handkerchief and cologne from Martha when she returned to his side. After sprinkling a bit of the cologne onto the damp square of cloth, he ran it lightly along Ailis's neck and then placed it upon her forehead. "Just rest quietly. Mrs. Fitch will return shortly, and I shall fashion a sling for you. Some ice will help ease the swelling. I'll apply it to your wrist and shoulder once we're through getting you settled."

Within the hour, she had been properly tended and fed, although nothing heavier than broth had been given to her, upon his orders. Mrs. Fitch had fetched a thick shawl and a pair of woolen stockings to keep Ailis's feet warm. In addition, his thoughtful housekeeper had set out extra blankets and a warming brick at the foot of the bed.

Jonas tossed more wood onto the fire in the hearth and stoked it to a blaze. As the sun set and darkness fell, the flames seemed to brighten and cast a glow about the room. That warm light wrapped itself around Ailis, enhancing the burnished gold of her unbound hair.

That lovely mass of curls took on a more amber hue by firelight.

Clearing his throat, he returned to her side and placed a cloth filled with ice on her wrist and another on her shoulder to ease the swelling. The cloths had to be replenished several times because the ice melted fast in the stifling heat of the room.

However, Ailis was still shivering and looked quite miserable. "I should move into the guest bedchamber," she said, her throat sounding dry.

"No, Temple. You'll stay in here. I don't mind being displaced for a few days." More to the point, he did not mind having Ailis occupy his bed.

She looked so right in it.

Of course, the notion was ridiculous.

Jonas quickly dismissed any amorous thoughts about her, since he had no intention of ever marrying and would never take Ailis on as his mistress. "Martha will remain with you this evening and throughout the night. She'll be here to take care of you, so let her know if you are not feeling well or need anything. Do not be stoic. There is no need for you to suffer in silence."

Ailis cast him a fragile smile. "You are being awfully nice."

He chuckled. "Completely out of character for me, I know. But it is my fault that I delayed you."

"None of us realized how quickly the roadway would turn icy. And I was rather stubborn about seeing you today when I could have waited until tomorrow or the next day." Her smile turned impish. "But I fully meant to pester you, and would have returned every day until I wore you down."

He gave a mock shudder and groaned. "You shall have these next few days to lay siege against me, because I must insist on your remaining at Langford Hall for now. Your uncle may be an excellent vicar, but he will be an inept nurse. It has not escaped my notice how much you take upon yourself at the vicarage. But you'll only cause more permanent damage to yourself if you return to your duties too soon."

This obviously worried her, as he could tell by the little nibble of her lip. "I cannot stay. How will he manage without me?"

"He'll just have to make do until you are better, Temple. Besides, he has a housekeeper who can take on extra chores for the week or two until you are recovered."

She tried to sit up, winced, and fell back with a breathy moan. "I cannot possibly remain here for an entire fortnight."

"You cannot possibly return to the vicarage until you are able to move your arm. We'll take it day by day," he assured her. "No sense getting worked up about it. If your uncle requires more assistance, I'll send one of my staff to help him out. How does that sound to you? Your regular housekeeper and one of my maids or footmen in addition…or I can send him both."

"That is very generous," she admitted. "It would ease my mind greatly."

He shook his head. "It is the least I can do. I know I have been more insufferable than usual lately. Not that I will change, since I fear this is my nature. But I am not completely lost to honor and must insist on taking responsibility for my mistakes."

"Is this what I am? A mistake?"

He gave her chin a gentle tweak. "A lovely mistake. It troubles me that you might have lain in the snow for hours, or worse, lain there throughout the storm and frozen to death had I not happened to be glancing out the window at the very moment you fell."

"The angels were looking out for me," she said earnestly, then cast him another of her delicate smiles. "See what happens when you get in their good graces? You ought to try it sometime."

He laughed. "I am taking care of you, aren't I? Is this not my good deed for the day?"

Taking care of the lovely Ailis.

Miss Temple of Virtue.

Gad, if all good women looked so tempting, he might not mind being more of a saint and less of a sinner. But that brought him back to the reason he had been even surlier than usual these past few weeks. He could not think of that blasted betting book opened at White's by his own traitorous friends without steam pouring out of his ears. Now, all of London had their attention on him, declaring him another of those Silver Dukes.

This explained the surge of invitations he had been receiving lately. His own mother was threatening to come to Langford Hall with a party of her friends at Christmastide. He had a letter from her delivered just this morning that he dreaded opening. It was still sitting on his desk with its seal intact.

"I'll leave you to rest now, Miss Temple. Martha can summon me if anything urgent comes up."

"Such as this morning's breakfast?" she teased, referring to her earlier bouts of nausea.

"Try not to deposit that gift in my bed." He grinned as he folded his arms over his chest and stared down at her. To his dismay, it was so hard to draw his gaze away from Ailis. "I have a bit of work to do. But I will look in on you before retiring for the night. Martha, make certain our Miss Temple is kept warm, and give her only light fare if she gets hungry later."

"Aye, Your Grace. I'll take good care of the lamb."

Jonas strode out and returned to his study, where a pile of work awaited him in addition to his mother's letter that he still did not wish to open. Ever since his friends had anointed him the next Silver Duke, the *ton* had gone into a frenzy.

Even his mother had taken up the gauntlet and was now determined to see him married. He knew what this latest letter contained, because as dowager duchess she felt above obeying his command to stay away from Langford Hall.

He cared for his family, but refused to have them and their friends descend on him like a plague of locusts for the purpose of matching him to some dimwit heiress.

All he wanted was to be left alone.

She was going to ignore him.

He sighed and set aside the document he was attempting to read, for concentrating on anything now was a useless endeavor. Between his mother's meddling and Ailis looking beyond lovely in his bed, how could any man think straight?

In truth, Ailis had lately been putting his heart in a twist.

What was it about this impertinent spinster that seemed to affect him?

He thought his heart had become an impenetrable fortress over the years, a consequence of the war and a year's imprisonment in one of the harsher French prisons, until he'd made his escape. His third escape attempt was the charm, and he had managed to get a few soldiers out along with him. But too many others had been caught or simply left behind because they were too weak to run.

He had worked tirelessly to negotiate their release upon his return to England. However, little was accomplished until Napoleon was captured and sent into exile.

The war had ended two years ago, but only recently had his nightmares occasioned by regret and frustration begun to abate.

"Ramsdale, leave the past alone," he muttered, knowing Ailis's injury and the pain she was enduring had brought back those memories.

He rose, took a moment to stretch his stiff body, and then crossed to his bureau to pour himself a brandy. With glass in hand, he sauntered to the window to watch the snow still falling hard upon the ground. He had wasted hours thinking of Ailis and all the reasons why he should keep his distance from her, and still had no idea what he was to do about her.

Do nothing.

Not only had the war years left him bitter, but they'd left him physically scarred as a consequence of those two failed escape attempts.

How did one regain one's civility after experiencing so much cruelty?

This is why he hated moving about the *ton* so much. There was so much fakery. All those useless rules and *faux* morality. But here in Broadmoor, people were open about who they were. This made him more appreciative of those rare beings driven by kindness.

This was Ailis, was it not? She was no meek violet, but she had a big heart and offered it sincerely.

However, she was fully capable of standing her ground. She had a lot of fight in her, yet was one of the kindest people he had ever met.

He liked this mix of strength and gentleness about her.

Perhaps this was why they got along so well, although he was often purposely curt to keep her from getting too close to him.

A man with an empty heart should not be so attracted to a young woman with a full heart, should he?

Later that evening, Jonas stopped in to see how Ailis was faring. He had wanted to come up sooner, but refrained because he was already too drawn to her and did not like this surprising turn of events.

Martha was right about her. She was soft as a lamb. Soft skin. Soft curves. The softest smile.

"Ailis? Are you awake?" he asked in a whisper, noting her eyes were closed, those lovely, dark lashes resting on her pale cheeks as she appeared to be lost in sleep.

Disappointed, but not wishing to disturb her or Martha, who also had her eyes closed while seated beside Ailis, he crossed to the window and drew aside the heavy drapes. He had been staring out his study window only a few minutes ago, but could not resist looking out again. He found this snowfall particularly fascinating. A little magical.

Perhaps because it had brought him Ailis.

The wind howled and rattled the windows, for the blizzard remained at full strength and probably would remain so into the morning.

Now that night had fallen, the moon's glow reflected off the icy white of the snow and caused it to shimmer.

"Your Grace," Martha said in a whisper, yawning as she rose from her chair beside the bed, "may I run downstairs for a moment? I'd like to gather some food for Miss Temple should she recover her appetite. She's hardly eaten all day."

Jonas nodded. "I'll stay until you return. Prepare another pack of ice for her shoulder, too. We need to keep the swelling down."

Ailis's eyes flickered open as he settled in the chair beside her that Martha had vacated. "Ah, you're awake."

She cast him the sweetest smile. "Yes, just needed to close my eyes for a few minutes. But I do not think I will sleep much tonight."

He nodded. "Your shoulder will be sore."

"Quite," she said with a sleepy sigh. "Pain shoots up my arm with even the slightest movement."

"I'm sorry for it, Ailis. Truly." He stretched his legs out before him, trying to get comfortable in the chair.

"I know. For all your frowning and grumbling, you have a good heart. What do you have in your hand?"

"This?" He stared at the envelope grasped in his fist, unaware he had brought it along with him until just now. "It is a letter I have been putting off reading all day."

"You do not seem pleased about it. Who is it from?"

"My mother."

"What?" Ailis's mouth dropped open and she laughed. "You have a mother? I mean...goodness. You have a mother?"

CHAPTER THREE

"OF COURSE I have a mother. What do you think I am? Some spawn of the devil created out of netherworld muck? I'm sure even *he* had a mother," the duke said, frowning at Ailis.

"Sorry," she replied, unable to suppress her bubble of laughter. "You surprised me, that's all. Of course you must have had one. But you never speak of your family and I have never known any of them to come visit you here. I would have thought… Well, it does not matter what I think, does it?"

He shrugged. "You are going to spout your opinion whether I wish to hear it or not, aren't you?"

She cast him a sheepish look and nodded. "Do you mind?"

"No, Temple," he said with a deep, rumbling chuckle that thrummed through her veins. "I rather like your impudence. It is a refreshing change from the fawning attention I receive from the parade of toadies who come to my door. Go ahead, tell me what is on your mind."

"Nothing of serious consequence," she said wistfully. "I had a family once and treasured them. Now it is just me and my uncle. He has been very good to me."

"As you have been for him, Temple." He cast her a rare and devastating smile. "Do not get too full of yourself when I tell you this, but you have been very good for all of Broadmoor. It is a nicer place to be because of you. Never tell anyone I said so, for I shall deny it."

"That was rather a backhanded compliment." But she smiled at him, for she did not think he had ever noticed her work. She ought to have realized he would, for this duke was one of the smartest men she had ever met and had to be aware of everything that went on within his purview. "Your Grace, why is it that I have been here almost six years now and never seen any Langford family members in residence other than you? Is there something wrong with your relations?"

"Perhaps it is *they* who are sensible and know to avoid me." He arched a dark eyebrow, the gesture making him look impossibly wicked, and also incredibly handsome. "No, it is nothing so dramatic. They are quite normal. Busybody of a mother. Feckless brother who has the makings of a decent lord if he ever gets serious enough to try. He is likely to be my heir. Two married sisters who are busy producing offspring. They all reside in London and are quite content to remain where they are."

"As you are content to have them far away from you?"

He ran a hand through the thick waves of his hair. "I see them often enough on the trips I make to London whenever Parliament is in session."

"Why do you not invite them to come up here? It is beautiful in the summer."

He stared at the letter in his hand.

"Your mother must love you and be concerned for you. Open it," Ailis urged, trying to suppress another bubble of laughter. This man was fierce and daunting, and it simply was not possible that anyone, even his mother, could make him tremble in fear or ever tell him what to do.

"Why should I open it? I know what it will say."

"Then why did you bring it in here with you if you already know its contents? Admit it, Your Grace. You brought it along because you wanted to share it with me and get my opinion."

"Do not presume to know my mind, Temple."

"Fine, don't read it, then. Be a coward," she said, knowing she was purposely goading him. She thought it hilarious that his own mother could hold such sway over this big, brawny man. But this also softened him in her opinion, for he was always so dour and closed off in his feelings.

That he actually had feelings was a revelation.

Well, she always knew he had them. He had never shared them with her before.

She immediately liked the lady, for how could one not admire the dragon's mother? Not that the duke was a dragon, but he behaved like a prowling menace at times. Whenever he got a fierce, frowning look on his face, everyone would scramble away.

Ailis never would.

There was something in his manner that did not frighten her. Perhaps he was gentler with her than with others.

But she had never noticed any significant difference in the way he treated her, until now. This usually curt and surly man was being quite wonderful in his care of her.

He sighed and opened the missive his mother had sent, taking a moment to peruse it. "Botheration. She and my brother are threatening to come here for Christmas."

"Good," she said, trying to hold back her mirth, "you should not be on your own at this time of the year."

"How is it different from any other time of the year?" He emitted a soft growl, a deep, sensual sound that shot tingles through her. "Bloody nuisance—this is exactly as I feared. They are bringing along a small party of their friends."

Honestly, did this man have to be so curmudgeonly? "But that is wonderful."

He frowned. "It is a disaster, and all because of that stupid betting book. They now think I am on the hunt for a wife."

"Shouldn't you be? You know, ducal duty and all. Keeping up the family line. Popping out heirs."

"That would require me to attach myself to one of those giggling geese. Not to mention, I would also have to deal with the goose's anxious mother."

"By 'giggling geese,' I suppose you mean *ton* diamonds. Poor man, to be surrounded by all that elegance and beauty. The loveliest women in all of England swooning over you. How absolutely awful for you. My heart bleeds."

He arched an eyebrow, looking wickedly appealing as he cast her a stern look. "It *is* awful. This is my home. My sanctuary. I do not want it invaded by people who drink too much, party too much, and cannot shut up."

She burst into laughter. "Oh dear. Stop being such a curmudgeon. And stop making me laugh. It hurts."

"Do not chide me, Temple. This is a terrible turn of events."

"I'm sorry. It is just surprising to see you so…upended." She had not realized quite how much of a lone wolf he was. Or lone dragon. Well, he was this magnificently forbidding beast, big and gorgeous, and unfortunately trusting no one. "Have you always been this way, Your Grace?"

"Reclusive?" He shrugged. "Not always. A man's preferences change over time. I happen to like my peace and quiet."

"And I have now turned your household upside down. Indeed, I am truly sorry."

He shook his head. "No, Temple. Wasn't your fault. Nor are you an imposition. And you do not grate on my nerves."

"Oh, goodness. You have put me in a swoon with such an irresistible compliment. Do you hear yourself? Is this how you go about seducing a woman? 'My dear,'" she said in a deep voice to mimic his own, "'you are tolerable, and do not make me grind my teeth as you blather. Come into my bed.'"

"I like to think I have a smoother delivery than that," he said with a genuine smile. "However, most would leap into my bed without my ever having to say a word. A mere nod would be enough. Not even names exchanged."

Her eyes widened.

"Temple, you are quite naïve. Do you doubt me?"

"No, I suppose it is true enough. You are handsome, wealthy, and titled. What is there not to adore?"

"The thing is, women would surrender to me even if I looked like a toad. It is all about the title, you see. I am a duke." He grunted. "And therein lies the problem. How am I to trust anyone, man or woman, when they all come at me with their hands outstretched?"

"And I am among the most shameful," she admitted, knowing how eager she was to collect his thousand pounds for the vicarage coffers.

"No, you are honest and forthright. You do not pretend to want something other than my money…and another eight kisses."

She blushed, for she did want them.

He cast her a knowing grin.

"We could end the farce and you could just give me the remaining eight hundred pounds," she suggested.

He glanced at the door as Martha approached, which meant their chat would come to an end soon. "I could, but I am not going to do it," he said quietly. "Temple, you shall have your eight kisses, and I am going to kiss you with enough heat to melt every delectable bone in your body."

He rose and left her with her mouth agape, casting her a wicked smile as he bade her and Martha a good evening.

Ailis's heart was in an untamable flutter. Her face was aflame.

She was glad he did not remain in the room, for she would have made a fool of herself in front of him.

Martha hurried forward with a worried frown and put a hand to Ailis's brow. "Your cheeks are quite pink, but your forehead feels cool."

"I'm sure I have a little fever," Ailis said, silently praying for forgiveness for the small lie. A mere fib. A slight exaggeration. "This shoulder injury is wreaking havoc with my body. First I am too cold, and then too hot. Then hot and cold at the same time. It is most disconcerting."

Martha did not appear to be fooled, and grinned. "His Grace has a way of disconcerting young ladies."

Ailis felt another flutter of her heart. "Oh, Martha. I am almost thirty. I hardly count as young anymore."

"Lamb," Martha said sternly, "you are a match for any of those fancy London lasses making their debuts. If His Grace ever got his head out of his arse, he might see you for the gem you are."

Ailis laughed. "Martha! That is quite an outrageous remark. Do not ever let the duke hear you say that."

"Oh, I shall never be that foolish. I need my position at Langford Hall and would not risk it for anything. But is it not fun to dream of a match between the two of you?"

"No, I would never dare think of it, even dream of it. My father was nothing more than a village solicitor. In fact, our village's only solicitor. He handled deeds and testaments mainly. We had no grand connections and there were years we barely made it by on his earnings."

She glanced around the duke's elegant bedchamber. "Just look at this room. The mahogany wainscoting alone is worth more than the entirety of the home where I grew up. If His Grace ever decides to marry, he will choose one of his ilk. A duke's daughter, perhaps. If the girl is very pretty, he might be persuaded to offer for an earl's daughter or that of a viscount. I doubt he would ever look lower."

Martha sighed. "I suppose you are right. But he is above forty now and graying at the temples. Still quite handsome, but growing more set in his ways with each passing year. I don't know if he will ever marry, so it is all idle consideration."

Ailis pursed her lips. "Has he always been this reclusive? You've been with the family a very long time. What was he like when he was younger?"

Martha walked over to the tray she had brought in and set on a side table. She began to fuss with the fare, cutting a soft bun, putting it on a plate, and then pouring a cup of tea for Ailis. "These are for you, lamb. Get a little sustenance in you before you fall asleep for the night."

"All right, but will you not tell me a little about the duke in his younger days?" Ailis took a sip of the offered tea and nibbled on the bun, sparing a smile for Martha when she took a seat beside her bed.

"Oh, he was quite the dashing lad. Handsome as sin. Always the handsomest boy, even as an infant. He used to laugh more often than he does now."

Ailis nodded. "He so rarely laughs."

"He used to enjoy parties and was considered quite the rake. But all that changed when he returned from the war."

Ailis set aside her tea. "The war changed many men, as I expect all such brutal conflagrations do. But he was already here when I first arrived, so he did not stay on and fight to the end at Waterloo."

"His years of service were mostly in Spain, in the earlier years of the war. His father was alive and duke at the time. You ought to have heard the row when his son came to him and said he'd bought his commission. As eldest, he ought to have stayed home and prepared to take over the Ramsdale holdings, but he had been working alongside his father for years and claimed he already knew what needed to be done."

"Still, it would all go to naught if he died."

Martha nodded. "This is exactly what his father argued. But I think His Grace enlisted because he was afraid his younger brother would be sent off. You know, first is the heir. Second is for the military. But Edward, the younger boy, was too gentle a soul and His Grace feared the lad would never survive."

"I see. He enlisted to protect the younger sibling." Ailis was not surprised to learn of this, for the duke did have keenly protective instincts. She had berated him about his lack of involvement with his subjects when scrounging for his contributions, but it was not completely true. He was not socially involved, but did take good care of those in his demesne in most other respects. The problem of absorbing all the unemployed soldiers returning from war was something almost every town in England had to deal with and would not be quickly solved.

"He returned to Broadmoor only a few weeks before you arrived at your uncle's vicarage. The duke won't ever talk about his years abroad, but he was taken prisoner toward the end of his tour of service in Spain. It was during one of those awful, bloody battles to claim a bridge that was vital to Napoleon's army."

Ailis was quite familiar with the efforts it took to push the French out of Portugal and Spain. Indeed, painfully aware.

"Several of our village boys died over there, although a few made it home and credited His Grace for their survival."

"This should have pleased him."

"I'm sure it did. But that year he spent as a prisoner of the French took a terrible toll on him. He managed to escape after several thwarted attempts, and then reported straight to the War Office in London. Only after giving them all the information he had gathered did he come home to Langdon Hall. He has never spoken a word about his time in captivity or his battle wounds that must have run deep. It has been six years since he came home and closed himself off to one and all."

"No wonder he knows so much about mending bones. How badly was he injured while in the army?"

"Quite badly, Miss Temple. Indeed, we were all so worried about him."

Ailis inhaled sharply. "Oh dear."

"It is not something we spread about. The duke is entitled to his privacy. I think this is why he will not retain the services of a valet. He does not like anyone to look at his scars."

"How awful are they?" How stupid of her not to realize that, of course, he must have quite a few of them. One did not spend time in captivity without incurring injuries both physical and spiritual.

"Quite bad, it is rumored."

Ailis had never seen physical signs of them, but they were probably hidden beneath his clothes.

"This is why he always bathes and dresses on his own. Always keeps to himself."

Ailis cleared her throat. "But he has a reputation with the ladies. Do they not... Surely they must have seen...*him*." She cleared her throat again. "You know...*naked*."

Martha rolled her eyes. "You are an innocent lamb, aren't you?"

Ailis pinched her lips, refusing to acknowledge the comment. The duke had remarked much the same.

"Men do not have to remove their clothes to do the deed," Martha went on, no doubt deciding that Ailis needed to be educated. "They just unbutton their falls and lift the lady's skirts. Quick. Done."

Perhaps Ailis was more innocent than she realized. "And that's it?"

"For those sort of encounters and that sort of woman ready to slake his urges. He might tug down her top to get at her bosom, too. But—"

"Oh, Martha! That is more than I need to know. Is there no hugging or sharing of hearts?"

"Hugging? Sharing?" She gave a trill of laughter. "No, lamb. Not for him or those women. That's just how he wants it to remain."

"It sounds awful, quite sad and lonely."

"His Grace does not seem to mind. He does not want any deep connection, just a quick tumble whenever the urge strikes."

"I think I would mind very much. What is the point of giving yourself away for nothing in return?"

"I agree, but not everyone can afford to be principled. A coin goes a long way when one is starving and needs to buy food. Not that he is one to seek out brothels or a lightskirt off the streets. No, he has plenty of elegant ladies eager to perform this service just for the sake of having him."

"Ugh. That still sounds horrible."

Martha shrugged. "We are fortunate in being so well settled. I have a good position here and I have my Henry. He's more than enough for me, so who am I to judge what others do? Henry's a funny-looking soul, but he's mine, and that's more than most others have. He's a hard worker, too. Well, each finds their own measure of comfort."

Ailis gave Martha's words some thought.

What if she died without ever finding any comfort? Were her standards set too high? She wanted to marry for love, but no man had come along to win her heart. What if she never found him and never experienced the wonder of love?

Perhaps this was the reason she looked forward to the duke's kisses. If true love was to escape her, then why not indulge in a harmless pretense of it?

Perhaps he felt it, too. And wanted the distraction of sharing kisses with his Miss Temple of Virtue.

Despite his claiming he would melt her with his kisses, she knew there would never be anything serious between them.

However, she had to be careful not to lose her heart to him. This game would end quite unhappily for her if this ever happened.

She closed her eyes and tried to fall asleep to the crackle and hiss of the warming fire. It took her a while to finally find a comfortable position and feel something other than excruciating pain. Once she was able to rest, other sensations filled her senses.

The first was the sandalwood scent of the duke on his sheets. It was a nice, soothing aroma, a blend of earthy wood and light citrus that put her heart in a flutter. Perhaps this was why her heart misbehaved every time she was near him lately.

He always smelled so good.

In truth, all the ladies noticed this and spoke of it whenever they gathered in church. These discussions were always in hushed tones, of course. The duke must have thought it quite odd when ladies started sniffing as he walked by. Even she had done it on one or two occasions, for the mix of his maleness and the woodsy scent of his skin was too enticing to resist. "So good," she muttered. "So good."

"Temple, what is so good?" the duke asked.

Her eyes flicked open in alarm.

What had she said in her dream? "What?"

"You were smiling and muttering about something being 'so good.'"

Heat shot up her neck and into her face. "I have no idea. Perhaps the ginger cake you offered me yesterday when I stopped in to pester you for a donation. It was delicious."

He grinned. "If you say so."

"What time is it?" She tried to sit up, but he placed a hand lightly on her uninjured shoulder to stop her.

"Almost noon. I was beginning to think you would sleep through the entire day. Not that it matters, because it is still snowing hard and you are not going anywhere. Let me help you, if you insist on sitting up. I don't want you hurting yourself." He leaned in close and circled his arms around her body to gently shift her into an upright position.

His hands felt divine, so big and warm and rough.

"Better?"

She nodded.

And tried hard not to inhale his magical scent that also held a trace of male heat. But she could not stop herself from breathing him in.

She sniffed, trying to mask it as more of a sniffle.

He frowned. "Are you coming down with a cold?"

"No, just clearing my nasal cavities." *Dear heaven.* "As I do every morning. Do you not do the same?"

"I suppose. Sometimes."

"It will pass shortly and I'll be right as rain." *Sniff. Sniff.*

Good grief, this man was too delicious and ought to be outlawed.

He regarded her oddly, and then shook his head. "How did you sleep?"

"I got through a few good hours without too much discomfort. But mostly I drifted in and out of sleep until finally managing these solid hours this morning. I am still tired, however. The pain has taken quite a bit out of me."

"We have laudanum. Why don't I give you some now?"

"No, I did not want it last night and will not need it now." Laudanum given in a dose strong enough to alleviate her pain would also loosen her tongue and reveal secret thoughts and desires that were better left unsaid. She would die of mortification if he ever discovered how much she liked him.

No, she could never give herself away.

He sighed as he sank into the chair beside her. "Let me have a look at your wrist."

Since she could not move it without feeling pain, he gently took it in his grasp and unwound the bandage he had put around it last night. "The swelling has gone down quite a bit."

She nodded.

"Does it hurt you as I touch it now?"

"Only a little," she said, knowing he was being very gentle. "Mostly, I feel pain when I move it around. So I am trying hard to hold it still."

"We'll give it another day before I have you exercise it." He released her carefully. "Are you hungry? Care to dine with me?"

She glanced around the room.

The curtains had been drawn back to allow in the morning light, as much of it as there was in the midst of this ongoing blizzard. But she liked to watch the snow fall and felt calmed by the graceful swirl of those beautiful snowflakes as they were tossed about in the wind and softly smacked against the windows. "Where is Martha?"

"Mrs. Fitch relieved her several hours ago. But a housekeeper has daily duties that cannot be put off, so she had to leave you alone for a few minutes. She'll send up another of the maids to sit by your side."

"Meanwhile, you have taken on the task?"

"That's right, but only for a few minutes. I am serious about not leaving you without a chaperone for any length of time. Do you mind?"

"No, how could I ever? Besides, this is your bed and your chamber that I have now usurped."

"I insisted upon it. It is the most comfortable room in the house and the least drafty. So, will you eat with me?"

"Yes, I would be delighted."

"Good." He smiled. "Not that you really had a choice. I have already instructed Mrs. Fitch to bring our meals in here. She'll be up shortly."

"How did *you* sleep, Your Grace? I hope the butterflies-and-flowers wallpaper was not too jarring to your senses."

He groaned. "I wound up sleeping on the sofa in my study. I'm more of a leather and wood sort of man. Flowers and butterflies are not my style."

"I wish you had let me move into that room. Now I feel awful that you could not sleep comfortably in your own bed."

"No, Temple. You needed it more than I. Besides, I've slept on much worse."

She recalled what Martha had told her about his military service and being captured by Napoleon's troops. He must have spent the year in squalid conditions, perhaps receiving better treatment than ordinary men because of his rank, but it still had to be a miserable experience.

She wanted so much to ask him about those war years, but it was too sensitive a topic.

However, she never hesitated to push him on matters of charity, because that was a completely different topic, and did he not have a duty to his subjects? Nor did she hesitate to prod him about his family, because he had been the one to bring her the letter he'd received. "Did you write back to your mother?"

He groaned again. "No, what is the point when it will do no good? She'll be here within the fortnight along with my brother and an entourage of giggling geese and their families. There is no stopping her once she sets her mind on a thing. Unfortunately, I happen to be that *thing* she has now fixed on."

"I think having family around will be good for you."

"No, Temple," he said, his smile fading as he turned earnest. "It is the last thing I want or need. But how can they ever understand when..." He rubbed the back of his neck. "Never mind; it is not worth discussing."

But this was just the opening she'd hoped he would provide. "Are you certain? Why should we not discuss it? I have nowhere else to be and I am a good listener. It is something I learned as I lost my loved ones...one by one, and helpless to do anything about it, although I tried so hard. Two older brothers and my parents."

"Temple, I'm so sorry."

She felt the sincerity in his tone and nodded to acknowledge it. "My brothers were far more adventurous than I was and both enlisted in the army to fight on the Iberian Peninsula."

"They must have enlisted about the same time as I did," he said.

She nodded again. "One died in the retaking of Oporto in Portugal and the other in the Battle at Talavera. The news broke my parents.

They were healthy and smiling until those letters came reporting of each brother fallen in battle. I tried to keep their spirits up, but I was devastated too. Still, I tried hard to help them through the loss. Listened to them, tried to put some joy in their lives. Nothing I ever did was enough. That was it—no matter how hard I tried to unburden them, nothing worked. All those long talks. All our plans. They were done with life. So, within the span of three years, I lost all my family."

"And came to live here with your uncle."

"I'm glad I did. Working alongside him has given me a renewed purpose, one I sorely needed. After living through three grueling years of feeling helpless, I had received a reprieve. I vowed I would never take anything or anyone else for granted."

"Nor do I take my loved ones for granted," he assured her.

She pursed her lips. "But you have spent years putting them off instead of embracing them. Do you not think this hurts them?"

"Temple, I am not engaging in this conversation. They are coming out here, aren't they? And have completely ignored my attempts to put them off because of that idiotic Silver Duke gossip. It has lit a fire under my mother that I will have a bloody hard time extinguishing."

She struggled to contain her laughter, but was it not so ridiculously amusing that this daunting beast should be taken to task by his own mother?

"You do have a lovely touch of silver in your hair," she remarked.

He grunted. "Perhaps I will take a razor to it and shave it all off, make myself as bald as a billiard ball."

She laughed again. "Don't you dare. Every woman wishes they had hair as perfect as yours."

He surprised her by giving her cheek a light caress. "Ah, Temple. Without a title, I am no one special. But you are quite something. I'm sorry if I am sometimes difficult with you. I'll try to be on better behavior, knowing now how much you have lost."

"Others have been through worse. I count my blessings, for I had many pleasant years growing up with the love of a good family. I appreciate what I have been given. And even now, I have an uncle who loves me and has treated me kindly. I have made a nice life for myself here in Broadmoor, helping him out with the vicarage duties. When that comes to an end, as it inevitably must, I will still be able to take care of myself."

"How so?" he asked, frowning.

"I was left a small inheritance that I have yet to touch because my uncle insists upon providing everything for me."

"And why should he not? You do so much to assist him in his parish duties." His expression softened. "Including reaping in the donations. They must have tripled since you arrived. No man is going to resist your smile or the sparkle of your eyes."

"Actually, they have increased *four*-fold."

"Ah, Temple. This does not surprise me. But what does surprise me is the fact that you are not married yet. Surely you must have had offers."

"I did," she said quietly, not wishing to think of the past. "I was even betrothed once."

He appeared startled by the notion. "You were betrothed?"

"Yes."

"But you never made it to the altar."

She sighed. "No, never was a blushing bride."

His stare was intense, as though he were hoping to read her mind. "What happened to end it?"

Chapter Four

"What happened to end your betrothal?" Jonas repeated when she hesitated to respond. He was not certain why Ailis's having a beau should affect him as it did. Nor did he understand how she could have had a beau and still never been kissed.

He was merely curious and not judging her.

After all, *his* two kisses would not have been nearly as special if others had come before them. But having been the first and only man to kiss her had left a searing impression on his heart.

"It was a mistake," Ailis said with a hint of defiance in her otherwise gentle voice. "One I'll readily admit was partly my fault. I thought if I accepted one of the gentlemen who offered for my hand, my parents might be cheered in the planning of the wedding or the prospect of their having grandchildren."

"But?"

She crumbled before him. "They did not care at all. It was at that moment I realized how irrelevant I had become to them. They did not love me enough to want to live for me."

Jonas suppressed the urge to reach out and put his arms around her, although he dearly ached to do so.

How could anyone *not* appreciate Ailis?

"They must have been in so much pain after losing your brothers," he said, noting the hurt she was still feeling after all these years, "that it just blinded them."

"I was in pain, too."

"But you never lost hope. That is the difference, I think. They had lost the will to live, yet you retained your hope throughout your struggle. In truth, you shine with your lovely strength. Why do you think everyone smiles when they see you? You are a ray of sunlight to brighten their day."

"I am going to swoon if you continue to pay me compliments," she said with a sweet but fragile smile.

"Ah, then I shall make every effort to remain cantankerous," he teased.

"You are the nicest cantankerous person I have ever met."

He laughed.

"And I shall forgive you even though you never smile when you see me. I suppose it is because I only ever approach you to ask for donations. But I've never dared come up to you simply to start a casual conversation."

"Nor do I ever encourage anyone to approach me. Perhaps this is something I ought to work on, but I am far more comfortable being left alone." He paused to study her, stifling yet another urge to take her into his arms.

She was wrong about his not smiling whenever he saw her.

It was often an *inward* smile. Still a smile, and one he felt in his heart but dared not show to others. And was he not inwardly smiling right now? The girl was irresistible with her bright eyes and soft lips that were a temptation for any man.

"Temple, how could you have been betrothed and yet never been kissed?"

She blushed. "It was not a love match, merely a matter of convenience. My beau was a young solicitor fairly new to our village who wished to consolidate ties with my father."

"And hopefully take over his practice?"

She nodded. "He'd moved to the village a year earlier and was eager to establish himself in our small community."

"What went wrong?" Jonas shifted closer, eager to hear. For the life of him, he could not imagine anyone breaking a betrothal to this girl.

She cleared her throat. "Turns out he was having relations with the blacksmith's daughter and got her with child."

"What?"

Her eyes widened. "Oh, I did not blame him. Truly, we had no feelings for each other, and it was becoming painfully evident that we each wanted out of this poorly conceived arrangement. I had only done it for my parents."

"To give them hope."

"Yes, but there was not a glimmer of it from either of them. This is what hurt most. I did not care that the young solicitor preferred the blacksmith's daughter over me. Nor did I care that he got her with child, although I strongly urged him to do the right thing and marry her."

"Did he?"

"Oh, yes. Her father would have come after him with his hunting rifle otherwise."

"As any good father should to protect his daughter. Although she was quite the fool to give herself to a man who was already betrothed to another."

"I suppose people do stupid things when they are in love."

"I wouldn't know," he grumbled.

"She did love him, truly and sincerely. They are married now, and I hope he cares for her as much as she does him. As for me, I was relieved to end it. What I found harder to accept was that I no longer mattered to my parents."

She took a deep breath and then let it out in a ragged sigh. "I had always dreamed of marrying for love. But I let go of that dream in the hope I could restore my family to a semblance of what it once had been. Feeling their sudden lack of love made me aware of how important love is in one's life."

"I can see that it is vital for you," Jonas said, but he knew that he could live without it. He was better off on his own, with only his demons to keep him company.

"I had no objection to ending the betrothal, and sincerely wished them every happiness. The blacksmith's daughter was certainly in love with him. I could see it in her face. And I think he cared for her, too. They won't do so badly together."

"This is what you want for yourself," Jonas remarked.

She winced. "I think it is too late for me to fall in love now. Hence, this ridiculous bargain of ten kisses with you. I plan to take full enjoyment, because this is likely to be the last exciting thing ever to happen to me."

"No, Temple. Do not ever give up on the hope of love."

"Why not? Have you not done the very same thing?"

He tensed, not wanting to discuss his situation. "It is different."

And it *was* different. He had come to a truce with his demons and was comfortable with his isolated existence.

"No, it is completely the same," she insisted.

"Ailis, leave it alone," he warned.

Of course, his ire was not with her but with himself. With the ugly things he had seen and experienced, horrors and hardships he could not get out of his mind. She was the town's angel of light—sometimes an annoyingly persistent angel, but he found her quite delightful even when she was being irritating.

That he could tolerate her was a good thing, he supposed.

There was no question she needed to stay at Langford Hall these next few days, something he would have found intolerable had he not found her company so pleasant.

In truth, he liked being around her more than was wise.

This troubled him, for he would miss her when the moment came for her to leave. She would return to the vicarage. Not so far away.

Still, not *here* with *him*.

Mrs. Fitch bustled in with their meal, bringing an end to their private conversation and his wayward thoughts.

Ailis insisted on getting out of bed to dine while seated at the small table. He often took his meals alone in his bedchamber, but having her company felt nice.

"You cannot sit here in nothing but your chemise and shawl," Mrs. Fitch insisted, and turned to him. "She needs a proper covering."

"All right," Jonas muttered, allowing his housekeeper to assist Ailis into one of his woolen robes that was much too big for her. She was drowning in it.

He did not see the point of all the fuss when she could not place her injured arm into the sleeve because her shoulder dislocation was too fresh and best left untouched to nestle in the sling.

The end result of properly dressing Ailis was a mess, an utterly adorable mess that had him silently laughing and had his heart in a roil.

Gad, she was delicious.

Ailis's hair was unbound and loose curls fluttered about her pixie ears. She had on a pair of borrowed woolen stockings that were too big for her small feet and would trip her if he did not keep hold of her.

The sleeve of his robe had to be rolled up and clipped in place to hold it firm. Atop the robe, she had wrapped the woolen shawl that also had to be held in place with one of her hair clips.

The garments were a clash of colors—red stockings, and he had no idea who had chosen this garish color or where Mrs. Fitch had ever found them stored. Black wool robe, under which lay hidden Ailis's white chemise and sinfully luscious body.

Atop the robe, she had a plaid shawl in light earth tones. The robe dragged along the carpet as he helped her into her chair.

One would think she had just scaled the Alps for all the pride she showed in her accomplishment in getting out of bed and walking across the room.

Ailis was an utter fashion mess.

And Jonas had never beheld a more fetching sight.

Ah, this vicar's niece could be a danger to his heart if he weren't careful.

He took the seat across from hers, but dismissed Mrs. Fitch when she offered to serve them. "I'll take care of myself and Miss Temple. Go about your duties, but send one of the maids up here to chaperone the naughty Miss Temple."

Ailis choked on the tea he had just poured for her and laughed. "Naughty? Me?"

He grinned. "All right. Perhaps I have it backward. It is possible I am the naughty devil from whom you need to be protected. Leave the door open, Mrs. Fitch."

"Of course, Your Grace." The housekeeper nodded and bustled out, leaving him once again alone with Ailis.

He should not have been left alone with her even for these few minutes, but where was the harm? Circumstances had already placed her in a compromising position. The mere fact of her spending the night in his home was enough to set tongues wagging.

If word ever got out she had spent it in his bedchamber... Dear heaven, what had he been *thinking*?

His staff could have managed caring for her in any of the guest bedchambers. Knowing Ailis, she would have liked staring at butterflies and flowers on the East Room's papered walls.

But no. He'd had to put her in *his* bed.

Fortunately, his household staff consisted of reliable, longtime retainers who had been in service to his family for generations and could be trusted to keep their mouths shut.

After serving Ailis her broth, he ladled a hearty stew into his bowl, and then tore each of them a chunk of bread that was warm because it was fresh out of the oven.

He studied Ailis as she sipped her broth and tried to avoid wetting her sleeve every time she dipped her spoon in the bowl.

She looked up and smiled at him. "This is delicious."

He could say the same about her. She looked good enough to eat.

Or kiss, if he managed a stolen moment alone with her later.

But no. He dared not kiss her today. She had suffered a bump to her head in addition to a dislocated shoulder. The newly formed bruising was hardly visible, only a slight purplish discoloration at her brow. However, she exhibited all the signs of a mild concussion, and he was not going to take this lightly.

Nausea and a slight case of vertigo were symptoms of her falling and striking her head. She had suffered a little from both overnight, Martha had reported to him this morning.

Despite being a bit wobbly as he led her to the table for their repast, Ailis now seemed in fairly good spirits while they ate and chatted. No sign of dizziness or stomach discomfort.

And she was a talkative little thing, but not overly so. He spoke almost as much as she did, and they did not seem to lack for interesting conversation. Jonas was surprised how easily they shared each other's company, neither one minding if they fell into a silent stretch.

"I have an extensive library," he mentioned, swallowing a bite of his stew and glancing out the window to check on the snowfall that had yet to abate since starting yesterday afternoon. "I could have Mrs. Fitch bring up a few books for you to read if you are bored."

"That would be lovely. I suppose they are mostly books on history or the sciences. Art, perhaps? Philosophy? Poetry? Military tactics and ancient battles? My brothers particularly loved those."

He nodded. "Yes, all of those."

"So, nothing improper or too scandalous?"

His lips twitched at the corners in the hint of a smile. "Nothing that I would ever dare show you. I do have some adventure stories that might interest you. What exactly are you looking for?"

"Oh, nothing in particular."

"Ailis," he said softly, "I can see by the glint in your eyes that you would like something more lurid than the history of cattle farming. Something along the lines of an Ann Radcliffe novel, perhaps? I have the complete volumes of *The Mysteries of Udolpho*. Heroine in peril. Ominous castle. Dark and stormy night. Handsome and valorous hero to rescue the fair damsel and declare his undying love for her? Although the fair damsel might have rescued herself in that story."

She smiled with genuine mirth. "And what is wrong with that?"

He shrugged. "Nothing. Did I say there was?"

"Yes, you spoke with your laughing eyes."

He grinned. "I'm sure I did not."

Perhaps he did find the notion of such a dramatic love quite amusing.

But he was not trying to condescend. He liked this quietly passionate side to Ailis.

Well, he always knew she had passion. But it was all directed toward helping the poor and nothing to do with her own pleasures. She would be quite something if he ever took her into his bed.

Of course, she was there already.

But *he* wasn't in it with her.

Nor could he ever think of sharing a night with her, of stripping off those ugly layers of mismatched clothes and kissing every inch of her soft skin, inhaling the scent of her warm body, and—

Dear heaven.

He would enjoy tasting Ailis. She made him think of apples and autumn spices whenever he was around her.

Had he gone demented?

"You wouldn't happen to have some gossip rags, would you?" she asked, unaware of the path his thoughts had taken him.

He arched an eyebrow. "In fact, I do. Not that I believe most of that drivel, but one must keep up on what is happening in Society."

"Oh, *must* one?" She cast him an impish grin. "You surprise me. I thought you had removed yourself from all the fuss and scandal."

"I have," he replied, "but I still want to know what others are doing around me. And what about you, Miss Temple of Virtue? Seems you are not above gobbling up the gossip. Not quite as pious as you let on, are you?"

"Piety and curiosity are not mutually exclusive." She tipped her chin up and cast him another impertinent smile that made him want to wrap her in his arms and kiss her endlessly.

In truth, he was almost of a mind to give her the next eight kisses tonight, because he found her remarkably enticing.

However, he did not want this bargain to end so quickly. Ailis's lips were to be savored.

For this reason, he was in no rush to end their arrangement.

This troubled him, of course. But he dismissed the danger of prolonging the game.

He listened as she continued to speak about the importance of reading gossip rags. "You must own that there is a lurid fascination in the horrendous choices some of your peers make. Your Grace, I do not mean to judge anyone. I am merely taking note of their mistakes in the hope of avoiding my own."

"I hardly think you are one to make mistakes of that sort, Temple."

"Oh, I think we are all at risk. Even you, Your Grace. It just takes the one person, the one forbidden fruit, and—"

"And we succumb to temptation?"

"Yes, think of Adam and Eve in the garden." She nodded to emphasize her point. "I saw it happen with the blacksmith's daughter and my former betrothed. It was shocking, but also wonderful in the way they found each other and could not be without each other. Well, I think she felt it more than he did. Even so, it is a lesson for us all.

Anyone can be tossed into circumstances they are helpless to avoid."

She glanced around, taking note of their surroundings. "Take us, for example. Did you ever think I would be taking up lodgings in your bedchamber?"

"No, I hadn't." Although now that she had, he could think of little else.

It should not feel so right.

"I am glad we are outside of London and the scrutiny of your peers," Ailis continued. "Our situation, as innocent as it is, would destroy my reputation if word ever got out. Thankfully, I am not important enough for anyone to take actual note of my name. The scandal sheets would report it something like this: *The Duke of R. is rumored to have a secret bedmate sequestered at his country estate. Is this why the dashing Silver Duke has not returned to London?*"

Jonas grunted.

She set down her spoon and studied him. "I jest, of course. But am I so far off the mark? This is why I need to return to the vicarage as soon as the roads are passable. I cannot be found here, nor should there be any trace I was ever here. I would be so embarrassed if your family ever found out."

"I doubt they will arrive before the end of the week at the earliest, probably longer in this inclement weather. There is nothing for you to worry about. The roads will be impassable for several more days after a snowfall as large as this one. It is quite possible they will give up and return to London."

"They won't," she responded with a confidence woven out of thin air.

"How do you know?"

"Seriously? You are a Silver Duke, like it or not. No one is going to give up the chance to spend Christmas in your company."

"Hopefully, my mother will show some sense. Would it not be reckless to keep horses out in such foul, icy weather? Why risk having them break a leg and need to be put down? No, anyone with a brain between their ears would wait until the snow melts and the sun burns away the icy patches."

"This has to do with hearts, not brains."

"No, Temple. This has to do with status, alliances, and power. As I've mentioned, no one would give a fig about me were I not a duke. And to now label me a Silver Duke? This only happened out of a desperation for gossip now that my three friends, the *real* Silver Dukes, are married and the *ton* was frantic for a replacement."

"And there you were, just ripe for the picking."

"Utter nonsense."

She cast him an impish smirk. "True or not, it is still fun to read."

He set down his spoon and leaned back in his seat. "I'll have Mrs. Fitch bring up some of those gossip rags for you, if you insist on lowering your intelligence."

"Says the man who reads them too."

He chuckled. "All right, I concede this round, Temple. Unfortunately, I do not have any of those romantic adventures you seem eager to consume, other than the Ann Radcliffe volumes that it appears you have read."

"They were very good."

"Mrs. Fitch can bring them up, too. But I'll get on it and add a few of your favorite books to my library once the snow clears and I can get to the bookshop to place my orders."

The notion obviously surprised her. "Surely you would not do this for my sake."

He shrugged. "I'm sure my mother's tastes run similar to yours."

One of the maids entered his bedchamber, her presence putting an end to their conversation. Since Jonas had finished his meal, he remained only long enough to assist Ailis back into bed, and then retired to his study.

There was always work to be done.

He could work in peace if he was of a mind to do so. No one would be foolish enough to ride out in this dangerously foul weather to call upon him today.

But his mind insisted on wandering back to Ailis.

What was it about her that tugged at his heart?

He truly was sorry she had lost her family, and even sorrier that her parents had failed to appreciate how good and kind she was. She had so much love to give.

Did he dare take some for himself?

He snorted and dismissed the possibility immediately. How could he ever shame Ailis by professing interest in her? What could he offer her but ruination? He had no intention of ever marrying. It was not merely a question of his scarred body. He did not think Ailis would ever feel revulsion for that. Many of those scars had faded over time, anyway.

But the burns on his legs and back never would. Nor would the memory of how they came about.

How could he commit to another person when there was so much damage inside of him?

Ailis would insist that love would heal him.

Perhaps.

A marriage where there was love might do it.

Or not.

He dared not make the mistake of marrying and finding out it could not work.

Yet the thought of marrying someone like Ailis did not frighten him, someone with a big heart and the competence to be his duchess. But that perfect woman would also demand his heart and soul.

Therein lay the problem, for his heart was empty.

As for his soul? That had been lost in a French prison years ago.

He went to the stack of newspapers piled in a corner of his study and riffled through the latest ones. After taking out a few he thought might interest Ailis, he summoned Mrs. Fitch to bring them up to her.

"At once, Your Grace," his ever-efficient housekeeper replied with a nod. "She'll like these."

He chuckled. "Yes, she's a little busybody. These gossip sheets will keep her amused and out of trouble."

"She's delightful, and not at all difficult."

He glanced out the window at the snow still coming down hard. "Glad to hear it, because she is going to be with us for a while if this blasted snow does not let up. At this rate, she could be trapped here the entire winter."

"Would you mind terribly, Your Grace?"

He did not bother to respond, nor did he berate his housekeeper for daring to ask such an impertinent question. Mrs. Fitch, along with Grimes, Martha, and several others in the household, had been in service to his family since he was a child. They knew him well enough to sense that he held some interest for the vicar's niece. He never would have given up his own bedchamber for anyone else. "Just take those newspapers up to Miss Temple."

"Of course." She bobbed a curtsy and scurried out, closing the door behind her.

Jonas let out a breath and settled in the chair behind his desk once he was alone again.

There were several investment proposals awaiting his review that had been sitting on his desk for several weeks now. He also had certain grain contracts to read over that his London solicitors had prepared and now awaited his signature.

The work took the rest of the day to complete.

As the last rays of sunlight began to fade and the sky turned a darker shade of gray, he rose and stretched his aching back.

Soon, the sky would turn black as ink and there would be no light save for the moon's silver glow, or as much of it as could filter through the clouds. He walked to the window and stared out of it as he had done several times over the course of the afternoon.

He noticed the outline of a moon visible against the sky. Were the clouds breaking up? Did this signify the blizzard's end? Or was this just a pause?

Surprisingly, he wished the snowfall to continue. He was not ready to lose Ailis yet, and not only because he still owed her those eight kisses.

Ah, kissing the mouthy spinster.

The taste of her still lingered on his lips.

He had eaten several meals since those kisses, and yet…the sweet taste of her was still on his tongue and in his memory.

He shook off the thought. Having accomplished a solid amount of work for the day, he set the rest aside and walked upstairs to look in on Ailis.

She looked up and cast him a beaming smile as he strode in. "I hope you had a productive afternoon, Your Grace. Can you believe it is still snowing? I wonder when it will let up."

"Probably soon. The sky cannot be holding much more snow. I expect we will wake up to blue skies and brightest sunlight tomorrow morning."

"I hope so. I need to get back to my uncle."

"Why? You cannot move that shoulder without the risk of damaging it. Has my staff not been taking excellent care of you?" He studied Ailis, who looked snug as a little bird nestled in his big bed. She was huddled under the covers and had the woolen shawl wrapped around her shoulders. A few gossip rags were strewn atop the covers and others were piled on the chair beside her bed. A fire crackled in the hearth, casting the room in a familiar amber glow.

It all felt rather cozy.

Splendid, too.

"Oh, yes. I have been treated like a princess." Ailis's hair was drawn off her face and fashioned in a loose braid down her back. Her bright eyes held his gaze and captivated him. "Here, do sit down, Your Grace." She reached for the newspapers on the chair and attempted to remove them with just one hand.

He quickly came to her side and took them all before they fell to the floor. "I have them." Grumbling, he handed them to Martha to set aside on the table for now. "But this proves my point, Miss Temple. Does it not? You are going to hurt your shoulder if you insist on doing things for yourself."

She let out a breath. "Admonishment received, Your Grace. By the way, thank you for the reading material."

"Have you read all the scandal sheets?" he asked, settling into the chair beside the bed.

"Just the ones I had piled on the chair. These others are for tonight."

"Have you come across anything particularly lurid or tantalizing?" he asked with a grin.

She cast him the prettiest smile. "Oh, yes. Lots. There's even mention of you and the ladies who people are betting on to win your heart."

He snorted and stretched his legs before him. "They are all going to lose their bets."

"Oh, you mustn't say that. Lady Viola Carstairs is the daughter of the Duke of Carstairs and reputed to be not only this year's *ton* diamond, but the diamond of the decade. I think she will be among the party coming to Langford Hall with your mother for Christmas. Lady Willa Montroy is another candidate for your affections. She's the only daughter of the seventh Earl of Montroy and another young lady much coveted for her beauty."

"Temple, do not indulge this nonsense. I have escorted both of them around London before and found them deadly boring."

"How can you say such a thing? They are witty and polished, and I am certain they have dozens of men falling at their feet."

"Well, I am not going to be one of them. As I've said, I am not interested in either young lady. My brother can have them both, if he wishes."

She set aside the newspaper she held in her hand and cast him a chiding look. "Imagine the stir you would cause if you chose one and your brother got the other. The *ton* would go wild with excitement. Everyone who was anyone would be biting their fingernails awaiting an invitation to these weddings. And what a fall from grace if their names were overlooked!"

He lolled his head back and groaned. "It isn't going to happen, so stop making a thing of it."

"It is harmless jesting. But I am not jesting about wanting to see you happily matched."

"Should you not be more concerned with your own happy match?"

She sighed. "I am firmly on the shelf and there is no help for me."

"That is nonsense, Temple."

"It is the truth."

"I do not believe it," he said, growling because Ailis was joyful and enthusiastic about everything, so why not her own wellbeing? He did not want her giving up on love or marriage.

"Your Grace, I am a spinster. This is an indisputable fact. I have accepted my lot. You needn't frown or fret—or even growl," she said when he growled again. "I am not worried about my future, so why should you be? I will admit to being a little sad, for certain. I wanted a husband and children and a bustling home life. But I will make do. As I've mentioned, I have a small inheritance to tide me over into my dotage."

"And when the time comes, you shall get yourself a cat and a cottage and live comfortably by the sea?"

"Yes, exactly, although I think I will enjoy having a dog more. Cats will not take long walks along a sandy beach with me. Perhaps I shall acquire one of each."

"You will do no such thing, Temple. You are not on the shelf. Far from it. And how can you think to get a cat when you sneeze whenever they are around you?"

She regarded him with some surprise. "You noticed?"

"Yes. You may believe I am detached and reclusive, but you would be wrong. I miss very little of what happens around me. Those fresh-faced young bucks might be interested in the younger ladies, but any man of any substance will notice you and desire you above them all."

She snorted.

"To prove my point, I shall invite you and your uncle to dine with us once my mother and her party arrive. Shall we place wagers on how many gentlemen find you to their liking?"

"Don't you dare. My uncle and I will be occupied preparing for the church's Christmas ball. I hope you will attend with your friends and family."

"I'll make certain we do," he said with a nod. "But you and your uncle must also join us. I will not take no for an answer."

"But—"

"Ah," he said, holding up a hand. "I have decreed it. You cannot refuse a duke."

"Seriously?"

He arched an eyebrow. "Yes, I am playing the duke card here and ordering you to join us…please."

She laughed. "Well, put that way…my uncle and I shall be delighted to accept your invitation."

"Good, that's settled. I'll send my carriage to pick you up when the time comes."

She rolled her eyes. "*If* the time comes. Your family is not even here yet."

"But they will be, for my mother can be quite stubborn once she gets an idea into her head. I have never met anyone as determined as she can be." He leaned forward and cast Ailis a dangerous smile. "Are you prepared to meet the dragon?"

Chapter Five

Ailis stared out the window of the duke's bedchamber the following morning and shook her head in dismay. The blizzard was still going strong for a third day, and there was no sign of its clearing. Not that she minded being stranded with the duke, for she enjoyed his company immensely.

When would she ever get the chance to know him better?

Nor was she worried about her uncle. The duke had sent young Leo Curtis to advise the vicar that she was safely ensconced at Langford Hall and would remain here until the storm passed. Leo's mother happened to be the vicarage cook, laundress, and housekeeper all in one, and would see to the vicar's meals and any household chores.

The Curtis family lived next door to the vicarage, so Ailis knew her uncle would not be abandoned. Leo was there to lend assistance if additional hands were needed.

"You're finally awake." The duke's deep voice slid over her like warm cream.

She turned to the doorway where he stood staring at her. "I slept late again, but I had a decent night's sleep," she assured him in response to the questioning arch of his eyebrow. "In truth, I have been doing little other than resting and reading these past three days."

He strode to her side and followed her gaze out the window. "I'm surprised it hasn't stopped yet."

"It is most unusual," she agreed, trying to remain composed while he stood so close to her. This was hard to do. Her heart was aflutter and her nose was twitching because she wanted to put her face to his freshly shaven jaw and inhale the delicious scent of lather and sandalwood on his skin.

To make matters worse, the duke had not bothered to wear a jacket, waistcoat, or cravat this morning, appearing before her dressed in a crisp white shirt of durable linen, buff breeches that molded to his long, powerful legs, and Hessian-style riding boots.

The shirt seemed to go on for miles across his broad chest and shoulders, and down the rippling length of his muscled arms.

Honestly, was this fair? He was beyond forty now, even graying at the temples. How could he still look this good?

He gave her a knowing smirk and smiled. "You're looking quite lovely this morning, Temple."

She glanced down at herself and groaned.

He was jesting, of course. She had on the same bright red stockings that were too big for her feet and that came to a point at the end so that they looked like elf stockings. For this reason, she had refused to wear the matching red cap for her hair that Mrs. Fitch had also found in storage.

She absolutely refused to look like an elf.

It was bad enough she had to wear his big black woolen robe that was enormous for her body, and a plaid shawl whose colors clashed with everything else she was wearing. Not to mention, her arm was in a sling.

"Yes, I'm sure I am irresistible," she said dryly.

"You are." He tucked a finger under her chin. "I meant it."

"I would be tossed into an asylum if I walked out looking this way."

"Yes, that is also true," he said with a grin. "By the way, your gown is dry and the mud stains have been washed out of it. Your stockings, too. I also took the liberty of having your boots polished. One of the maids will bring everything up to you shortly. However, I think you ought to wait another few days before you dress."

"But I ought to go home as soon as the snowstorm clears."

"I'd like you to stay on for a few more days, Ailis. I want to start you on some very light movement exercises, nothing strenuous because your shoulder is going to take another month or two to properly heal. It won't fully mend for another six months."

She stared back at him in dismay. "That long?"

He nodded. "You'll also need to keep the arm in a sling for another week or two. Believe me, you'll howl in pain if you attempt to go without it any sooner."

She let out a deflated sigh.

"However, a little exercise is important. I've noticed that keeping the blood flowing through your limbs helps to heal a dislocated shoulder faster and reduces the pain."

"Whatever you think best," she said, offering no protest. "I would have spent these past days in agony had you not known how to fix my shoulder. So I am in your debt and willingly remain in your capable hands."

"Good." He gave a nod of satisfaction. "Glad to be of help. Have you had your breakfast yet?"

She glanced at the side table that had nothing on it but a few of those gossip rags she had read the night before. "No, Martha went downstairs a few minutes ago to put a plate together for me. Have you eaten yet?"

"No, I've spent the better part of this morning checking on my horses and making certain my grooms are all right in their quarters above the stable."

She glanced out the window at the heavily falling snow. "Are the men not too cold?"

"They claim they are fine with their braziers for warmth. They'll head to the kitchen if the weather gets to be too much for them. Most have sense enough to avoid frostbite, but some of those fellows are stubborn and would rather sleep in the cold with the horses rather than come inside with the rest of the staff."

"How are the horses faring? You have some prize thoroughbreds stabled here."

"They're managing quite well. The grooms have cleared off much of the paddock area to allow the horses to walk around. We'll see about having them actually run through their paces once the snowfall begins to ease."

"I'm glad they are all safe, grooms and horses."

"Yes, it is quite dangerous outside."

"Are you here because you intend to join me for breakfast?"

"Yes, if you don't mind."

She nodded. "I have nothing else pressing, as must be obvious. I would be honored to have you join me."

In truth, she was ecstatic.

However, she tried to school her features in order not to appear too obvious.

To her dismay, he tossed her another knowing grin. "Admit it, Temple. You enjoy my company."

How was this man able to recognize her every feeling and expression?

"You are useful to have around," she said with a casual air, "since I can do nothing with a busted shoulder and am quite bored."

He gave her chin a light tweak. "As I am enjoying your company," he said with surprising earnestness.

Ailis doubted this reclusive duke was as eager for her company as she was for his. She hardly considered herself scintillating, since she had been groggy and dazed for most of these past few days.

He left her side to start rifling through his wardrobe, and had just taken out a waistcoat for himself when Martha lumbered back in with a tray in hand. "Your Grace, I wondered whether you would join Miss Temple."

"I shall. Do you mind bringing up a plate for me? And some coffee, too."

"At once, Your Grace." She set Ailis's breakfast on the small table and then scurried off again.

He shrugged into his waistcoat, a brown leather and wool vest designed more for a day of field work than gentlemanly elegance. "Well, Temple. What do you think?"

She eyed him curiously. "What do I think of your waistcoat?"

"No, of our next kiss. Number three, to be precise. Are you ready for it?"

Her mouth gaped open.

He tucked a finger under her chin and nudged it upward to close her mouth. "Ah, and your eyes are growing wide again. Too soon for you?"

"No, it's just… I look a mess. How can you want to kiss me now?"

He cast her an indulgent smile. "It is only your lips that matter, and they look rosy and sweet."

"They do?" She gave them a nervous lick.

"Yes, Temple." He stepped closer and gently cupped her cheek. "Unless you do not want me to—"

"Oh, I do. The charity business, you know. And we are only at three kisses if you count this upcoming one, and still have seven more to go after this."

He smiled. "Close your eyes, love."

She squeezed them tightly shut.

The butterflies in her stomach were in a wild flutter and she felt heat rush into her cheeks. She wanted the kiss, but was disconcerted because she hadn't expected him to kiss her before breakfast.

Was this something usually done?

He chuckled. "You will burst veins in your eyeballs if you do not ease up. Try to relax. And do not pinch your lips together so fiercely, either."

He ran his thumb lightly along the line of her jaw, and then gently along her lower lip.

Oh, heavens.

"Breathe, Temple."

She let out a gust of air.

"That's better," he murmured with a chuckle, leaning in closer so that she felt the heat of his body and the strength pulsating from it.

His breath was warm against her lips.

In the next moment, he captured her mouth in a scorching kiss, the pressure gloriously deep and fiery.

Heavens, heavens, heavens.

That man's mouth was a dangerous weapon. Sinfully effective.

He drew her up against the hard wall of his chest and held her in his protective embrace, all the while careful to avoid knocking into her sling.

When she remained unsteady, her legs turning to water so they could no longer hold her up, he wrapped his big hands around her and drew her even closer.

She could no longer tell where her body ended and his began, for they were melting into each other.

She had never felt so secure, so safe in anyone's arms, and yet still wildly out of balance because of their intimacy and the heat ignited between them.

This had nothing to do with her shoulder, still healing and tender. This was all about her heart.

Did the man have to kiss her with such exquisite ardor? Did he put such heat into all his kisses? Melt every woman he touched?

He was a rake, after all.

However, she was a novice and could not possibly hold any significance for him.

She accepted their blazing kiss for what it was, a torch that would quickly die out, and allowed herself to revel in the pleasure of the moment.

His tongue probed against the seam of her lips and nudged them apart.

She held on to him, closing her hand over the bulging muscle of his upper arm to steady herself, but she could not get her fingers even halfway around its circumference.

Oh, this is why he had been acclaimed as the next Silver Duke. His was a mature and manly body, all meat and muscle.

He held her with gentle strength and confidence, displaying utter perfection as he slowly ground his lips on hers and sank them deeper to plunder her soul.

And this was only kiss number three.

How was she ever to survive the next seven without falling in love with him?

"Open your eyes, Ailis," he whispered against her ear, his lips still temptingly close.

It took her a moment to realize he had drawn his mouth off hers because her lips and even her tongue were tingling.

Dear heaven.

Their tongues had tangled.

"How was it?" he asked.

She opened her eyes and stared up at him.

Unable to speak, she made a mewling sound somewhere between an *eep* and a *meow*. It was an appallingly kittenish sound that had him grinning in smug conquest.

"Ailis?"

She took a deep breath as he released her. "It was all right for a third kiss."

He laughed. "Your blush gives you away. Admit it, number three was a *great* kiss."

She nodded. "All right, you insufferable man. Yes, it was sheer perfection. I had no idea kisses could involve tongues as well."

An odd look came over him as he studied her.

"Is something wrong, Your Grace?"

"No, it's just... Gad, Ailis. No, nothing's wrong."

She ought to have known he would never confide in her.

"But I think we are beyond the need for formality now. You may call me Jonas whenever we are in private."

She inhaled lightly. "Jonas? Oh, no. I couldn't."

"Why not?" he asked, frowning.

"It is too familiar, isn't it?"

He arched an eyebrow. "And *that* kiss was not?"

She blushed again, as she often did because he had a way of disconcerting her. "Well, yes. It was thoroughly shocking…and fun."

He laughed.

"But our kisses are for charity. That's all they are ever meant to be, is this not so?"

"I'll write out that third bank note for you after breakfast." He appeared suddenly tense and sounded brittle.

Was he possibly disappointed?

She sighed. "May I call you something less intimate than Jonas and not so formal as Your Grace? A suitable compromise?"

He let out a soft breath and his tension appeared to ease. "Ramsdale will do, I suppose. I truly hate being called that, however. Even my mother insists on calling me that."

"Why does it displease you?"

"It signifies my title and has nothing to do with the man I am."

"What about my calling you Langford? You were Lord Langford for most of your life. Did they call you that when you were in the army? Or were you Colonel Langford? Or Colonel Lord Langford?"

He rubbed a hand along the nape of his neck and stepped away from her. "Does it matter? I am not the same man who came out as went into the army. Ah, never mind. Just keep to Your Grace."

Now she felt awful. "The name suits you. *Jonas*. It is strong and succinct, just like you. But it saddens me."

"Saddens you?" The admission obviously confused him. "Why?"

"Because our friendship is momentary. A mere illusion. It will all come to an end once I have received my ten kisses. To be honest, your kisses are affecting me more than I ever expected."

He smiled and gave her cheek a light caress. "Why is that bad? I want you to enjoy them."

"I am enjoying them quite a bit too much," she admitted with a mirthful laugh that was also tinged with regret. "But I am one of many to you while you are my one and only. You will likely remain the only man I have ever kissed."

"And you think I will move on to kiss others?"

"Won't you? Do not deny that you will. So, for us to take these charity kisses further by allowing me the privilege of calling you by your given name... I think this will hurt me all the more when I return to the vicarage and am soon forgotten by you."

"I am hardly likely to forget you, Ailis."

He was looking at her in that smoldering way he had looked just before kissing her. But this was just the way of rakes, wasn't it? They had a natural ability to make every woman feel desired.

"Sadly, that is not true," she said. "You will forget me. The memory of the kisses we shared will melt away just as this snow will melt away once the sun comes out."

"And you? How will you remember me?"

"Quite fondly, Your Grace. These kisses will always remain a beautiful dream for me."

His expression turned odd again, perhaps a bit wounded. "I see. I never thought of it that way. You are right, Temple."

Ah, he had gone back to thinking of her as the priggish vicar's niece, his Miss Temple of Virtue.

But her name...*Ailis*...had sounded awfully sweet on his lips.

Martha returned with his breakfast plate and pot of coffee, effectively ending their conversation.

After setting out the cups, silverware, and table linens, Martha asked the duke if she should leave. "Stay," he ordered her.

"Of course, Your Grace." She took the chair beside the bed and waited quietly while he ate his eggs and kippers, and Ailis had some warmed bread with jam. She hardly managed a bite, for the effects of his kiss lingered and left her unsettled. Her shoulder began to throb, but it tended to do so constantly throughout these past days, so she ignored it.

"You are looking pale again," the duke said, frowning. "Have you finished? Shall I help you back into bed?"

"Yes, I would appreciate it. Do you mind?"

"Not at all." He rose and set his table linen aside.

"Could we postpone those exercises, too?" she asked, for she was starting to tremble and her stomach was suddenly roiling.

"Of course. Nothing needs to be done today. We can start tomorrow. And only very mild exercises. There'll be no serious stretching or rotation movements for a month at the least. Your shoulder is still too raw and needs to rest in that sling for another week or two."

He wrapped his arm around her waist and assisted her in standing up, for getting to her feet was the worst and caused her the most pain.

"You are wobbling, Temple," he said, and lifted her in his arms to carry her to bed. He set her down gently on the mattress as soon as Martha turned down the covers.

"You've had enough of an adventure for the morning, lamb," Martha said.

Ailis grumbled, "I hardly moved."

"Nor should you," the duke said, stepping back while Martha tucked her in and settled the pillows at her back and under her arm to make her comfortable. "A dislocated shoulder is no small injury."

"Are you serious about my having to wear a sling for another week or two?"

"Yes. You'll do yourself permanent damage if you think to take it off earlier."

"This seems a bit extreme. Just by taking it off?" How was she to prepare for the Christmas charity ball?

He folded his arms across his chest and frowned at her from the foot of the bed. "Do not even think to lift anything, or raise your arm to string holly or place mistletoe above an entryway. You won't be able to do it. Do you wish to spend Christmas in agony in bed? Because that is where you will be while everyone else in Broadmoor enjoys themselves at your charity ball."

"Fine," she said, knowing she was pouting like a child.

She never pouted. But this was due to her frustration. How would anything get done in time for the day of celebration?

"Stop making faces at me, Miss Temple," he said with a rumble of laughter. "It will do nothing for your recovery. Resign yourself to taking on a supervisory role. Write out a list of all that needs doing. I will have my staff assist you."

"Most generous of you," she said, still grumbling when she knew she ought to have been grateful. "But will they not be needed here once your mother and her party arrive?"

"Perhaps, but we shall work it out."

She tried to settle in a more comfortable position but yelped as pain shot through her.

"Ailis! Blast it, let me help you," he said, settling her more securely.

"Thank you, Your Grace." She tried not to let him see that she was still in pain. "My greatest concern is the baking. Just about everything else can be done earlier, but the baking itself must be done that morning."

"Do we not have an excellent bake shop in Broadmoor?"

She nodded. "But we cannot afford to have them make all the cakes and pies for us. They are expensive and—"

"I'll pay for the baked goods. Hire them. Tell them what you need. Have them put it all on my account."

She and Martha gasped.

Then Martha had the biggest grin on her face.

Ailis sighed. "Thank you, Your Grace. That is very good of you, and most appreciated."

"Then what still troubles you, Miss Temple?"

She cast him a wincing smile. "Only my own stupid pride," she assured him. "I love preparing for our annual charity event and especially setting up all the booths and games for the children. I love decorating the rectory, and having the scent of warm apples, cinnamon, and cherries fill the air as we bake all those cakes and pies. I love the dancing throughout the day and the more formal dance at night. But this year, I can only watch as all of it is accomplished without me."

"Oh, lamb," Martha said sympathetically.

"Miss Temple, you will still be directing others," the duke added. "I am sure you will have no lack of volunteers who will pitch in to help. But you are and shall always be the heart of this event. It is your ideas, your planning. Your organization. Your direction. This celebration does not happen without you. All you will miss out on is the dancing. Unfortunately, that is something I cannot fix for you. But I must stand firm on this. You cannot risk damaging your shoulder while hopping about to a lively reel. No dancing."

She closed her eyes and nodded. "No one will want to partner with me anyway, not while my arm is in an unsightly sling."

She heard his release of breath, for her eyes were still closed and she suddenly felt too tired to open them. Not that she had done anything but walk to the window to look out upon the snow still falling and piling up in drifts upon the ground. Then she had eaten breakfast—another exertion, apparently.

She hated feeling weak.

"I shall look in on you later, Miss Temple. Count on my joining you for an early supper."

"All right." She would apologize to him then for her petulance. However, for now, she wanted to wallow in pity. It was a completely indulgent and petty thing to do, but their third kiss had left her undone.

What had seemed fun—kissing a duke—no longer felt so harmless.

She hoped the butterflies still fluttering in her stomach were merely a sign of indigestion.

But what if they were a sign of something more? Would it not be a disaster if they signified she was falling in love?

With the duke?

Chapter Six

The following day, after going through a morning's worth of correspondence and other business matters, Jonas left his study, grabbed his cloak and gloves, and marched to the stable. He had already checked on his horses this morning, but he needed to be out in the fresh air again to clear his head. "Silas," he said, striding toward his head groom, who was leading several of his horses to the nearby paddock, "how is Avalon faring?"

Avalon was his prize thoroughbred, a beautiful beast with speed and endurance enough to win all of his races at Newmarket.

"He's a bit restless, Your Grace. I thought to let him out for a run along with the others. Snow's piling fairly high, but the horses I took out earlier have trampled it down for these others. He'll be fine. A bit of snow won't hurt him. And look at Sheba," Silas said of Jonas's prize filly, who had red bows in her hair to keep her white coat from disappearing against the white of the snow. "She's loving this cold weather."

Jonas remained with Silas and the horses for a full hour, enjoying the bracing cold and gently falling snow as much as his horses did. But as the snow began to thicken again and mix with ice, he blinked away the icicles sticking to his eyelashes and knew it was time to seek shelter. "Let's get them back into the stable, Silas. The snow's turning to sleet now. Can't have them slipping and damaging a leg."

Silas called over two young grooms, and they all hurried into the field to lead the horses back to their stalls.

Jonas was covered in snow and little shards of ice by the time he returned to the house and stomped in through the kitchen. Mrs. Fitch hurried forward to take his cloak and gloves. "Your Grace, your hair's soaking wet," she admonished him, because he had not worn a hat.

He raked his fingers through it and felt the icy crystals melt in his palm. "No cause for alarm," he teased. "It'll dry."

"Shall I bring some tea for you into your study?"

"Make it a pot of hot cocoa, and bring it up to my bedchamber. Cups for me and Miss Temple. I want to look in on her. She looked a bit pale for much of yesterday."

"Yes, Your Grace."

He climbed the stairs and marched down the hall toward his quarters, his mind on Ailis and his foolishness in showing off to her with that kiss designed to make her melt. He knew she was a novice and would have no idea the impact a scorching kiss would have on her.

And kiss number three had been scorching. Blazing hot.

Even he, despite his cynicism and experience, had been singed by the heat of it.

Perhaps this third kiss would not have worked had she been an icy spinster, but she was warm and caring, an untapped font of passion.

All she needed was someone to draw it out of her, to stir those fires hidden inside her.

Blessed saints.

What a sweetly hot response he'd elicited from her. But to what purpose? Simply to prove to himself that he could conquer her?

He ought to have realized that kiss would change the game, for he now knew he had the power to break her heart.

He cursed himself for a fool and resolved to make amends as soon as possible.

The door stood ajar, so he did not think to give it a knock before peering in. "Martha, how—"

Heat roared through him and seared his lungs.

His heart stopped pumping and the breath rushed out of him.

"Temple, why is this door open?" he said with a growl, hardly hearing himself while lust roared through him.

He struggled to regain his breath and steady his pounding heart.

"What are you doing in here?" she cried. "You weren't supposed to come up here before midday."

Realizing he was gawking, he immediately turned his back on her. But the glorious vision of Ailis wearing nothing but her chemise, one sleeve dangling off her shoulder and slipping to the point of almost revealing one round, firm breast, could not be expunged.

Almost.

But he'd seen the lush, creamy swell of it.

Martha had obviously just given Ailis a sponge bath and *not* thoroughly dried her off, because in addition to the chemise being half off her, there were wet patches on the fabric that were transparent in the most indelicate spots.

Her arse, for one.

Gad, what a perfectly rounded bottom on the girl.

Martha must have also washed Ailis's hair, because it was wet and unbound, the droplets sliding down her silken skin and clinging to her delightful curves.

More visions of her glorious breasts and backside flashed before him.

Not only was his heart pounding wildly out of control, but his hands were trembling.

Trembling.

Him, of all people. He'd been through hell. And this slip of a spinster had him trembling?

"It is almost midday now," he said, hardly hearing himself because his traitorous heart was still pounding through his ears. "Where's Martha?"

"She went downstairs to fetch needle and thread. My gown had a small tear in it from my fall, so I wanted it fixed before I put it on."

"Why?" His eyeballs were still throbbing. "You are not going anywhere today, and likely not tomorrow, either."

"But I must leave the moment the snow stops falling," she insisted while grunting and huffing because she was trying to slip his robe on and it was three times her size and unmanageable.

"Why are you in such a rush to leave? Because I kissed you? Is this what your sudden desperation is about?"

She let out a breath. "Yes."

He felt awful about oversetting her with that kiss.

Truly, he had not thought it through as he should have done. Giving her a thrill, and proving to himself that he had it in him to give her that thrill, was not harmless.

Ailis *felt* the raw heat of it, the passion. Ailis *felt* everything. This was part of her charm, was it not?

"Shall I stop kissing you and simply give you the donation, Ailis?"

He felt the crackle of air between them as she pondered the question. Clearly, she wanted her ten kisses. Just as clearly, she was afraid of what might happen if they were as hot as kiss number three.

He stepped outside into the hall and closed the door between them, because he was going to sweep her into his arms and do more than merely kiss her again.

And that would be disastrous.

"I do not need your answer today, Ailis. Give it some thought. Nor can I leave you just now, because I asked Mrs. Fitch to bring us up some hot cocoa to share."

He heard her soft footsteps as she scurried to the door. "I love hot cocoa."

"I thought you might," he said, smiling in relief. Yes, bribe her with hot cocoa in order to make amends for the kiss both of them were still feeling. Not that gaining her forgiveness would really be that simple, but it was enough for now.

He heard more of her soft grunts as she tried to don his robe and obviously struggled because every slight movement had to be causing her pain.

"Temple, have you managed to cover yourself yet?"

"No. The robe keeps sliding off my shoulder."

"Shall I help you put it—"

"No! I'll wait for Martha to return. She won't be a moment. Just wait outside the door and do not dare come in."

He hadn't taken orders from anyone since he was in the army, and even then he was the one usually in charge. But he did not mind this snip of a thing telling him what to do, so he folded his arms across his chest and leaned against the wall while awaiting Martha's return.

Mrs. Fitch was the first to come up, bearing the pot of cocoa and other embellishments on a silver tray. "Your Grace?"

He took the tray from her hands. "Miss Temple requires assistance dressing. Help her into my robe and those garish red stockings. I dare not go in until she is presentable."

He said this for Ailis's sake, not to prove to anyone that he was a gentleman.

His thoughts were not gentlemanly in the least.

He'd gotten a dose of Ailis scantily clad, and his heart was still pounding. An intolerable heat was still thrumming through his veins.

How could one inexperienced spinster have him in such a roil? Had she somehow bewitched him with her enticing attributes? Shapely bosom, slender legs, graceful neck. Softest skin.

He was not liking the profound effect his Miss Temple of Virtue was having on him.

Why was she becoming so important to him? Could he see her in his future?

Standing in the hallway holding a tray of cocoa while his housekeeper assisted Ailis in making herself presentable was not the time to think more deeply about his life, about his bachelorhood, and the stark loneliness he would feel once Ailis was gone.

"Your Grace! I am not wearing those red stockings!" she called from the other side of the door, breaking his tension and making him laugh. "I shall put on my own when Martha brings them up."

"You are awfully demanding for a little elf who has usurped my bedchamber. Are you decent yet? May I come in?"

His housekeeper opened the door and took the tray out of his hands. "Miss Temple is now at home to visitors," Mrs. Fitch said with a mirthful air. She placed the tray on the small table and busied herself setting out their cups and pot.

Jonas approached Ailis, trying hard not to grin at the adorable sight of her.

She was securely tucked in the robe that was impossibly big for her. The sleeves alone fell to her knees. But the rich black of the wool seemed to bring out the lush gold of her hair, still unbound as it dried in the warm air.

She looked so pretty in that ill-fitting garment.

Perhaps it was the mix of impertinence and sensuality that he found irresistible about her. But these unexpected feelings were what had sent him out into the cold this morning. He could not run outside into the snow every time she heated his blood.

"Let me do up the sleeve, Miss Temple," he said, struggling not to take her in his arms again.

"All right." She studied him, her big green eyes wide as she watched him roll it up and then clip it in place. Her injured arm had remained in the sling, so the other sleeve remained empty and just flapped at her side.

"Did you manage to sleep at all after breakfast?" he asked, knowing he had to stop thinking of kissing Ailis again.

Kiss number four would have to wait. He needed to turn the heat *down* between them, not stoke it.

"I tried to close my eyes and rest, but couldn't. So I read instead."

"More gossip rags?"

"Yes," she said with a light laugh as they settled at the table. "These last ones had lots more to say about you."

He frowned.

"It was all about that betting book on you, of course. But as part of the story, they dug up names of all the young ladies you had escorted in the past."

"Anything to sell their bloody newspapers." He sank into his chair and poured each of them a cup of cocoa. "I'm sure most of those ladies are married now."

She cleared her throat. "Yes, and some of them were already married when you 'escorted' them around London."

"Are you chiding me, Temple?"

"No, Your Grace. I am keeping my opinion to myself because it is not really any of my business, is it? But it has not stopped your peers from placing bets on which of their husbands will be cuckolded now that you are back on the prowl."

"I am not on the prowl," he said in frustration. "I am not even in London. They must be low on news if I command so much attention in these latest scandal sheets."

"You seem surprised. Unpleasantly so, I might add. Have you not read these already?"

"No, didn't get around to these latest ones. Seems I had better catch up on them today. Not much else I can do while the snow has brought everything else to a halt."

"They say you like brunettes."

He arched an eyebrow as he handed over her cup of cocoa. "Is that so? What do you think, Mrs. Fitch? Does my taste run to brunettes?"

Mrs. Fitch had been fussing about the chamber, tidying up items that were already neat and did not need to be put in order. But Jonas expected she was too fidgety to sit still and pretend not to listen in on their conversation. "I am certain you favor blondes, Your Grace."

He stared at Ailis. "Perhaps I do."

"I'm sure you don't," she said, and took a gulp of the steaming cup. "Ooh, too hot." She set it down and blew on it to cool it.

"Perhaps I have no idea what I like," he murmured, "and this is what gives rise to gossip."

Ailis cast him a challenging look. "And whose fault is that?"

Mrs. Fitch coughed, no doubt to stifle a chuckle.

His staff liked Ailis. She spoke to him as no one else dared. He allowed it because she was always honest, even if some of her comments irritated him.

She suddenly gasped and shot to her feet. "Look! The snow has stopped."

Jonas rose along with her and went to the window to peer out. Disappointment overtook him when he saw that she was right. The sky remained overcast and gloomy, but appeared to be turning a lighter shade of gray.

How long before the cloud cover disappeared altogether and the sun came out?

Ailis looked relieved. That third kiss had scared her.

To be precise, her response to the kiss had frightened her because she had liked it too much.

How was he to fix this?

"Will you permit one of your grooms to escort me home, Your Grace?"

The idea did not please him, but he gave a curt nod. "Tomorrow, assuming the weather holds up and depending upon the condition of the roads. I won't risk my horses injuring their legs on an icy patch. Nor will I allow you to ride your mare even if the roads are clear. You cannot possibly manage it while nursing a dislocated shoulder. I'll take you in my carriage. Again, not before tomorrow and weather permitting."

He had barely gotten out the words when the sky darkened again and the snowfall resumed.

Ailis groaned. "Drat."

He silently cheered. "Seems we were premature in making plans to get you home."

She glanced out the window again. "In all my years, I have never seen such a snowfall. Some of those drifts must be above my waist."

"Probably higher. Come, Temple. Finish your cocoa and we'll make a list of all you'll need for your Christmas festivities."

"I hope your mother and her party will make it to Langford Hall safely. Do you think she is already on her way?"

"Yes, knowing how determined she can be. I'm sure she gathered her party and took off for Langford Hall as soon as she sent her letter, not caring that my response would be to tell her not to come out here."

Ailis grinned.

"However, she is also a sensible woman and will not put herself in danger by riding on perilous roads. She'll find a comfortable inn to wait out the storm with her party of friends. My brother will not be so cautious."

"What do you mean?"

"I would not be surprised if he shows up here before any of the others do."

Her eyes widened. "Then he cannot find me here. What will he think?"

"My staff and I will set him straight about you."

"What if he does not believe any of you? Forgive me, Mrs. Fitch," she said, turning to the housekeeper. "I do not mean to cast aspersions on your character, or that of anyone on the staff. But is it not likely he will believe the worst about me and think His Grace ordered all of you to lie to him?"

"No," Jonas replied, even though the question was addressed to Mrs. Fitch. "My brother will believe what we tell him because he knows I will never lie to him."

"Even about something that appears as bad as this?"

"Temple, you are worrying over nothing."

She tipped her chin up. "My good name is *not* nothing."

He sighed. "I realize it is precious to you, and I will do all in my power to have it remain so. Even if my brother does not believe us, he does have a smidgeon of sense and knows to keep his mouth shut. I would not worry about him."

"Easy for you to say. But this possibility firms my resolve to leave here as soon as possible."

"Not before the snow lets up," he insisted.

"As it just did," she pointed out.

"But it has now resumed," he pointed out in return.

But this got him thinking about what he would do if Ailis's good name *was* tarnished. The blame for her downfall would fall squarely on him, would it not?

He shook his head, not wanting to give thought to the consequences. Surely she would be gone before any of his family or their party arrived.

And if not?

Despite his Silver Duke reputation, he could never abandon Ailis to ruination.

Her good name was priceless to her.

Would he mind all that much giving up his freedom to marry her?

Chapter Seven

Jonas had now spent that last four nights sleeping on the sofa in his study, a fact that engendered great consternation in his loyal staff, since it meant their sleeping accommodations were finer than his own, at present. But he dared not move into any of the guest bedchambers because they were not far enough away from Ailis, who was proving to be more of a temptation than he ever expected.

The pretty spinster should not have made any significant impact on his life. Yet here she was, ensconced in his ducal bedchamber and making him yearn to keep her there far longer than the course of this snowfall.

For this reason, he dared not have her remain once the skies cleared and the roads safely reopened. He needed to take her home. She was already in a fret over the Christmas charity ball as she had fallen behind in the preparations.

"Your Grace," Grimes said, silently crossing the study to draw aside the velvet drapes and allow sunshine to flood into the room. "The snow has stopped and the sun is shining."

Jonas blinked to accustom his eyes to the morning light that seemed brighter than usual because of the sun's reflection off the snow. "I can see that, Grimes. Botheration, it's blinding."

"But is it not a relief? I was beginning to fear the snow would never stop falling."

"Yes, it is positively marvelous," he replied, his voice laden with sarcasm as he groaned to a sitting position and stretched his stiff back.

Lord, he missed his own bed.

He would miss not finding Ailis curled up in it even more.

After taking another moment to stretch, he strode to the window and peered out. The sky was the most vivid blue he had seen since last spring, unmarred by a single cloud. However, with the weather now clearing, he could also see the snow was hard packed. The blanket of white on the ground was itself covered in a sheen of ice that glistened under the sun. Icicles had coated the tree branches so that they shimmered like crystal prisms and created a magical effect.

Ailis would love this. He wondered whether she was awake and looking out onto this view. It was as though his estate had been transported into the realm of the Winter Queen of local lore.

Everything was covered in gleaming ice.

"Will you be taking Miss Temple home today, Your Grace?" Grimes asked, regaining Jonas's attention.

"No." The word slipped from his lips without a thought, for he was not ready to send her back yet. Not that he would ever keep her against her will, nor did he wish to have her with him a moment longer than was necessary. But was it not wise to give her another day or two of rest in order to ensure her shoulder properly healed? "Everything is covered in ice and nothing is melting. The roads must still be treacherous. Common sense requires she remain with us until we are certain they are safe to travel."

Grimes nodded. "Shall I have your shaving gear brought down here?"

"No. I'll see to the horses first, and then ready myself for the day in the East Room." He was getting used to staring at those butterflies and flowers on the wallpaper while he groomed himself. "Let Mrs. Fitch know I will take my breakfast with Miss Temple afterward."

"Very good, Your Grace," Grimes said, and left to carry out his instructions.

Once alone, Jonas went to his desk and wrote out two bank drafts for one hundred pounds each, representing kisses four and five, which he was determined to give Ailis before he took her home.

These needed to be soft and wholesome kisses, a necessity to erase the surprising ardor of that third kiss. Numbers four and five were to be without heat. Just sweet and tender.

He grumbled in frustration, for he did not have a sweet and tender nature.

As a duke's heir, he had been raised to take charge, fight for what was his, and hold on to it fiercely. That he took care of all those in his demesne arose from an ingrained sense of duty and not from a soft heart.

Ailis was the one with those gentle traits of kindness and compassion.

Therein lay the problem, for she could be so easily hurt. So deeply hurt by him, if he weren't careful.

The simple solution was to lower the heat for Ailis's sake. Under no circumstances could he allow their hearts to become involved. He would apply the same rule to fending off the debutantes brought along by his mother—not that he expected those young ladies half his age to feel anything for him, even if he wooed them in earnest.

Those young ladies would quickly get over the disappointment of not winning his heart, and move on to make more suitable matches for themselves.

But Ailis… The two of them had already established a rapport over the years, a lively, bantering friendship that could easily turn into something more with little effort.

She lived in Broadmoor. He would constantly run into her while on his errands, and there was no avoiding her when he attended church every Sunday.

If she lost her heart to him, there would be no moving on for her.

She was that sort of dangerous temptation, the sort to give her heart fully and love faithfully for all the days of her life.

There was nothing for it but to assure this game of ten kisses remained only a game.

After preparing the drafts, he set them in the top drawer of his desk and marched down the hall to grab his cloak and gloves.

A blast of cold air struck his face the moment he stepped outdoors, making him glad he'd thought to wrap a scarf around his neck before heading out. The wind was surprisingly strong and chilling as it swooped down from the north.

Not even the brightly shining sun could warm the earth today, which meant this deep freeze that settled in one's bones would not melt the roadways, and they would remain dangerously icy.

A trail of vapor spilled from his mouth as he let out a breath.

For medical reasons and weather conditions, the decision was easy. Ailis would have to stay at least one more day.

"Morning, Your Grace," Silas said as Jonas met him and his grooms walking Avalon, Sheba, and several other horses—including Ailis's little mare—out of the stable for their morning run in the paddock.

"Good morning." Jonas took Avalon's reins and led the beast himself. "How were the horses overnight?"

"No problem," the leathery-faced head groom said, giving Sheba a pat on the nose. "Snug as bugs, they were."

"How about you and your grooms?"

"No complaints, Your Grace. Those braziers do the trick to keep us warm. But it is cold as a witch's heart out here, isn't it? We dare not keep the horses outside too long."

Jonas nodded, for he was already feeling the chill despite being fully wrapped in a cloak, scarf, hat, and gloves. This unpleasant cold could not be good for the horses either.

Since Silas and his grooms appeared to have all well in hand, he left after fifteen minutes and returned to the house to wash and dress. He had taken several sets of clothes from his bedchamber the night before and did not need to disturb Ailis by rummaging through his wardrobe this morning.

But once he had readied himself for the day, he was eager for her company. Since his staff was up and stirring, he expected Ailis might be awake, too.

He knocked at her door. Martha opened it, and then stepped aside to let him in. "Morning, Martha. How is our patient today?"

She bobbed a curtsy. "See for yourself, Your Grace."

Ailis, still wearing his black robe and those seriously garish red stockings, stood at the window amid a circle of light. Her hair, once again that beautiful, burnished gold in the sunlight, was drawn back in a loose braid that fell below her hips. Clearly, her hair had not been brushed yet, for stray wisps fell on her brow and curled at her ears, the result of a night's sleep.

Whether it had been a *good* sleep had yet to be determined.

His heart seemed to open up when Ailis turned and cast him a brilliant smile. "The snowfall has stopped, Your Grace. Did you see?"

"Yes, I noticed," he said, striding to her side to join her at the window. "Did you sleep well last night?"

She gave him an emerald-eyed look that did odd things to his heart again. How was he to keep kisses four and five soft when the mere sight of her had his body in a roil?

And she was not even *trying* to be alluring.

"Yes, an excellent slumber," she proclaimed, although he did not believe her because she looked a little pale despite the cheerfulness of her greeting. The pursing of her mouth and shadow of strain in her eyes revealed she had passed yet another uncomfortable night. "Will you take me back to the vicarage today?"

He felt like an ogre in having to deny her.

This had been their constant push and pull, each knowing she had to leave as soon as possible. Yet her need to heal, as well as the dangerous road conditions, required her to stay.

"No, it is freezing outside and the roads will be too slick."

"Oh, were you out already this morning?"

He nodded. "To check on my horses and yours, and make a determination as to the safety of the roadways."

She nibbled her lip.

Ah, her lips would be his undoing. They were the loveliest shape, so gracefully curved, and that lower one was enticingly plump.

"But the day might warm up and melt the ice," she said with a frown.

"It might. However, it hasn't yet." He gave a casual shrug, trying not to stare at the face that he found so endlessly fascinating. Ailis was beautiful in a quiet way that snuck up on a man and left him helpless to resist. "Not even the birds have dared come out of their nests yet. They are the harbinger. I'll consider taking you home once they come out."

"But you took the horses for their run."

"They are very hardy beasts and needed their daily exercise. We usually leave them out in the fields for hours, but no animal could handle the deep freeze for long today."

"I see."

Ailis did not look pleased, but she was not going to change his mind about this. She would have to accept remaining another day at Langford Hall.

Conversation done. Decision affirmed…or so he thought.

"So, you will reconsider if the birds come out?" she asked, still negotiating with him.

He sighed. "If they come out today, then I will consider taking you back to the vicarage first thing *tomorrow*. Are you going to stare out the window all day, looking for birds?"

She turned to him, her laughter light as she said, "It had crossed my mind. I do not wish to sound ungrateful, for I owe you more than I can say. You have been so kind and generous to me, but my uncle needs me and there is so much I must do for—"

"For the charity ball, I know," he said, trying not to sound impatient. She had made her concerns clear. But had he not also made it clear she was in no fit condition to exert any effort whatsoever? "As for your uncle, your return will only be an added burden for him and your housekeeper. I will send you back to him very soon, Ailis. I promise. And you shall also have one of my maids and a footman for extra help these next few weeks. But I am not sending *them* out in these dangerous conditions just to accommodate you."

"I do apologize. You are right, of course. It is just that I am not used to being idle."

"Nor am I, but it is foolish to ignore the obvious." He turned to Martha and asked her to have breakfast sent up for him and Ailis before she went off duty. Knowing Martha, she had stayed awake all night to watch over Ailis and not slept a wink. The less reliable, younger maids would have dozed through the night. They were fine for daytime duties. But he trusted no one other than Martha or Mrs. Fitch for the nighttime hours. "Send Jane or Ruby up here to serve as chaperone for Miss Temple."

"At once, Your Grace."

He sighed again and raked a hand through his hair while watching her scurry off. This gave him a few minutes alone with Ailis. "I've written out drafts for another two hundred pounds."

"Does this mean I am to get two more kisses today?"

He nodded. "If you want them. They will not be a repeat of kiss number three."

Gad, her beautiful eyes widened to emerald pools as she stared back at him.

"How will they be different?" She blushed as she asked the question.

"They'll be softer."

She glanced toward the door. "May we try one now?"

He would gladly give her a dozen. "Yes, Ailis. Close your eyes."

He caressed her cheek when she did so, and kept her sweet face cupped in the palm of his hand while he leaned forward, their breaths mingling, and pressed a whisper-soft kiss to her lips.

When he heard her sigh, he sank his mouth deeper onto hers because kissing her softly did not mean that he was to give her a weak or tepid kiss. She needed to feel the pressure of his lips on hers and their reassuring warmth.

What he dared not repeat was the heat of that incendiary third kiss, for the ardor between them still bubbled just beneath the surface like a hidden pool of lava, silent and waiting to scorch them both upon the slightest misstep.

It was up to him to control their dangerous desires because he understood the consequences.

Ailis was inexperienced and would follow his lead. She trusted him to guide her and would follow no matter where he took this kiss because she was too curious for her own good. There was now an undeniable attraction between them that neither of them had ever wanted or expected.

He chose not to take her in his arms and merely cradled her lovely face in his hands.

He dropped his hands to his sides when he ended the kiss.

What he did not count on were her tears.

"Ailis?" He ran his thumbs along the slender trails upon her cheeks to dry them. "Why are you crying?"

"Because kiss number four was so wonderful."

"And this made you sad?" Why could she not stop *feeling* everything and just have fun? Was it so difficult to treat this adventure as a lark and stop putting her heart into each kiss?

"Yes...no. It is hard to explain. Your kisses make me happy. But a little sad, too."

He sighed, for he understood the feeling. "We are doing this to give you an enjoyable experience, not to hurt you."

"I am not hurt by it at all," she insisted.

"But your tears, Ailis. This is no longer a harmless game."

"Are you suggesting it must end?" She looked as though he had just plunged a sword through her heart.

"Should we not end it? I may be arrogant and often insufferable, but I refuse to be cruel to you."

"I would never consider you cruel," she said, tipping her chin up because she was going to be stubborn about this. "I have no illusions or *delusions* about what will happen afterward. You mustn't blame yourself because of my foolish feelings. Frankly, what business is it of yours how I choose to absorb your kisses?"

"Are you serious?" He laughed. "It is completely my business."

"Actually, it isn't. You have clearly set forth the rules. Kisses only. Ten of them. And I expect you to do a decent job with each one."

He laughed again. She was a bossy little thing.

"Then we shall each go our merry way," she continued. "So why deprive me of the pleasure of your expertise? I want each kiss to be splendid and memorable. In truth, they probably will be magnificent no matter how much you try to undermine them. But the entire point of our bargain is to have me experience the wonder of this relatively innocent intimacy. So, are you going to keep them splendid or will you sabotage them?"

Did she not realize that she was the one making them splendid? They were exactly that because of all the heart Ailis put into them.

This was also what made them so dangerous to him as well. He had not helped the situation, being too prideful to ever give her a bad kiss.

"I am not sabotaging anything. You are getting caught up in the idea of a *duke's* kiss and making too much of it. I expect it is my reputation—that Silver Duke business—that is adding to the excitement and making you think they are more splendid than they really are."

"What utter rot." She cast him an impudent frown. "You dislike being referred to as one of *those* dukes, don't you?"

"Yes, immensely. But this is who the *ton* believes I am, a thoughtless rake with a dash of silver in his hair, one who knows how to seduce women and does not care if he leaves behind a trail of broken hearts."

"I know this is not you," she said, putting a hand lightly over his heart. It rested there only a moment before she drew it away and took a step back with a heavy sigh. "Why do you think I agreed to these kisses from you and no one else before you? It has nothing to do with the fact you are a duke," she said, sounding quite indignant.

"It doesn't?" Ailis was fooling herself if she denied that this was part of his allure. They would never be having this conversation if he were the local blacksmith. "Enlighten me."

"This is not about your wealth or title, but all about the good man you are." She smiled up at him. "Although you sometimes need to be coaxed and prodded to do the right thing. I do not enjoy being the one to have to drag you by the ear to—"

"Ailis, you have gone off the topic."

She sighed. "I know you are the opposite of a rake. In truth, you are the most honorable man I know. Yes, you are also handsome, and I will not deny that was also a factor. But you could be as handsome as Adonis and I still would not want to kiss you if you had the morals of a toad."

He chuckled.

"I want these kisses from you because I know you will never intentionally hurt me or ever take advantage of me. I trust you to protect my good name because this idea is rather foolish and dangerous. But I am the one putting myself at risk here. Yet how dull my life would be if I never put a toe out of line. In the scheme of things, are these kisses really so daring?"

He gave her cheek a light caress. "They could be to you."

"But never to you," she said, casting him a wry smile. "I am sure you consider me rather meek and pathetic."

"No, Ailis. Never that." Her words surprised him, for how could she ever think of herself as anything less than lovely? Lacking in romantic experience in no way detracted from her allure. In truth, her innocence enhanced the attraction for him, because men were apes at heart and did not want to share what they considered theirs.

And was not Ailis his, even if only for the span of ten kisses?

But she would never understand how special they were for him as well, because Society shunted spinsters aside as useless and forgettable, and she believed he would do the same.

These made-up rules and conventions were utter codswallop.

"Despite the risk, I also need to be who I am," she said, once again tipping her chin up in defiance. "I want to know how it feels to be kissed by someone wonderful, someone I can trust and respect."

"Ah, you think me wonderful?"

"In your own cantankerous way, yes." She smiled up at him. "I always liked you, even if you were incredibly irritating at times."

"Careful, Temple. You'll have me in a swoon with all your compliments." But was this not precisely the reason he liked her? She was no one's toady.

"You must admit that you often give me a difficult time." Although she did not appear offended and was still smiling at him.

Ailis always had the sweetest smile. One felt its warmth and sincerity.

"Perhaps, but that is because you are so easy to tease. Childish of me, I know. But you are not like the others who come knocking at my door. I enjoy the way you challenge me. You are not afraid to stand your ground whenever we disagree. It is refreshing to be spoken to with candor. It is also refreshing to see you fight with passion because you sincerely believe in your causes. However, you are also very sentimental, and that is a concern to me."

"But this is entirely the point of my wanting these ten kisses with you and no one else. I can respond genuinely and know I will always be safe with you. Might I suggest we strike a bargain?"

He arched an eyebrow. "Another bargain beyond these ten kisses?"

"A modification to that bargain. I will not turn weepy again...and you need not pour your full heart into them again as you did with number three."

"Only part of my heart will do? Or none of it, so long as I can fake the ardor?" He frowned. "Ailis, I'm not sure I can have my kisses reflect nothing at all. What is the point of giving you the experience if I must hold back more than I already do?"

She regarded him thoughtfully. "Did you hold back even with that third kiss?"

"Yes, I had to. More would have happened between us otherwise. But not every kiss needs to be the same. Whether they are soft or steamy, or fiery to the point of volcanic, they are all a necessary part of the experience. They each have value."

"Are the fiery ones the most valuable?"

"That is entirely up to you to decide. Who is to say what you will or will not like? Just do not start ranking them from best to worst. The point is for you to enjoy the experience, not make a test out of it."

"But shouldn't some have more value than others? Let me assure you, they have all been excellent so far."

He laughed. "I know. You needn't flatter me."

"It wasn't meant as flattery. I thought you would like my honest thoughts."

He gave her cheek another light caress. "I do like your honesty. Did I not just admit it?"

"What are your thoughts about *my* responses to your kisses? This is something important for me to know. If I am wrong about my future and actually do find someone to marry, should I not know whether or not I am putting him off?"

Jonas could not imagine any man resisting Ailis.

Nor could he imagine her married to anyone but *him*.

However, that was absurd. He had no plans to marry. And even if he did, how could it possibly work out between him and a vicar's overly sentimental niece?

Of course, this assumed he was of a mind to marry and upset the natural order of his existence…his barren existence, as these past few days having Ailis in his home had shown.

He was relieved when Jane, one of the younger maids in the household, wheeled in the breakfast cart and brought an end to their conversation.

Ailis appeared frustrated because she wanted to know his thoughts about her kisses.

He, on the other hand, was desperate to *stop* thinking about her sweet, supple mouth and how irresistible he found her.

How would he rank her kisses among those of the more experienced women he had seduced?

Easily at the top of the list, because hers were given with the fullness of her heart.

This was what he loved and also dreaded about Ailis. She was a lovely, sweet thing, and he felt the full impact of her kisses. They shot straight to his heart because she gave all of *her* heart in response. He did not think he would ever grow tired of kissing her.

But was he not making too much of it?

Perhaps kiss number five or six would turn him sour.

He reached into the breast pocket of his jacket and withdrew the bank drafts earlier written out, handing them to her. "Ailis, add these to the other donations safely stored in your reticule."

She studied them a moment before looking up at him. "Both?"

He said nothing while Jane was obviously listening in as she set out their plates. He thought to send her away, but that would be worse for Ailis. Then Jane suddenly realized she had forgotten milk for Ailis's tea and excused herself to retrieve it.

Alone with Jonas again, Ailis regarded him expectantly and repeated her question. "Both? But we've only gotten to number four and you have just given me the fifth of these bank drafts."

He shook his head. "Hold on to it anyway. I fully intend to get to number five today."

This seemed to please her. "Then we are proceeding to ten?"

"Yes, the charity donations shall remain as agreed upon, but you must promise me you'll stop them if they are hurting you more than helping."

"I am not going to stop them. Will you kindly *stop* worrying about me?"

But he could not.

What was it about Ailis that brought out his protective instincts? She was also bringing out his possessive urges. When had he ever felt possessive of any woman?

The answer was never. Quite the opposite—he was usually relieved to walk away.

But he felt differently about Ailis.

She was not *his*, even though he was apishly considering her as such during this string of kisses.

But what was to happen once they reached ten?

Did he want to make her *his* beyond them?

Chapter Eight

Jonas had been so busy concentrating on Ailis that he did not realize someone was standing at the door and watching them until he heard a gentleman clearing his throat. "Why would the lady put a stop to your charity donations, Jonas?"

Blessed saints.

"What are you doing here, Edward?" Jonas's brother had his arms folded across his chest and was casually leaning one shoulder against the door while grinning at him and Ailis. "More to the point, how did you get here?"

Edward winced. "I will admit to rather foolishly riding out in the midst of the worst blizzard in recent history, but I only did it for your sake."

Jonas stared at his youngest sibling, noting his dark brown hair was quite windblown and his ears were still red from the bitter cold. "Let me see your hands," he ordered his brother, leaving Ailis's side to stride toward him.

"Whatever for?" But Edward held them out for Jonas's inspection.

"You could have gotten frostbite, you idiot," Jonas said with a growl, but was relieved that his brother's fingers showed no sign of damage. "Whatever possessed you to put your life in danger this way? And what have you done with our mother?"

"Not to worry, I did not abandon her in a snowdrift. She is several days behind me, and cozily settled in one of the more elegant coaching inns until the storm passes. However, she is most eager to arrive here with her bevy of *ton* beauties for your perusal, so I expect she will resume her travels without delay as soon as the storm passes. You know, *tempus fugit*, and all that."

Yes, time was flying by, and what did Jonas have to show for it?

Edward walked toward Ailis, his leering gaze ever on her. "And who is this delectable morsel?"

Jonas cursed under his breath.

Ailis looked incredibly lovely with her hair in a loose braid that fell below her hips, not to mention she did look delectable wrapped in his too-big robe.

Her eyes widened and she gazed at Jonas in alarm.

He made matters worse by placing his arm around her waist and drawing her closer to him, but how else was he to convey that she was *his* to protect and his brother was not to touch her?

As for Edward, he was enjoying Jonas's discomfort immensely. "Ah, but I now understand why you did not want us coming here. Seems you are already having your own private party. Will you introduce me to this charming gift so temptingly wrapped in *your* robe?"

Jonas growled. "Not another word, you dolt."

Ailis looked like she wanted to bury herself under a mountain of snow.

He knew there was no help for it but to explain the situation to his brother. "Miss Temple, this is my wayward brother, Edward, the current Lord Langford. Edward, I suggest you apologize to Miss Temple immediately. She is the vicar's niece and here only because she fell off her horse while paying a call on me on behalf of the vicar. She has dislocated her shoulder and suffered a mild concussion, as you might have noticed had you not been too busy ogling her."

His brother, now noticing her arm was in a sling and her forehead had the lingering traces of a bruise, had the good grace to look embarrassed. "Do forgive me, Miss Temple. It's just that I never expected to find any young lady ensconced in my brother's bedchamber, especially one as beautiful as you, and wearing his... Well, do forgive my mistake."

She nodded, trying to remain poised, but her embarrassment was obvious to both brothers, since her cheeks were ablaze. "Your Grace, you and your brother must have much to catch up on. Jane will return with my milk in a moment, and she can assist me with my breakfast. I do not mind eating alone."

"Nonsense," Edward blurted. "I shall join you both. I am fascinated to learn more about you, Miss Temple."

"Oh, I think you shall find me eminently forgettable."

He glanced at Jonas and cast him another irritating grin. "I doubt that. Let me see where Mrs. Fitch has put me for the duration of my stay. I'll wash up and join you in two shakes of a lamb's tail."

"Let me escort you out." Jonas wanted to box his brother's ears for the smirks he was tossing at Ailis. He grabbed his brother firmly by the elbow and dragged him down the hall toward the room farthest from his own quarters.

No one would get near Ailis tonight but *him*.

Oafish? Yes.

Possessive? Without question.

However, this little incident proved Ailis could not stay beyond tomorrow. His mother's friends would destroy her if they ever found her here.

Fortunately, his brother had come ahead to give him warning. And Edward, despite his annoying smirks and leers, could be trusted to keep quiet about Ailis.

"Where are you taking me?" he asked. "Not to the castle dungeon, I hope."

"Shut up," Jonas grumbled. "I'm putting you in the West Room."

"As far away from the lovely Miss Temple as possible," Edward remarked, casting him a knowing grin. "I have never seen you behave so possessively over a woman. What are your intentions toward her?"

"I have none. Nor should you."

"Why not? What is wrong with her?"

Jonas gaped at his brother. "There is nothing wrong with her. Can you not see she is a lady in every way? You are not to trifle with her affections."

"I would never be so disrespectful," Edward said, then held back further remarks as a footman entered the room carrying his travel pouches. "Thank you, Williams. I'll unpack them myself."

"Very good, my lord," Williams said, and then bowed and walked out.

"You already know the names of my staff?" Jonas was surprised his brother had bothered to make the effort.

"Of course—why would I not take interest in them, since I stand to inherit this place if you refuse to get about the business of marrying and siring an heir? You really have been most neglectful. Mother carps about it all the time."

"And that stupid betting book has set her on the warpath," Jonas grumbled.

"Oh, yes," Edward said, laughing. "Prepare for the siege. Cry havoc! And let slip the dogs of war. This is all-out war your Silver Duke friends have unleashed on you. But you mustn't blame them. They do this because they wish to see you happily settled."

"And they've told you this?"

Edward nodded. "Mother and I had the pleasure of dining with Bromleigh, Lynton, Camborne, and their charming wives shortly before departing London. I've never seen more blissfully enraptured men in all my life."

"Oh, Lord. This is going to be worse than I ever imagined, isn't it?"

Edward winced. "Afraid so."

Well, if any good had come from those stupid bets, it was that

Edward had proven smarter than Jonas had ever given him credit for. Obviously, his brother had been paying attention in his literature classes if he knew the lines spoken by Marc Antony in Shakespeare's *Julius Caesar*.

Havoc, indeed. Just what Jonas wanted at Christmastide.

"Competition will be fierce for your affections. Possibly, blood will be shed. Hopefully not yours," Edward teased. "The young ladies our mother has brought along are quite determined."

"How delightful." But this meant Ailis would be eaten alive if caught here, even if she did not consider herself in the competition.

Jonas's mother would not partake in Ailis's downfall, of course. She was meddlesome but never heartless or manipulative.

However, winning a duke was a high-stakes game to be played by these *ton* diamonds and their families. Cheating was not out of the question.

Once Edward had unpacked and quickly washed up from his trek in the snow, he turned to Jonas. "Here, take this letter. But do not open it until I give you the nod."

Jonas frowned. "What is it?"

"I'll let you know when the time is right."

"That's it? You won't give me any hint?"

Edward grinned at him. "No, you'll just have to be patient. Promise me you won't open it until I say you may."

Jonas shrugged and stuffed it in his breast pocket. "All right. You have my word."

The two brothers marched back to the ducal chamber, where Ailis was no doubt fretting and hopefully not in tears.

On their way to his chamber, Jonas noticed the door to the East Room was open, since the maids were cleaning it after his use. This was where he had been washing and dressing these past mornings.

Edward stopped in his tracks and peered in. "Did you stay in here while giving the lovely Miss Temple your bed?" he whispered so as not to be overheard by the maids bustling about the room.

"I slept downstairs in my study," Jonas responded quietly, "but readied myself for the day in here."

"Ah." Edward adjusted his spectacles to properly set them on the bridge of his nose. "You did not trust yourself to remain too close to her. I cannot blame you. That is one delicious crumpet you've—*Ack!*"

Jonas yanked him out of the chamber and continued to his bedchamber. "Stop making those crude remarks about Miss Temple."

Edward grinned. "You like her. What is going on between the two of you?"

"Nothing. She'll be returning to the vicarage now that the snow has finally stopped. I would have taken her back today, but I thought the roads would be too treacherous."

"They are," Edward confirmed. "Mother thought I was mad to set out amid the ongoing storm. She was right. I almost landed headfirst on the icy ground at least a dozen times along the way. My horse will no longer speak to me."

Jonas laughed despite wanting to be angry with his brother for ignoring those dangerous conditions and invading his home. "You are such an arse."

"I know, but you love me anyway." Edward turned serious a moment. "You spent a year as a prisoner of war because of me. Do you think that is a sacrifice I will ever forget?"

"I did not enlist to fight in the war because of you," Jonas insisted, for he would have purchased his commission at some point to join the battle against Napoleon even if his brother had not been the one expected to serve in the military.

"Yes, you did it all for me. We both know you signed up first because you wanted to protect me. I would not have survived a day if I was the one shipped off. So, I am forever grateful and will keep your little *tendre* for Miss Temple a secret."

Jonas sighed. "There is nothing between us, Edward."

"Your eyes say something different." Edward held up a hand to stop Jonas's protest. "I will hound you no more on the matter. Just make sure your servants do not let slip that she was ever here. But bloody blazes, Jonas. Did you have to put her in *your* bed?"

"Her shoulder had to be fixed without delay and the other rooms were not made up yet."

"Very poor excuse, and you know it. But go ahead and deny the truth all you want. Mother will be quite put out when she realizes she dragged these lovely diamonds all the way out here in the midst of a blizzard for nothing. She will demand explanations."

Jonas raked a hand through his hair. "How far back did you leave her?"

"Oh, you needn't worry that she will arrive today with her entourage. She plans to wait in her comfortable inn lodgings for another day or two before daring to make the last leg of the journey north."

"Are you certain?"

"Well, no. She does want you to meet the lovely ladies and their rabidly eager families. On second thought, perhaps it is wisest to get Miss Temple back to the vicarage at first light tomorrow morning."

Precisely what Jonas had been thinking. "Who is in our mother's entourage?"

"Several diamonds you have escorted around London previously. Lady Viola Carstairs, for one. She's come along with her father, the Duke of Carstairs. Lady Willa Montroy, for another. Her parents, the Earl and Countess of Montroy, will be chaperoning her."

"Chaperoning? Or conniving to have me compromise her?"

Edward shrugged. "I won't deny this is going to be a battlefield for you. The betting book has Lady Viola and Lady Willa down as the favorites. But our mother has also brought along Viscount Tenney, his wife, and their two daughters, Faith and Hope. Watch out for them."

Jonas arched an eyebrow. "Why?"

"My friends and I refer to them as Faithless and Hopeless. Those two young ladies might look sweet, but they are completely without morals and vicious schemers."

He groaned. "What possessed our mother to invite them?"

"I don't know. Perhaps she thought their presence might sooner push you into the arms of Lady Viola or Lady Willa."

"Stupid idea."

"Well, I shall leave it to you to tell her that."

Jonas laughed. "Oh, no. I value my life. You will stay on for the duration, won't you?"

Edward cast him another of his irritating grins. "Is that a plea or a demand?"

"Take it however you like, but I will cut you off without a farthing if you dare leave me alone to face that pack of hounds."

"I braved the snow and ice to get here, did I not? I'll remain for the duration. I've even taken the liberty of inviting two of my friends. You remember Lord Pomeroy and Lord Whitcomb, don't you?"

"Yes, your university friends. I found both to be amiable, although a little dimwitted. Have they improved with age?"

Edward winced. "Well, we all managed to graduate from Oxford without being sent down. Depends on what you mean by *improve*. They do not get drunk nearly as often as they used to when we were at Magdalene College, nor do they gamble as frivolously as they once did. But will they ever achieve scientific breakthroughs or write brilliant poetry? Doubtful. However, they have wagered on your *not* marrying, so I think they will be quite useful to you."

"Then I may count on them as allies?" Jonas asked, easing a little upon hearing that news.

"Yes, for they will not hesitate to sabotage the plans of these young ladies and their parents. Frankly, their bets seemed awfully foolish, considering what happened to Bromleigh, Lynton, and Camborne. All three were felled within weeks of each other. The *ton* is still reeling over that. And now, their attention is turned on you."

Jonas frowned. "I was never a Silver Duke."

"Brother, dear. You are presently *the* Silver Duke whether you like it or not. The ladies are going to swoon and flutter like butterflies around you once they catch sight of that glorious sprinkling of silver at your temples."

"What utter rot, Edward. That dusting of gray just proves I am old enough to be their father. If they swoon, it will be over the title. Never the man."

His brother gave him a friendly slap on the back. "You underestimate your appeal. Just ask Miss Temple—she'll give you an honest appraisal."

"Keep her out of this." Jonas shook his head. "I am fully aware of what these young ladies are after. As I said, it is my title."

"And your wealth," Edward added with a shrug. "But take heart. My friends are going to undermine these young ladies because they cannot afford to lose their bets."

"Oh, excellent," Jonas said, his voice dripping with sarcasm. "Just what I need, an entire party of schemers with me for the Christmas holidays. What could be more joyful?"

Ailis was seated at the small table still looking embarrassed when they returned. But Jane must have brushed her hair and braided it again, because it was nicely styled and there were no loose strands of gold wrapping about her ears.

In truth, she looked soft and lovely.

Three place settings had been set out, and a cart with salvers stood beside the table. "I'll serve," Jonas said, feeling rather proprietary about Ailis.

Jane took a chair in the corner of the room and sat quietly, but was avidly watching him as he placed eggs and ham on Ailis's plate, then piled larger portions on his and Edward's plates. When he realized Ailis could not cut the slice of ham on her own, he did it for her.

This had his brother grinning.

Ailis merely looked perplexed. "Jane could have done this for me."

"I know," Jonas said, wondering why he was still behaving like a territorial ape and fussing over her.

This was not in his nature at all. He would not have done this for anyone other than Ailis.

Well, he might have done it for Edward or his mother, had either of them required assistance. He loved them very much, even though he was monumentally irritated with them just now.

Ailis smiled in gratitude, making him lose the trail of his thoughts.

Ah, yes. His inexplicably proprietary claim on her. What was the point when he had every intention of keeping away from her while his mother and her entourage were here?

Sadly, this meant he would not be around to assist her with the Christmas decorations or setting up the booths for all the events planned for the charity ball.

Not that she needed him to do anything but open up his coin purse. The vicar, the villagers, and the few of his staff he could spare would help Ailis put everything in order for the big day.

"Miss Temple, tell me a little about yourself," Edward said, sounding sincerely interested.

Ailis cast him a shy smile. "Oh, there isn't much to tell. I live at the vicarage with my uncle. He's been the vicar in Broadmoor for ages. I came here about six years ago, after my parents died. It is a lovely village and I have enjoyed every moment of my stay. My uncle is a dear, kind man, and I find working with him quite rewarding."

"I gather you organize the church events," Edward said. "What other duties has he assigned to you?"

Jonas chuckled. "She's his secret weapon when it comes to gathering donations."

"What do you mean?" Edward asked.

Jonas arched an eyebrow. "Is it not obvious? No man in his right mind is going to turn her down."

Ailis frowned at him. "But you did. It took me ages to—"

"Miss Temple…"

"Never mind." She sighed and shook her head, turning to his brother. "It is all settled now, Lord Langford. Although your brother did give me a hard time at first."

Edward glanced from one to the other. "How much are you seeking in donations? And to what purpose?"

"I was collecting for the needy to get them fed, housed, and clothed for the winter. My uncle and I estimated it would take about a thousand pounds to get them through the winter. But we've met our goal now."

"Thanks to my brother?" Edward asked.

She nodded. "He has been most generous—as well he should be, since all the land in the village is his anyway. And should he not take proper care of all those who rely on him for their survival?"

"Miss Temple," Jonas said again in a tone of caution, "I do not need you to box my ears. My brother was merely asking a general question and does not require elaborate explanations."

Edward laughed and leaned closer to Ailis. "On the contrary, Miss Temple. I am eager to know exactly what you think of my brother. Do spill every lurid detail."

Jonas set down his fork and pushed his seat slightly away from the table. "I forbid you to speak about me."

This was exactly what he had hoped to avoid by remaining at Langford Hall and well away from London. But it seemed the meddlesome gossips, including his curious brother and stubborn mother, refused to be daunted.

"Gad, Edward. Stop grinning or I'll toss you back out in the cold."

"You *forbid* me?" Ailis frowned at him.

"Yes, Miss Temple. For it is in my power to do so, lest you forget." He sighed and sank back in the flimsy chair that squeaked whenever he leaned back on it. "Edward, stop snooping into my affairs."

"It is all innocently done," his brother insisted. "I need to be informed in order to best protect you."

"I do not need anyone's protection, and certainly not that of my younger brother."

"How wrong you are," Edward grumbled. "Do you think our mother or any of her entourage will wait five minutes before shamelessly prying into your business? I'm merely trying to protect your flank from the advancing horde." He turned to Ailis. "I am a very loyal brother, but he can be hardheaded and does not appreciate all I do for him."

She laughed. "You are a saint to put up with him. He can be quite tyrannical."

"Ailis, for pity's sake," Jonas grumbled. "Not you, too."

She cast him a remorseful smile. "Sorry, I could not resist teasing you just this little bit. But like your brother, I am on your side. He wants to see you happy and so do I."

"I'll be happiest when I am no longer invaded by guests. I shall dance a jig once everyone has returned to London." He rose and strode to the window to peer out, for the weather should have warmed a little by now.

He noticed the icicles were indeed beginning to melt and the birds had come out from the shelter of their nests. Some were singing in the trees while others poked about on the frozen ground in search of seeds or worms.

He met the sight of this thaw with mixed feelings, for it meant that Ailis could go home today, if he were of a mind to escort her home.

But the sight he saw next had him tensing. "Edward, just how much of a head start did you say you had on our mother's party?"

"About two days, I would guess."

"Two days? And you did not stop anywhere along the way?"

"Well, I did have to stop whenever the wind and deep freeze became too much for me. Nor could I ride at night. You must own that this would have been the height of folly. And then Conqueror lost a shoe the other morning, just as I was about to depart the coaching inn. Took some time for the blacksmith to get around to replacing it. By then, I'd lost precious hours of daylight. Why are you asking me these questions?"

"Come have a look," Jonas said, studying the string of carriages slowly making their way up his drive that was now a mix of icy patches and slush.

Ailis rose along with Edward and rushed to the window with him, but Jonas held her back. "Careful, you might be seen."

She frowned. "By whom?"

"Oh, hell," Edward muttered. "How in blazes did they get here so fast?"

Ailis poked her head around him and gasped. "Your mother and her entourage? Oh, no! How is it possible?"

Jonas wrapped an arm around her waist to steady her as the color drained from her face. Could this morning turn any more disastrous?

"Ailis," he said with a piercing ache to his heart, "where are your clothes?"

CHAPTER NINE

AILIS TRIED TO control her panic.
This isn't happening.
This cannot *be happening.*

But it was, and the dowager duchess along with the bevy of *ton* beauties she had brought with her would be at Langford Hall's front door within minutes! "I'll be destroyed if they find me here." Where was her gown? And stockings and boots? And gloves, cloak, and scarf. What was she forgetting?

Oh, her reticule.

Of course, she had placed the duke's donations in it.

She raced to the duke's wardrobe and found her gown and stockings neatly folded on a shelf. "Jane, help me dress!"

Edward grinned. "I suppose that is my cue to leave."

Ailis's eyes widened.

The duke raked a hand through his hair. "Edward, help me stall them."

His brother nodded. "I'm so sorry, Miss Temple. We'll do all we can to protect you. Keep this door shut. In fact, barricade it. Do not under any circumstances come out until either my brother or I return."

"I wasn't planning to," she assured him, her heart racing as the duke and his brother hurried out.

She heard the duke issuing commands to the maids who were

cleaning the nearby rooms, and then heard him shout to Grimes.

Leaving the duke to do whatever it was he needed to do, Ailis returned to worrying for herself. Her shoulder began to throb painfully as she moved too fast when removing the duke's robe. Twinges as sharp as lightning bolts seared through her body.

Each slight movement hurt, and she thought she might faint by the time Jane had finished helping her into her gown. The effort of removing the sling and getting her injured arm through the sleeve, which was too tight because of the swelling, proved more excruciating than she ever thought possible.

"Give me a minute, Jane," she pleaded, sinking onto the bed while her dizziness and an unexpected wave of nausea passed.

She now understood why the duke was so insistent she rest in bed and keep her arm propped in that sling.

After taking several deep breaths, she got to her feet and allowed Jane to finish lacing her gown. "Not too tight. As it is, I can hardly breathe."

"Oh, Miss Temple..." Jane's hands were trembling and so was her voice.

Ailis realized they both needed to calm down and be ready to move quickly when the time arrived to make her escape. "His Grace and Lord Langford will see me safely through this little crisis," she said, feeling more hopeful than certain. "If I do not have the chance, will you thank Mrs. Fitch and the staff for me? I am so grateful for the care all of you have given me."

"It was our pleasure, Miss Temple. Never you worry. None of us will give you away."

Ailis sat on the bed once more while Jane helped her with her stockings and boots that had been polished and... Had the worn heels been replaced? They looked as good as new. More reasons to be grateful to the duke and his staff.

But she could not dwell on this, for Jane had sensed her panic and now needed to be calmed as well.

"What a coil! What a coil," the girl repeated as she began to sob.

"Hush, Jane. His Grace's guests are about to enter the house." Ailis heard their voices carrying up the stairs from the entry hall.

The warning only served to scare Jane worse. "Oh, Miss Temple! What shall we do if they walk in here?"

"No one would dare," Ailis assured the weeping maid. "Nor do I think any of them will be escorted up here just yet, since they arrived early and Mrs. Fitch does not have the guestrooms readied." The noises they heard close by in the hallway had to be mostly household staff rushing about while preparing the bedrooms. "His Grace is a capable host and will have ordered refreshments served in the drawing room. He'll stall them down there while he figures out a way to get me out."

Jane nodded. "He's very clever."

"Smartest man I know," Ailis replied, and she spoke the truth. He was also battle trained and probably excelled in military tactics that he had put to use in surviving the war. Was this not an accurate description of him? A clear-eyed man. Full concentration on his objective. Icy calm. Ready to strike fast.

Indeed, planning her escape would not be all that hard for him.

Dear heaven.

What if there was no escape until nightfall?

"Jane, we must be quiet as mice. We may be here for hours yet." Ailis hardly dared breathe for fear a guest might overhear their whispers and be so bold as to peek into the duke's bedchamber. It was unlikely, but who could think logically at a time like this?

Edward had described these *ton* diamonds and their families as brazen, conniving schemers and, in general, ruthless in their quest for marriage. Ailis could not imagine they would be so foolish to attempt such a breach of etiquette as peering into the duke's bedchamber, but what if they did?

His mother might. Ailis got the sense this woman was quite formidable, and no one, not even her daunting son, could tell her what to do. If she suspected something was amiss, no place would be out of bounds for her search.

The breakfast plates clattered, drawing Ailis's attention with a start. "Jane, what are you doing? Stop clearing the plates."

"But they cannot stay here, Miss Temple. The room will start to smell."

Oh dear.

This was Jane being overset and not thinking clearly.

First of all, the duke and his brother had scarfed down their breakfast and left hardly a crumb on their plates. Ailis had mostly finished her meal, leaving a little bit of the ham uneaten.

But so what? The ham was hardly likely to rot quickly.

Jane was now fussing with their cups and creating more noise as they clattered.

Ailis sighed, knowing she was safest with the maid gone before she spilled the entire cart and brought everyone running up here. "Jane, I think you ought to get these plates back to the kitchen."

"And leave you here on your own, Miss Temple?"

Ailis nodded. "They need to be cleared away, as you wisely pointed out. As fast as possible, before the maids or valets brought by his guests start running up and down the servants' stairs. We cannot risk one of them being sharp enough to spot *three* place settings on your cart. This will immediately raise questions about a mysterious third person at the table."

Jane nodded. "I'll take care of it, Miss Temple," she said with a sniffle. "I'll do it right now."

As Ailis turned away, she caught her reflection in the mirror and realized something had to be done with her hair. She could not leave it with the one fat braid down her back. "Oh, my clips. Jane, can you—"

But the overset maid had already disappeared through the hidden doorway.

Ailis heard the rattle of cups and plates along the servants' stairs as Jane made too much noise in her haste to be discreet. She dared not call the girl back. Doing up her hair properly was not all that important and could wait until Jane or one of the other maids returned.

And was she not better off left here on her own? She knew how to be silent while removing all trace of her presence in the room. The first thing she did was sweep her clips into her reticule, which proved much harder than expected because she only had the one hand available while the other was bound at the wrist and resting in the sling.

Besides, the braid was neat, since Jane had brushed it out and rebraided it while the duke was showing his brother to his guest quarters.

However, Ailis had to get all the blonde hairs out of the duke's brush. This was another thing someone with a sharp eye would notice.

Perhaps she was being ridiculously fretful, for who would ever look so closely at a duke's hairbrush? But did it not make sense to remove the minutest trace of her existence from this bedchamber? What if the duke chose to take one of those beautiful diamonds into his bed? She knew such things went on at these *ton* house parties.

The possibility saddened her profoundly.

Sighing, she dared to peek out the window. The footmen were still unloading trunks from the coaches and there was quite a bit of activity going on in the courtyard.

No one looked up, but she moved away from the window out of caution.

Whenever Jane returned, Ailis would have her be the spy and peer outside. It was safest to have Jane do the scouting for her, since the girl had bright red hair and was plumper than Ailis. No one was going to mistake one for the other.

A few moments later, she peered out again. The duke was out there now to greet more new arrivals.

Dear heaven.

Were they moving an entire army into his home? She had never seen such a long string of carriages waiting for their turn to unload. This would keep the duke and his brother busy for an hour yet. "Herd them in already," she grumbled, knowing she could not make her way out until all the new arrivals were indoors and their conveyances driven to the carriage house beside the stable.

They were taking their sweet time, weren't they?

Or was she being too impatient?

The duke helped an older woman down from her elegant carriage. The woman, wearing an exquisite fur-lined cloak and matching hat, patted his cheek and then turned her own cheek to him so that he could place a kiss on it.

She had to be his mother.

"She looks a bit of a dragon," Ailis said to herself, watching as he dutifully tucked the older woman's arm in his and led her inside. Several young ladies who had been helped down from their carriages by attentive footmen followed after them like little ducklings in a row. Ailis grinned. "How funny."

But she knew the duke would not find it quite so humorous, for those young ladies were never going to leave him alone.

The walls would feel as though they were closing in on him, and that was not funny at all.

Another thing Ailis did not find humorous was the way these young ladies treated the duke's brother.

In short, they ignored him. It was as though poor Lord Langford did not exist.

"And they call you *Polite* Society," Ailis remarked with a grunt, knowing they were only polite when it served their interests.

Lord Langford suddenly glanced up and caught her spying. She hastily ducked out of sight, but not before she'd caught his frown.

Dear heaven. Who else might have seen her?

Likely no one, for he was the only one who knew the duke had a lady in his bedchamber, or even knew where the bedchamber was located. But she'd caught Lord Langford's expression just before he had looked up and noticed her.

It was one of sadness and hurt.

This was how he must have spent his entire life, unseen within the expansive shadow of the duke. And yet he clearly never blamed his brother for the constant slights he must have endured throughout the years. Quite the opposite, he seemed to adore and worship Jonas, and the affection was obviously reciprocated.

It was not the duke's fault that the *ton* regarded him as valuable while a second son was not. These diamonds might have preferred Lord Langford as a husband rather than the duke, but would any of them ever admit it? They were expected to make a successful match, although their definition of *successful* was not at all the same as Ailis's.

Love was not a requirement in *ton* marriages. In fact, it was forcefully discouraged. Wealth, rank, and consolidation of power were deemed most important. Affection and warmth were longings left to be fulfilled by their paramours. This was why so many scandals broke out among these elite.

Still, who would not fall in love with this duke? Was he not the handsomest man in all of England? One of these fortunate ladies would have it all if he chose her.

"Ah, lucky girl," Ailis said, taking a seat beside the hearth. There was a fire blazing in it, so she held her hands out to warm them while waiting for someone to return for her.

Her idle mind drifted once more to the duke.

If the man had any faults, it was that he frowned a lot and kept too much to himself. But his distancing himself from others, that quality of aloofness, also added to his allure. He was obviously handsome and considered dangerous because he maintained an aura of mystery about him.

But why was he so completely private about his life and experiences? Had the war changed him? Or was he always like this?

The walls around his heart were so firmly constructed that she did not know if any of those young hopefuls would ever break through and win his love.

What a pity. She sensed he would make a wonderful husband and father.

Ailis shot out of her seat when the servants' door, hidden among the opulent rosewood paneling, opened and Jane returned. "What's going on?"

The girl shook her head. "Mrs. Fitch sent me up here to tell you to sit tight and not move a muscle. The house is completely invaded and it is a madhouse downstairs. I cannot stay with you, Miss Temple. I'm needed to help settle the guests in their quarters. None of those ladies are as nice as you."

"They must be tired after their long journey."

"No, they are just petulant and full of their own importance."

Ailis grinned. "Hush, Jane. One of them might be the next duchess."

The girl rolled her eyes. "Oh, no. The duke is already eager to be rid of them."

Ailis did not think this was really true, but she did not bother to comment on it.

Left alone once again, she let out a heavy breath and settled back in her chair beside the hearth. This was going to be a long wait.

Would the duke be able to sneak her out once everyone retired to bed? That would not happen until the wee hours. The Upper Crust were known to party until dawn. But the maids and valets these guests had brought along would start to rise by then, would they not? There might never be a moment she could leave unseen.

What if she never made her escape?

No, this situation could not remain as it was.

But what if her uncle came around asking questions once the snow melted sufficiently to travel about?

Jane crept back in through the hidden door an hour later.

"Miss Temple, the duke insisted we feed you." She carried a basket and drew aside the cloth covering to reveal some bread, cheese, and fruit. Also in the basket was a bottle of lemonade. "It is the best we could do without attracting attention."

"It is perfect, Jane. Leave it here and I'll manage. Oh, but open up the bottle for me, would you?"

Jane nodded and immediately did as asked.

"And I've been giving my escape some thought," Ailis said. "I could pretend to be one of the maids on staff. I would only have to leave my arm out of the sling long enough to walk down the servants' stairs."

"Won't it hurt you?"

Ailis nodded. "Only for a little while. Next time you come up, bring me an apron and a mobcap. Make it large so I can tuck it low and hide as much of my face as possible."

Not that any of these elites would ever bother to look at a household maid, but why take the risk?

"I'll suggest it to Mrs. Fitch and she will find a moment to mention it to His Grace. It isn't a bad plan, Miss Temple. I think it could work," Jane said, and disappeared through the hidden door again.

After spending another hour sitting and waiting, Ailis was more convinced than ever that something had to be done. What was to stop her from sneaking down the back stairs right now? Wouldn't the maids and valets have tended to their duties by now? And she could carry a pillow on the pretense of needing it to be replaced. A big, fluffy one would help cover her face.

"No, that won't work." She needed to walk out with her cloak, gloves, reticule…unless Jane carried those down to the kitchen first.

But Ailis had five hundred pounds of bank notes in her reticule.

She could not leave it unguarded... Well, she could stuff them in her bodice.

Yes, she had her escape plan firmed up now. A mobcap to hide her hair and face. Carrying a pillow or linens. Mrs. Fitch could send a crew of maids in here to tidy the duke's room. Did it not need to be tidied anyway? And who was going to keep count of how many maids bustled in or out?

Feeling quite smug about her plan, Ailis tossed a few logs onto the fire, ignoring the twinges that shot through her body even though the logs were small and she only lifted them one at a time using her good arm.

With the fire now blazing to her satisfaction, she settled again in one of the big chairs by the hearth to await Jane's return...*anyone's* return.

The time stretched interminably.

Where was Jane? What was taking her so long?

Ailis jumped to her feet in relief when she heard the bedroom door click open. "Jane, thank goodness! I was beginning to despair you—"

Her heart stopped beating. Simply stopped, for the dowager duchess stood in the doorway with Jane trembling behind her.

"I knew my sons were hiding something from me," the formidable woman intoned. "Leave us, Jane."

The girl was in tears. "I'm so sorry, Miss Temple." She bobbed a curtsy and dashed away.

Ailis's heart had yet to resume beating as she gaped at the duke's imposing mother, who now closed the door and turned toward her. She was not a tall woman, more or less Ailis's height. She had dark brown eyes like her son, and her hair had obviously once been dark but was now mostly gray.

However, this was no meek old woman.

Ailis curtsied and waited for the dowager's insults to come spilling out of her mouth.

But the proud woman said nothing and merely approached Ailis, touching her injured shoulder with surprising gentleness. Even that slight pressure was painful, and Ailis winced. "What happened to you, my dear?"

Ailis was amazed by the softness in her tone. "I fell off my horse several days ago while riding home as the blizzard began, and dislocated my shoulder."

This really was not much of an answer, because it was obvious that falling off one's horse outdoors in no way explained how she ended up in the duke's bedchamber.

"And?" the dowager prompted her, motioning to the two chairs by the fireplace where Ailis had been seated only moments ago. "Sit," she commanded. "Tell me all of it."

After taking her seat, Ailis properly introduced herself. "I am the vicar's niece and actively assist him in all church functions. I came to collect donations for the charity Christmas ball from your son. You see, we desperately need these donations to help the destitute families in the parish, especially now that the war has ended and so much of the population is unable to find work."

The dowager nodded. "It is just as bad in London, perhaps worse because so many of those poor souls are preyed upon by villains and criminals. Some of my friends and I are working with the Home Office to establish houses for our injured soldiers, as well as those for destitute mothers and orphans."

"How lovely of you, Your Grace," Ailis said with sincere admiration. "I worry the same for our villagers. This is why this year's Christmas ball is so important to me. It is a daylong affair with games for the children, and food and dancing for all. I tried several times to explain this to your son, but he gave me such a hard time and…" She cleared her throat, realizing she should not be criticizing the duke. "But rest assured, he is a very kind and generous man."

The dowager laughed. "My son? Kind?"

Ailis could not help but smile. "Well, he can be difficult. Quite irritating, at times. But he does have a strong sense of duty. It just took me longer than I would have liked to convince him to pay up. Which he has done. Generously, too. But in the time wasted on…I mean, in the time spent discussing the matter on my last visit, I delayed too long and got caught in the midst of the snowstorm."

The dowager frowned. "Did my son purposely delay you?"

"Oh, no. It was my fault in choosing to pay a call on him when I did. You see, I had finished my morning rounds and could have returned to the vicarage as the skies began to turn gray and threatening. But I thought I had time to squeeze in one last call. His Grace generously gave me tea to warm me up and ginger cakes to eat because I must have appeared hungry and bedraggled."

The dowager smiled. "I did not realize my son was so considerate."

Ailis tried not to grin, but Jonas's mother knew how much of a curmudgeon he was and had hit the mark with her comment. "I left as soon as we noticed it had begun to snow hard. But I made it no more than halfway down the drive when my mare slipped on a patch of ice and off I tumbled."

"Landing on your shoulder and badly injuring yourself," the dowager said with genuine sympathy.

"Yes. The fall left me stunned and I was in too much pain to even lift myself off the ground that was already covered in snow and ice. The next thing I knew, your son was at my side and comforting me to keep me calm. He carried me into the house and…"

Ailis sighed, for this explanation sounded awful, even though what happened next was completely innocent. "Your Grace, none of the bedchambers other than his were made up at the time. So he put me in here while he fixed my dislocated shoulder. He was brilliant, and I would have been in utter agony had he not known what to do. I also had a mild concussion from the fall, and—"

"Oh, you poor dear!"

"It was not my best day, I will admit. Your son decided it was best that I remain in here, since I would need watching around the clock for those first few days. Mrs. Fitch, or one of the household maids, was with me at all times. Your son was a complete gentleman, I assure you. Nothing..."

Well, he *had* kissed her with hot desperation.

She cleared her throat. "No one could have provided better care." But she groaned inwardly, knowing her face was now aflame, because how could she ever forget his exquisite kisses? "I wanted to go home, but he refused and insisted on waiting until the snowfall stopped. He would not place his staff in danger, you see."

His mother arched an eyebrow but said nothing, so Ailis pressed on. "The snow went on for days, as you well know, since you were forced to take refuge in one of the coaching inns for several days yourself. He had planned to deliver me home tomorrow, perhaps even this afternoon if there was enough of a thaw."

"But we arrived early."

Ailis nodded. "So I am now stuck here, poised to ruin my reputation because I am found where, under normal circumstances, I should not be. My good name is the dearest thing to me. In truth, it is everything to me."

She dared to meet the dowager's gaze and held steady. "Nothing untoward happened—I give you my word of honor. Your son is noble in every way."

The dowager remained silent, giving little of her thoughts away.

Ailis felt compelled to continue, although she really did not have to convince a mother about the qualities of her own son. "Your Grace, how did you manage to get here so quickly? The storm only ended this morning."

"It only ended in the Broadmoor valley this morning, but it had cleared out over a day ago where we were staying, just south of here.

Poor Edward rode on ahead and needlessly faced the tail end of the storm the entire way. He should have stayed put and come with us, but he insisted on getting here first. He says it was to give Mrs. Fitch time to ready the rooms and have meals prepared for us, but I'm sure his reasons had mostly to do with warning his brother."

"He only arrived a short while ahead of you," Ailis said. "I wanted to leave as soon as the snow stopped, but His Grace was concerned the roads were still too hazardous. Apparently, Lord Langford was wrong in confirming they were too dangerous to cross."

"Was this the only reason my son wanted you to stay?"

"He was not keen on having me here any longer than necessary. But he also had a medical concern about keeping me here an extra day or two. You see, he did not want me to resume my duties at the vicarage just yet. He was worried that I would start working too soon and strain my shoulder."

"Sounds reasonable," the dowager mused, casting her a sympathetic look. "Your uncle must be worried about you, however. Has my son sent word to him?"

Ailis nodded. "His Grace sent one of the grooms to tell him of my injury as soon as it happened. The lad's mother is the vicarage housekeeper and resides close to the church. Since the snow had only started a short time beforehand, he thought the boy could deliver the message and just stay home with his family to wait out the storm."

"Most considerate of my son."

She nodded again. "Yes, it was. He really is a fine man. It sometimes takes some doing to draw his good nature out of him. One must be persistent and tug hard."

Jonas's mother arched an eyebrow. "You seem able to do this."

Ailis gulped, realizing she might have been too casual in describing the duke. "Me? Oh, I am the worst at it. It often takes me three or four tries before that icy shell of his starts to thaw and he gives in to my requests." Now that she had poured her heart out to the dowager, she was not certain what would happen next. "Your Grace, I must leave. This must be obvious to you. But your son dares not have me go yet because…this innocent situation looks so bad."

The dowager's eyebrow was still arched, and yet revealed nothing of what this daunting woman was thinking.

Ailis pressed on. "Everyone will think it outrageously funny that the Duke of Ramsdale was caught with a young woman in his bedchamber. But I will be the one condemned and ruined for the mere sin of falling off my horse. I don't know how to protect myself from such infamy. Your son understands my concerns, and I hope he can come up with a plan to get me out of here quietly. I had a plan of my own. But what is the point of any of it now that you've seen me?"

The dowager had it in her power to destroy Ailis.

Would she do it?

The worry got to Ailis, and she began to cry.

The dowager took Ailis's hand in hers. "My dear, no one beyond me and my sons will ever know of your presence. Please do not fret about this. But you must realize you cannot be around him while these young ladies are here."

Ailis felt overwhelmed with relief. "I fully understand, Your Grace. I have no intention of interfering with your attempts to marry him off to one of those diamonds. In fact, I heartily agree with your efforts to see him happily settled. He should have attended to this years ago."

The dowager's expression turned wistful. "I know, but he's been through so much… I could not add to his burdens back then. However, I think enough time has passed and his awful wounds ought to have healed by now."

Ailis wished she knew more about the duke's past beyond the snippets of gossip that were probably distorted and false for the most part. She was about to commiserate with the dowager when the door suddenly burst open and Edward hurried in. "Miss Temple, I—"

He blanched upon seeing her seated beside his mother.

"Oh, hell." He adjusted the spectacles on his nose. "Jonas is going to be mad as blazes about this."

"Indeed," the dowager intoned. "*Jonas* is not the only one going to be mad as blazes. What was he thinking to leave Miss Temple in his bedchamber? Or put her in here in the first place? Fetch him for me, Edward. And kindly refer to your brother as Ramsdale. He is the duke now and has been for many years. He deserves to be addressed with due deference."

"He hates being addressed by his title," Edward muttered, but gave a curt bow and left to do her bidding.

It was not long before both brothers returned.

The duke was livid. To say that he was breathing fire was an understatement. His eyes were dark as ink. His expression was raw rage.

He looked dangerous, quite simply fearsome and frightening.

Despite everything, Ailis melted at the sight of him.

But he was not looking at her—his attention was fixed on his mother. "Give me one reason why I should not toss you and that gaggle of squawking geese in the parlor out on your arses right now," he said with a low and lethal growl. "Who gave you permission to enter my quarters?"

Ailis drew in a breath, surprised by the force of his anger. It was not aimed at her, but she did not want him taking it out on his mother, either. On impulse, she reached out to put a protective hand over the dowager's slender fingers.

The duke noticed the gesture.

So did his mother, who cast her a smile in response.

Ailis drew her hand away, realizing how inappropriate it was to touch the duchess, even if it was only meant to be a kindly comfort. "I'm sorry."

"Miss Temple, my mother does not need you to protect her from me," the duke said, his voice still low and dangerous. "But she does need to give me an explanation for invading my bedchamber."

Ailis swallowed hard and nodded.

The four of them were now enclosed in his bedchamber, for he had made certain to firmly shut that door behind him and close them all in the large room that had suddenly become as stifling as a tomb.

Wouldn't all his guests notice his absence? And especially think it odd to hold a family meeting in his bedchamber?

Had anyone followed him up here? Perhaps that someone already had their ear to the door.

The duke, looking quite fierce and imposing, folded his muscled arms across his chest. "Mother? Have you anything to say for yourself?"

The dowager tipped her chin up in defiance. "A mother can sense if something is troubling their children. I was merely worried about you and had to know if something bad was going on."

"Bad?" He glanced at Ailis, still scowling fiercely. "I am no child. You could have just asked me."

"And you would have lied to me, Ramsdale. Admit it. You were never going to tell me about Miss Temple."

"Because it is none of your business. It is no one's business," he shot back. "And now, I need to get her out of here and back to the vicarage with no one the wiser. If I hear so much as a whisper bandied about her among your entourage, I shall toss you all out in the cold."

"No one is going to hear about Miss Temple from me," his mother assured him. "She's a delightful young lady and explained her circumstances to me. Yes, I agree she must leave as soon as possible and keep well away from here. Now, how are we going to sneak her out?"

The duke raked a hand through his hair. "I haven't quite figured out a plan yet."

"I have one," Ailis offered, and told them about her mobcap idea and slipping out with the maids. "I could carry a pillow and use it to hide my face if anyone looks too closely."

The duke growled. "You are not to carry anything."

"But then—"

"Men!" his mother said with a sniff. "Here's what we are to do. Once everyone has come down to tea, Mrs. Fitch shall escort Miss Temple down through the servants' stairs into the kitchen. From there, Grimes will be summoned to escort her into your study."

"Why?" Edward asked.

His mother rolled her eyes. "Because Miss Temple has only just arrived to collect the charity donation Ramsdale has promised her uncle for the Christmas charity ball. Seeing he had company, she went around to the kitchen door so as not to interfere with the entertainment of his guests. Of course, Ramsdale will order Grimes to see Miss Temple into his study, where he will hand over the donation."

"But he has already done that," Ailis interjected. "I have his bank drafts in my reticule."

"My dear, hand them back to my son. Ramsdale, you are to make a show of handing them over to Miss Temple. After which, you will instruct Grimes to have your carriage readied."

"Why?" Edward asked.

"Because Miss Temple has foolishly walked here and your kindly brother does not want her walking all the way back to town on her own." The dowager turned to the duke, the situation completely under her command. "You shall instruct Edward to see her safely home. You may also inquire in the presence of company about her injured shoulder and admonish her for coming out in this bad weather to collect your promised donation. But that is all you will say to her. You are then to completely dismiss her from your mind and attend to your guests."

The duke once more folded his arms across his chest, which looked quite massive as he stood there puffed up and glaring at his mother. "You are telling me what to say and do?"

"Yes, Ramsdale. I am. There. Done. Miss Temple is safely out."

She tipped her chin into the air. "No need to thank me. I do it freely, and with a mother's loving heart."

"First of all," the duke said, his expression only a little less fierce than before, "stop referring to me as Ramsdale. You know I hate it."

"But you are the duke, no matter how much you refuse to acknowledge the fact. You have a duty to the Crown and to your family to maintain our good name."

"Second of all, I have no intention of putting on a show for the amusement of our guests."

"But you will do it for the sake of protecting Miss Temple's reputation," his mother retorted, matching his glower with one of her own.

Ailis liked that his mother appeared to be just as implacable as he was. The pair looked so much alike as they stubbornly stared at each other.

Edward noticed it, too, and grinned.

"The *show*, as you call it," their mother insisted, "is for the sake of Miss Temple. Everyone has to believe she has just arrived, that it is strictly business, that you have efficiently addressed it, and you are now sending her on her way."

She took a moment to study Ailis. "My dear, you are too pretty."

Ailis did not know how to respond to the remark, for it did not sound like a compliment.

Both sons snorted.

Ailis did not quite understand what their snorts meant, either. But Lord Langford was once again grinning, and the duke's lips were twitching as though he were struggling to squelch a smile.

"We'll have to dig up a silly hat for you to wear. Something hideous that hides much of your face. Edward, have Mrs. Fitch find something appropriate. A black hat, since black matches with everything. It is quite a useful color."

The dowager gave another pointed look at her sons, then slapped her hands to her thighs and rose. "There, all solved. I shall enjoy pretending to make your acquaintance, should Ramsdale choose to introduce you to his guests. However, I advise against your making too much of a show of it, son. Better to treat Miss Temple as one of the many tradesmen who call at your door."

Ailis readily agreed. She had no desire to be introduced to any of the Upper Crust currently populating his parlor.

The duke did not look pleased, but he nodded.

"And I further suggest you return downstairs now," his mother added. "I shall take over from here."

He growled.

She ignored him. "And do be witty and charming, Ramsdale. At least keep up the pretense of enjoying your guests until such time as Grimes draws you aside."

He growled again.

Ailis coughed to smother her laughter. He was a man, fully grown and powerful, and yet was having his ears boxed by his mother.

He turned to Ailis. "Give me the donations."

"Oh, yes." She rose and scurried to her reticule, finding it difficult to draw them out with just one available hand.

"Here, let me do it," the duke said, coming to her side and making her insides melt again because he was being gentle and protective as he set aside her hand and dug the bank drafts out himself. "I'm sorry about this, Ailis."

"Not at all your fault, Your Grace. I am immeasurably grateful for all you have done for me."

He tucked the bank drafts in an interior pocket of his jacket. "I may not have time for a private word with you later, not if this farce of a donation exchange is witnessed by one and all. Take care of yourself. Will you promise me?"

She nodded. "I will."

"Do not overdo it, for your shoulder is not yet healed."

She smiled at him. "I will be very careful not to strain it."

He cast her a wry smile, not quite believing her. "I'll send a maid and a footman down to you as soon as possible. In the meantime, rely on Mrs. Curtis for your needs. Do *not* attempt to lift anything heavier than a lacy handkerchief on your own."

She placed a hand over her heart. "My sacred oath."

Only then did his smile turn full and broad.

But it lasted only a moment before he turned away and called to his brother. "Let's head downstairs and set up Miss Temple's prison escape. Mother? Or should I refer to you as Napoleon Bonaparte?"

"Do not be so insolent, Ramsdale. You are not too big to drag to the woodshed and thrash. Yes, I'll follow you down in a moment." The dowager turned to Ailis once the two men had walked out. "My son might invite you to dine with us or take tea with us during our stay."

"I fully expect he will," Ailis replied. "He has already suggested it. I thought it was a nice idea at the time."

"But no longer," Jonas's mother insisted. "Please, my dear. It is important that you decline his invitation. Please do so for the sake of the dukedom. I would not ask this of you were it just the family in residence. But you do understand my concern, do you not?"

"Yes, it is time for him to…move on." Ailis felt an acute disappointment, but knew the dowager was right.

"Then do I have your promise? If he invites you to dine with us, you will refuse him?"

"Yes, I promise. I would never do anything to interfere with his choosing the right sort of woman to marry."

But Ailis was curious about the ladies the dowager duchess had brought along with her. She expected they were beautiful and quite accomplished, but were their hearts just as beautiful? The duke required someone willing to stand by him and support him, yet also challenge him when necessary.

The duke needed someone who made him smile because he did so little of it now.

Would any of these diamonds make him happy?

Chapter Ten

Jonas was in ill temper when he returned downstairs and was immediately accosted by the four young ladies his mother had insisted on tossing at him. "Your Grace, what a charming little house you have here. So quaint," Lady Viola cooed, pretending to like his abode when she clearly did not.

He noted the disappointment in her eyes and knew this young lady was a Londoner through and through. Langford Hall was a pleasant home but would never be mistaken for a grand estate. Not that he had any interest in acquiring a larger or more elegant residence when he was just by himself and this house set in the countryside near Broadmoor served him perfectly well.

Where he saw comfort and tranquility, she saw boredom and isolation.

Did she even know what a chicken looked like other than what was served on a dinner plate?

He cast her a forced smile. "Yes, I am quite happily settled here, Lady Viola. Wouldn't ever leave my beloved sanctuary were it not for my duties in Parliament."

"But surely you must enjoy Town life," she replied with a faltering smile.

"Not in the least. Nor would I allow my wife and children to endure the noise and rank odors of the city. No, it is Broadmoor for me and my family."

How much clearer did he need to be?

Lady Viola, miffed as could be, took it out on a passing footman who carried a tray of glasses filled with champagne, a strawberry in each. When he paused beside her to offer her a glass, she brushed the man brusquely aside, not caring that he almost spilled the entire tray onto the floor.

Paling, the poor footman struggled to right it, and then quickly moved on to offer a drink to the other guests.

Jonas was not surprised by the actions of this petulant princess, for he had escorted her around London several months earlier and found her to be just as insufferable then. She was all smiles for him, and would likely continue tossing pretty smiles his way. But was she so foolish as to believe he would not notice her behavior toward others?

Ready and eager to be relieved of having to converse with Lady Viola, he gave the nod to one of Edward's friends, the always strapped-for-funds Lord Pomeroy, remarking on what a pleasure it was to see him again.

The man was quick to catch on and scurried toward him, taking the seat beside the petulant princess that Jonas had just vacated. "May I remark on how divine you look, Lady Viola," Pomeroy said, his expression enraptured as he commenced fawning over her.

Jonas excused himself as the dutiful lord compared Lady Viola's hair to the golden sands of Arabia and her lips to rubies.

Right, time to go.

He caught young Pomeroy's wink at him and knew his broad smile was because of the wager placed in that infernal betting book contrived by Bromleigh, Lynton, and Camborne, the friends Jonas intended to throttle with his bare hands once he saw them again.

Jonas did not experience an ounce of guilt for the subterfuge. Lady Viola was an heiress and Lord Pomeroy was an earl's son in desperate need of money. Was there ever a more perfect match created? Plus, Pomeroy would also have the winnings of that ill-conceived bet if

Jonas failed to marry.

A winning situation all around.

The other three ladies, all beautiful and elegant, were now flicking their fans at him flirtatiously and laughing with a witty air when he asked, as any dutiful host would, whether they lacked any comforts for their stay.

It was just small talk, for he knew Mrs. Fitch was a wonder and would see they all had everything they needed supplied to their rooms.

But Hope Tenney gave it more meaning than intended and openly propositioned him, suggesting he might provide her comfort tonight. "I shall leave my door unlocked for you, Your Grace."

The other two ladies were not at all appalled and merely giggled.

Lady Willa smacked her fan against his shoulder. "I shall give you the better sport, Your Grace. Come to me first."

Egads.

He politely declined both offers. But he could see these young ladies would not be so easily thwarted. He would have to make up some excuse, a matter of his lumbago flaring, should the need arise. He was old enough that these little geese would believe he suffered from that ailment. Didn't all old men suffer from inflammations of one sort or another? Or so these young ladies would be quick to believe.

As the minutes droned on, Jonas wondered what was taking Grimes so long to come and collect him.

Fortunately, Edward and his other friend, Lord Whitcomb, had swooped in to rescue him from the amorous advances of Lady Willa and Lady Hope. By this time, Faith Tenney had moved away to peer at the underside of the vases and decorative plates in the drawing room, no doubt attempting to determine whether they were made by an artist of any importance.

He turned around to avoid her and almost knocked over the sister, Hope, who had left Edward and Whitcomb to silently come up behind him. "Do forgive me," he said, catching her before she fell.

She propositioned him again.

Blessed saints. Would he have to barricade his door tonight?

The Tenney sisters were firmly ruled out as marriage prospects.

Lady Willa was also ruled out, and not only because she had propositioned Jonas within ten minutes of greeting him. She was another debutante he had escorted around London earlier in the year. He knew her to be just as petulant and spoiled as Lady Viola.

Why had his mother brought them along when she must have known he would dismiss all of them as marriage prospects? Did she think so little of him as to believe he would discount love altogether?

It saddened him that she might think so, especially since his parents had enjoyed a love match. But it seemed this was not to be for him, and he now had to protect himself from these little schemers until the blessed day of their departure.

In the meanwhile, he had a bit of work to do in making clear to the parents and their spoiled offspring that marriage was out of the question for him even if he were ever caught in a compromising position with one of these diamonds. No one was going to strong-arm him into doing the "honorable" thing.

Besides, how was it honorable for their daughters to steal into his bed and trap him into marriage?

No, their schemes were never going to work on him. Not to mention, where was the dishonor when none of these young ladies were virgins?

This made him ache for Ailis and the ridiculous fact that she was almost thirty and had never been kissed before him. The soft, giving way she had responded to his kisses, that sincere sense of wonder in her lovely eyes when she had looked up at him after each kiss… How could he not feel touched to the very core of his heart?

Lady Willa drew him out of his thoughts by calling him over.

"How may I be of help?" he asked, straining to maintain his polite façade.

"Lord Whitcomb is being quite beastly to me," she said, pouting. "He insists on partnering me for cards tonight."

Jonas arched an eyebrow. "And this is beastly how?"

"I was hoping to partner with you." The girl batted her eyelashes at him, playing the coy dove. But he had seen Lady Willa stick her dainty foot out to purposely trip Lady Viola not two minutes earlier, a stupid ploy to make it appear as though Lady Viola was awkward.

How was he to survive the week?

And how could his own mother, usually an astute and discerning woman, not have noticed how impossibly *wrong* these ladies were for him? As his lack of interest became apparent, he hoped they would all take the hint and depart early.

He almost fell to his knees in relief when Grimes finally approached. "Your Grace, the church lady is here to see you," he intoned with impeccable lack of expression.

"Church?" Lady Willa said, giggling with an air of dismissal.

"Ah, yes. The donations I had promised. Escort her into my study, Grimes. I'll be along shortly." He lingered a moment or two, hoping to appear indifferent to Ailis's supposed arrival. "If you will excuse me," he said as all four young ladies gathered around him again. "Duty calls."

He walked out of the drawing room and strode into his study, eager to see Ailis once again, even though it had only been minutes since he had last set eyes upon her.

"Gad, where did they ever find that hat?" he said with a chuckle.

She was supposed to look hideous. But as she turned to him and looked up at him with her big eyes, he thought she was the prettiest thing he'd seen in an age.

Big things looked very good on her. His robe. Those red stockings that would have looked hideous on anyone else but made her look adorably elfin. Now this big hat that enhanced the sparkling beauty of her eyes.

"Hush," she warned as he leaned against his desk to stare down at her so primly ensconced in her seat. "Just give me the donations and let me be on my way."

"All right." But he made no move to withdraw the drafts from his jacket pocket.

She studied his expression and frowned. "What's wrong?"

"They are all hideous, Ailis. Truly, altogether hopeless. Spoiled, scheming. How could my mother do this to me? And they'll be here through Christmas. What are these exclusive girls' schools teaching them?"

"Why, back in my day," Ailis teased, putting on the voice of a grumpy old man, "young ladies knew how to behave."

Jonas laughed. "I forbid you to mock me, Miss Temple."

She smiled back at him.

Sighing, he withdrew the bank drafts. "Ah, Lord Tenney is watching us. He's strolled by the doorway twice now."

"But that is good. Now is the perfect time to see me out the door."

His heart thudded as he handed her the bank drafts and watched her struggle to tuck them in her reticule. "Don't help me," she whispered when he reached out to do just that. She managed to stuff them in, and then rose. "Do forgive me for interrupting you when you have guests, Your Grace. I shall not delay your return to your party. It is getting late, and I ought to be walking back before nightfall."

"You walked here, Miss Temple?"

"Yes, Your Grace."

Lord Tenney listened attentively while strolling by a third time.

But Jonas knew he and Ailis had their scene well scripted.

"I must insist on your using my carriage to get you home. I'll have Grimes order it readied. Do you mind waiting here while it is brought around? Grimes will fetch you when it is brought to the front. I do not wish to be rude, but I cannot ignore my guests."

"Not at all, Your Grace. I am so sorry for taking up your time." But her eyes implored him to wait another moment.

"What is it, Ailis?" he asked in a whisper.

"My mare is still in your stable."

He nodded. "Ah, and as for that other matter," he said, louder, "I shall send one of my staff around tomorrow with the other donation I promised you. Will that do?"

"Yes, Your Grace."

"Then I bid you good day." He almost made the mistake of kissing her, for the gesture felt so right and natural. And did he not owe her kiss number five still?

She shot him a warning glance. "Get out of here...please, please, Your Grace."

He laughed and strode out without another word.

God, but his heart ached.

Lord Tenney was still lingering beside the study, so Jonas shut the door behind him as he walked out in order to keep the man from wandering in and questioning Ailis. One good look at her and Tenney would notice she was quite beautiful. "Come have a drink with me," he said, and steered the curious lord back into the drawing room, where the others were all seated.

It took a monumental effort to avoid staring into the entry hall to watch Ailis as she left.

Odd, but a piece of his heart seemed to be leaving along with her.

His heart was still in a tormented ache when he retired to his own bed for the first time in days later that night. It was shortly after two o'clock in the morning when the card games ended, for most of the travelers were tired and many had escaped to their guest chambers after a late supper, skipping the card tables altogether.

But they would be refreshed by morning and eager for full days and nights of entertainment. Gad, how was he going to keep them amused for an entire week, perhaps longer if his stubborn-as-a-boar mother dared invite them to remain another week?

An entire fortnight with these people?

Inconceivable.

He undressed and slipped naked under the covers, inhaling the lavender scent of the freshly laundered sheets in the hope that a hint of Ailis might still linger. He was disappointed to discover there was not even a trace of her feminine scent left on his pillow covers or upon the mattress.

It was as though she had never been here.

Yet she had been, and his heart could not bear the loss of her presence.

How was he ever to return to normal now?

Which got him thinking about what he was doing with his life. The stillness of the night, this haunting quiet of the dark, did that to a man.

Having Ailis with him had been a revelation.

Oh, he'd taken women to bed before. This was not the revelation. What struck him was the unexpected splendor of taking the *right* woman into his bed. That was Ailis…and he had not even touched her beyond a few kisses.

He had a choice to make as he entered his forties and found himself sleeping alone in his big, empty bed. That choice had been simple before Ailis tumbled off her horse and shook him out of his comfortable routine.

A week ago, he had been content in his solitude. Resolved to his fate and set in his ways. Perhaps it was because the scars that marked his limbs and torso had convinced him to choose that path of isolation and keep things simple.

Yes, simple. No involvement meant no hurt.

But how could it be right?

After having Ailis with him these past few days, what had once felt settled now felt aimless.

His solitude, which he once equated with freedom, was beginning to feel like a prison.

This was due to Ailis and the way she filled his house with warmth. She had done nothing but be here, occasionally keeping him company, offering opinions or merely speaking from the heart, but mostly just recovering. Nonetheless, her presence brought about a profound change in the way he wanted to spend his days.

Was this not significant?

Of course it was, but did he dare do something about it when he was so scarred in body and soul? Those hideous marks all over his body were hidden by his clothing, but they were there and would be obvious when he undressed before a wife.

Would Ailis feel revulsion upon seeing them?

If anyone were capable of overlooking them and showing him nothing but compassion and acceptance, it would be her. Perhaps he would summon the courage to show her one day, for it was easy enough to roll up his sleeves and reveal his scarred forearms.

His doorknob began to jiggle.

He was not particularly concerned, because he had locked his door and jammed a chair against it for added security. But how galling to have to protect himself within his own home.

Sighing, he rolled out of bed to hunt in his wardrobe for his robe. As he wrapped it around his torso, he realized the garment still held the feminine scent of Ailis, that apple and honey scent that made him ache to taste her...and in no place proper.

He paused by the door, hoping whoever was attempting to get in would simply go away.

The doorknob jiggled again.

Then a soft grumble: "Drat. Mama, I don't think he is in his bedchamber. Do you think he is visiting someone else?"

Botheration.

Lady Willa.

The mother muttered something he could not make out. Not that it mattered, for their plan to set up a compromising situation was clear.

What a pair of simpletons.

Apparently, *his* message to these debutantes and their parents had not been clear enough. What did they not understand about his warning that he would *not* do the honorable thing if put in one of those contrived situations?

Not an hour later, the Tenney sisters attempted the same thing. He heard their giggles along with the jiggle of the doorknob, and realized they were both offering to join him for the night.

This could not continue. He would have to lay down the law with his mother. She needed to control her friends and their marriage-minded daughters.

But what an indignity! A grown man having to scold his own mother—and having to lock his bedroom door because he was unsafe in his own home.

Lady Viola was the only one who had remained in her bedchamber. That might have been a point in her favor had Pomeroy not discreetly informed him shortly before breakfast the following morning that he had spent the night with the young lady.

"I'm going to offer for her hand in marriage, Ramsdale. Do you have any objection?"

Jonas gave him a hearty clap on the back. "You have my sincere congratulations. Not a single objection. However, it is her father you need to convince."

"Will you put in a good word for me?"

Jonas nodded. "I doubt he will care for my thoughts on the matter, but I shall certainly encourage the match should he ask."

One debutante out of the way.

Three to go.

He called his mother and Edward into his study shortly after breakfast.

When they arrived, he shut the door behind them and ordered them to sit in the chairs in front of his desk. He stood in front of them, leaning against his desk as he folded his arms across his chest and stared down at their expectant faces. "What in blazes were you thinking in choosing these supposed ladies to bring here, Mother? I thought perhaps I was being too cautious by barricading my door, but *three* of the young ladies came to my door last night. *Three.*"

"Which ones?" she asked, not in the least appalled.

"That is not important. The fourth, by the way, entertained a gentleman in her room, which is the only reason she did not come knocking at my door last night."

"They didn't waste time, did they?" Edward remarked.

Jonas shook his head. "No." He returned his attention to his mother. "Need I point out that their behavior rules them out as potential brides? The last thing any man wants is a wife who will make him a cuckold. How am I to trust any of them to be faithful?"

His mother nibbled her lip, fretting for a long moment before responding. "But I thought you did not want to be burdened by a wife who will actually live with you once she has given you children. Is this not a perfect arrangement? You get your heirs and she gets to set up house in London and leave you in peace."

Jonas grunted. "That sounds completely horrid."

His mother sighed. "Then what do you want, Ramsdale?"

"To be left alone. Have I not made this clear enough to you? If you have bet on my marrying, then you have only yourself to blame when you lose the wager."

Edward was sitting back, his long legs stretched before him as he listened to Jonas bickering with their mother. "I have placed my bet," he said, "but I am not going to lose."

Jonas nodded. "Then you know I will not marry."

"Quite the opposite, my dear brother. I wagered like our beloved mother. I say that you *are* going to marry."

Jonas turned to him in surprise. "Then you are certainly going to lose, Edward. Not to mention that in doing so, you will betray your friends who are counting on my remaining a bachelor."

"I'll make it up to them," Edward said, sounding not in the least contrite.

Jonas frowned at him. "How? You do not have the blunt to make them whole."

Edward laughed. "But you do. I plan to borrow it from you."

Jonas could not help but laugh, much as he wished to remain serious.

But honestly, were all men plagued by such families?

He loved his mother and brother, of course. He also loved his younger sisters, who were both quite happily settled in London, married to fine husbands, and giving said husbands a host of children.

In truth, he could not ask for a better family, even though they could all be quite irritating. They claimed he was even more so, but he was the duke and had every right to be insufferable.

"Mother, let's cut short this farce. You need to find a way to send those young ladies and their parents home."

"No, I am not going to do it. You need to stop your holier-than-thou attitude and see these young ladies for the prizes they are. Granted, they were not taught the importance of a love match such as I happily shared with your father. Nor did I ever expect to marry for love, since ours was a negotiated arrangement. And yet it grew into a beautiful marriage filled with love and respect between us. These diamonds are excellent matches in every regard. And who is to say they will not grow to love you?"

"They'll grow to *hate* me, is what they'll do. If I marry, it will be to someone I can trust to keep her legs shut to other men." He grunted as he raked a hand through his hair. "I am leaving the two of you in charge of entertaining our guests for the day."

"Where will you be?" his mother asked.

"Seeking refuge at the vicarage. I'm going to look in on Miss Temple because she is another one with a mind of her own and is going to damage her shoulder by attending to church business when she ought to be resting." He took a deep breath. "I am going to invite her and her uncle to supper tonight."

His mother shot to her feet. "You cannot."

"Why not?" Jonas asked.

"The other ladies will believe she is their competition and…" She emitted a defeated sigh. "They might not be very nice to her."

"Their competition? That is laughable," he retorted, even though she had perhaps struck too close to home. "Well, good. So what? Let them think I am considering her, and we shall see their true colors come out, won't we?"

"At the expense of Miss Temple's hurt feelings?" Edward frowned. "Is this the only reason you want her here? To give others the impression that she has captured your heart? But that is quite a low thing for you to do if she hasn't, and now you are making her think that there could be something more between the two of you. Giving her that hope is not only low, but cruel, especially if you are only using her to chase the others away. You do realize you would be tossing her to the wolves."

"I'll protect her," Jonas said with a stubborn set to his jaw, for he would never let anyone hurt Ailis, and how could his brother believe otherwise?

Edward seemed unconvinced. "You cannot repel their onslaught once it begins. I thought you had a better understanding of this Marriage Mart business. It is cutthroat. Ruthless. Miss Temple will be defenseless against their attacks."

"I am sending her the invitation. You underestimate Miss Temple's abilities. I will make it up to her if anyone insults her."

"And will you also make certain she understands you have no interest in her? That you asked her here to endure the mockery of others just for your convenience and nothing more?"

Jonas let out a heavy breath. "I'll see you later. I have to get out of here."

He strode out, leaving his mother and brother gaping at him. They began whispering between themselves before he had even made it out of the study. Obviously plotting something to do with him.

Were there not enough plots and counterplots going on already under his own roof?

"Grimes, have my carriage readied."

The reliable butler regarded him with some surprise. "At once, Your Grace. Will you be riding out with company?"

"No, I shall be blessedly on my own. My mother and Lord Langford will attend to the guests for the rest of the day."

"And should a guest ask where you have gone? What may I tell them?"

"It is no one's business, that's what you are to tell them."

"Very good, Your Grace," Grimes said with all solemnity, and remained watching Jonas as he climbed into his carriage a few minutes later.

"To the vicarage, Clarkson."

It did not escape Jonas's notice that Grimes broke into a wide smile upon hearing his destination.

Why? Merely because he was off to see Ailis? Why should he *not* see her when she was injured? And was it not his duty to see to her wellbeing?

Chapter Eleven

Ailis had just climbed onto a footstool in the vicarage's drawing room to give the shelves a light dusting when she heard a man's deep growl coming from behind her. In the next moment, big arms encircled her waist as she was scooped up and then gently set back on her feet, this time on the steady wood floor.

She turned to face the culprit, knowing exactly who he was, since she had recognized that delicious growl that sent tingles skimming through her body.

"Your Grace? What brings you here this morning?" It was a bright, sunny day, which was why she had felt the need to do a little cleaning, since sunshine seemed to expose the balls of dust gathered atop the shelves. "Your Grace? Are you just going to stand there glowering at me?"

He still had his hands on her waist, his touch warming her to the point of blushing.

"Temple," he said sternly, "did I or did I not tell you to take it easy when you returned home?"

Ah, he was irritated with her. Hence his referring to her as *Temple* rather than *Miss Temple* or merely *Ailis*.

She tipped her chin up and tossed him a stubborn look. "You did, and I am doing just that. Since when is light dusting—"

"You might have fallen off the footstool, especially as unbalanced as you are with a healing shoulder and your arm encumbered by a sling."

He had a point, but she refused to acknowledge it.

"What are you doing here?" He was not the only one who could toss admonishments. Was he not supposed to be at Langford Hall, reveling in the admiration of the *ton's* most beautiful women?

"Do not change the subject." He emitted another of those sensual, lionlike growls that shot more tingles through her. "Why are you doing any work at all?"

Instead of releasing her, he drew her closer.

She could not overlook that he still had his arms wrapped around her waist. His touch felt awfully nice, but she was never going to acknowledge this either.

Nor would she ever admit he had gained a firm hold on her heart, a grip she found extremely troubling and unexpected. She hadn't realized just how deeply she was drawn to him until spending last night alone in her bedchamber and aching for his company.

Really aching for him.

This was the true reason he had caught her doing light chores around the house today. She needed to keep busy in order to get her mind off him. And now, his coming around to the manse when he should have been entertaining his guests was not helping at all.

"Which of the ladies is your favorite?" she asked, ignoring his question, since she was never going to answer him honestly and reveal *he* was the reason she was too unsettled to rest in her bed. "Or is it too soon to select a favorite?"

"It isn't too soon. My mind was easily made up."

"Ah, after only a few minutes in their company? You are quite the decisive man. So, which diamond did you choose?"

"None of them." He frowned again. "Not a single one of them is suitable, as I believe I mentioned yesterday."

She noticed he was gritting his teeth as he awaited her response to this statement—an outrageous statement at that, since it had taken these young ladies a week to travel here, and he had already dismissed them before a full day had passed.

"I will not be a party to your bad behavior," she remarked. "You cannot escape them by pretending you need to see about my health."

"It isn't a pretense. I would be here even if I adored all four of those young ladies, which I absolutely do not. Each one is a complete and utter mismatch, a monumentally inconvenient waste of time for me."

"I see. Complete *and* utter. That is quite decisive." She attempted to take a step back in order to slip out of his grasp.

He tugged her closer instead, apparently not ready to let her go just yet. Not that she minded his nearness, for he was big and handsome, and his scent was always nice. A hint of fruit, spice, and maleness.

But someone might walk in on them and misconstrue the situation.

She cleared her throat. "As you can see, I am fine. You ought to return to your guests now."

"No, Temple. You shall not be rid of me so easily."

"No?" She placed a hand on his chest, intending to nudge him back a step, but his body felt so warm and solid beneath her palm that she scandalously allowed it to linger there. She enjoyed the strong, steady beat of his heart.

Was it beating that little bit stronger for her?

Hers was in a mad flutter.

Again, not something ever to admit to him.

She let out a soft breath and looked up at him. "May I speak honestly, Your Grace?"

He finally managed a smile, albeit a small one, and she could tell by the light twitch of his lips that he was struggling not to let it come forth.

A pity, for he had a divine smile.

Divine lips, too.

"You are asking my permission?" Now his smile fully burst forth. "Why bother to ask me now when you have never done so before? Don't you always speak your mind, Ailis?"

Ah, he was liking her again. *Ailis*. It felt so nice to hear her name come out in the deep rumble of his voice.

She cleared her throat again. "Well, yes. I do my best to always be honest with you. With anyone, in truth. But I also try to be kind, for I never wish to hurt anyone's feelings."

"Are you about to hurt mine?" He was still smiling, so she did not think he was overly concerned about what she was going to say.

"No, Your Grace. I never would."

He gave her cheek a light caress. "Go on, then, speak your mind."

She licked her lips and cleared her throat yet again, then took several deep breaths while trying to collect her thoughts.

He laughed. "Ailis, stop making sounds like a little chicken and just tell me."

She nodded. "All right, here goes…and these are my sincere and honest feelings. You must not mistake them for pandering or mere flattery. What I would like to say is that the world needs wonderful men like you. The world needs *offspring* from wonderful men such as you. This is why you must marry."

He arched an eyebrow. "Ah, that is quite the revelation."

"Why are you surprised that I think so highly of you? Most people do. My point is, who will lead us in the next generations if not the children and grandchildren of these rare men of intelligence and valor?"

"Such as myself?"

She nodded again. "They do not spring from the ground like wheat stalks or root vegetables. These exceptional people must come from somewhere equally exceptional—for example, from their forefathers. Oh, I am not saying you are the only source. But I think you are a vital and important influence."

He grinned. "And what of you, Ailis? Should such exceptional children not also come from exceptional mothers? Do they not need to be nurtured by intelligent, compassionate women like yourself? This is perhaps more important than any impression a father might have on their upbringing."

"Perhaps, and I agree that mothers are also vitally important. But how would I ever qualify as someone exceptional? My influence does not extend beyond the parishioners of this church, and it is merely one of several in Broadmoor. Your influence, on the other hand, impacts the entire country and even extends to other nations."

"You hold me in too high regard," he insisted. "And need I point out that siring offspring with a woman who is spoiled, short-tempered, and shortsighted is not going to create these splendid children you seem to think will lead us into the future?"

"Are all the diamonds visiting you so awful?"

He shrugged and finally took a step back, releasing her. "Perhaps not quite as bad as I make them out to be, but I am not so far off the mark. They are not right for me."

She set aside her feather duster and motioned for him to take a chair so they could sit and talk. "Surely you must have come across some intelligent, thoughtful, and compassionate young ladies in your time in London. I cannot believe there is no one out there who would suit you to perfection."

"There might be," he admitted, "but she is definitely not one of those four. In any event, all is not what it seems."

"What do you mean?" She frowned, for he was being mysterious suddenly. "What is it that I am not seeing, Your Grace?"

He took a deep breath. "Ailis, can I trust you?"

Her eyes widened. "Of course you can. I promise you this. Have I ever given you reason to doubt me?"

His expression turned thoughtful. "You earned my trust years ago and have never let me down."

Having said that, he remained silent a long moment.

But this extended silence only added to her confusion.

She became even more confused when he began to remove his jacket. Of course, he still had on his cravat, a lovely forest-green silk that looked quite elegant on him, a waistcoat also of forest-green silk shot through with threads of silver, a shirt of finest white lawn, and buff trousers that molded to his long legs.

Her heart beat a little faster as he undid the cuff of his sleeve. "What are you doing?"

He cast her a wry smile. "Ailis, stop fretting. I am not going to take off my clothes in front of you."

She let out a breath and chuckled. "Oh, how disappointing," she teased. "I was hoping you would put on a show for me."

She expected him to grin, but his expression suddenly sobered and a glint of pain shone in his eyes. "You would not say that if you had to look upon this for the rest of your life." He rolled up his shirt sleeve and exposed what appeared to be burn marks that ran up the length of his forearm. "It is the same on my other arm and my legs."

"Jonas," she said in a strangled whisper, unable to imagine the incredible pain he must have experienced when suffering those burns.

Her heart broke. It simply broke into a thousand pieces, and she wished she could say something or do anything to make his past anguish and suffering magically disappear.

"Jonas," she repeated softly, hoping he would not take offense by the familiarity, since he had asked her several times to refer to him by his given name. Was it not right that she should do so now? "Do these scars still hurt you?"

"No, Ailis," he replied as she reached out to gently touch his arm. "The physical pain has mostly passed."

But the cost to his heart, to his happiness, must have been insurmountable. This explained why he held himself off from everyone.

This was why he settled for quick entanglements to satisfy his urges, for he only needed to lower the falls of his trousers and…

She turned away a moment when she felt her cheeks suffuse with heat.

He believed there could never be any real intimacy between him and a young lady because of these wounds. But who would care when he had so many fine qualities? His scars would be insignificant when compared to his valor, his honor, and his intelligence. Not to mention his exceptionally good looks.

He also had a wonderfully wry sense of humor, which he displayed whenever dealing with her. He often made her laugh, even when he was being cantankerous and curmudgeonly.

But the grim, dour duke he presented to the world was not his true self. This was him being defensive and pushing others away to ensure they would never get too close and break his heart by rejecting him.

He released a heavy breath. "Ailis, I forbid you to weep over me. Why in blazes are you crying?"

The tears trickled down her cheeks, and not only because she felt an intense sympathy for his pain. She was crying because he was trusting her with this deep secret, with his weakness that he had hidden from everyone for all these years. That he would lay his heart bare before her meant everything.

"I cannot help it. Will you kiss me now, please?"

He shook his head and laughed softly. "Ailis, I cannot make sense of you. Why would you want to kiss me after I have shown you this?"

"Because I now understand you better, as you expected I would. This was entirely the point of your showing me this glimpse into your past and the suffering you endured, was it not? I thought you were a wonderful man before this moment, but now I think you are incredibly and amazingly wonderful. My heart is bursting with pride for you and in knowing you. My heart is also experiencing myriad other feelings that I cannot describe because I do not understand them all myself."

"Not pity, I hope."

She pursed her lips. "No, pity isn't among the feelings that have my heart in a roil. Admiration. Respect. Ache because of all you have been through and suffered. Sorrow because you chose to handle this enormous pain on your own."

"How else would I manage it? In truth, it was not hard for me to do."

"Because you desperately wanted to protect yourself from those who might revile and hurt you."

He cast her an indulgent look. "Do you truly believe I care what other people think? You ought to know me better by now."

She shook her head. "It isn't people in general that you are protecting yourself from. What you are doing is guarding your heart from the one special person you could love forever. That rejection would be the worst for you, so you have dealt with this problem by choosing to push every young lady away before you can ever develop feelings for her. But I cannot imagine their ever *not* loving you."

"Ailis, I do not need false flattery from you. I do not lack in confidence. Arrogant duke here," he said with a wry smile, "lest you forget."

"I am not trying to flatter you. In fact, I am angry with myself for assuming you were aloof and cantankerous when you are not this way at all. I also assumed you were full of yourself due to your exalted rank."

"Full of myself?" His look of surprise quickly turned to one of amusement. "Are you calling me a blowhard?"

She cast him a soft smile and sniffled as more tears fell. "You were never a blowhard. I am explaining myself all wrong. You have a strong sense of duty to those in your demesne, but we have never been a mere duty to you. You have never dismissed us…or dismissed *me*, even though I am often quite irritating."

"No, Ailis. You are persistent, but never truly annoying. I never minded your visits."

"I hope you know that I always liked and admired you. I think your humanity shone through despite the mask you always wore."

"And now, my mask has come down and you know the truth about me," he said in all seriousness. "You are among the very few who know."

"Among the few?"

"Well, my doctors know. Grimes does, out of necessity. Edward, too."

"This is why your brother admires you so much."

That he thought enough of her to reveal these deep wounds... Could she mean more to him than he had ever let on? She thought their ten kisses were merely for amusement, but had she been mistaken and they represented more?

"I thank you for this, for the trust you have shown in me," she said with all sincerity. "I will never let you down, I promise."

He took her hand in his. "You never have. I do not doubt your integrity. This is why I decided to show you who I really am and what compels me to act the way I do."

"But why choose to do this now?" She eyed him curiously, not certain what else he wanted of her. Was he merely seeking a friend because his house was presently overrun? Would he have confided the truth about his wounds had his mother not brought these *ton* diamonds to Langford Hall?

Well, she would see where this next step led. She would like to be friends with him, the reliable confidante he could turn to when he needed to talk about the torments hidden in his heart and know his confidences would never be betrayed.

Yes, a good friend.

Would he ever accept her as someone more?

And yet...was she completely misunderstanding his intentions?

Was he revealing his scars because he meant to push her away, just like he pushed away everyone else?

"Your Grace, did—"

"*Jonas.* That is my name and I want you to use it. You and I are not going back to that formal nonsense."

"All right. *Jonas*, why did you show me the burns on your arm? Did you think I would no longer want your kisses because of this disfigurement?"

He shrugged. "I wasn't sure. But this was the only way I could find out for certain. Odd, isn't it?"

"That you trusted me?"

He nodded. "However, rest assured that I will never hold you to our bargain if my scars do offend you."

"Offend me?"

"Yes, it is the expected response. Isn't it? Utter revulsion."

She gasped. "If that isn't the most foolish thing I have ever heard come out of your mouth in years. If you were not a duke, I would already be kicking your shin. Your scars do not repulse me. They will *never* repulse me. If anything, understanding you better now, I wish I had bargained for twenty kisses. Forty kisses. A hundred more!"

He shook his head, once again grinning. "Ailis, you do not have to say this because you think I wish to hear it."

"And you ought to know I would never simply say something I did not believe just to pander to you. Is this not my weakness whenever I am around you? That I cannot keep my mouth shut and must voice my *honest* opinion whether asked for or not. So, will you please kiss me now before others walk in and the moment is lost?"

"Gad," he muttered, "you truly are something else."

"Something good, I hope."

He drew her out of her seat so that she now stood before him. "Number five," he said with a husky rumble that turned her legs to water. "Close your eyes, Ailis."

She had been staring up at him, wondering how she was ever going to escape falling in love with him after this. Perhaps she was meant to love him, even if it was unrequited. But was his friendship not a valuable thing in its own right? "My eyes are closed and I am breathlessly awaiting magical number five."

His lips sank onto hers with just the perfect mix of scorching heat and soul-searing tenderness, a kiss that somehow retained all its power and yet was achingly gentle.

It was a kiss that demanded her surrender but did not force it.

He understood—perhaps on instinct, since experienced men such as he seemed to understand a woman's body and the cravings of a woman's heart—that whatever she gave of herself had to be done willingly, for that was the true magic of a kiss.

Of course, such men as this duke knew how to be quite persuasive. His kiss embodied all the confidence and arrogance that had made him the man he was, but with it, he was also giving her a secret piece of his heart.

Or was she misunderstanding this treasured fifth kiss?

Perhaps nothing of his heart was meant to come with the tantalizing thrill of his lips as they plundered and probed hers. But what beautiful lips he had, commanding and yet tender as they moved in that hot, slow grind over hers.

Nor could she resist the perfection of his muscled arms as he held her in his protective embrace.

How could there ever be a better man or a better kiss than this one?

Her head began to spin. She felt claimed and possessed, as though kiss number five had branded her as his forever and she belonged to him now.

But could he ever belong to her?

She did not think so.

She would dream of him and dare no more, for powerful dukes did not fall in love and marry the spinster nieces of a village vicar.

"Ailis," he whispered, ending the kiss with a groan, "join me tonight at Langford Hall. I would like you and your uncle to come for supper. I'll send my carriage around for you."

She took a moment to restore order to her reeling senses. "Oh dear. I cannot. Please do not ask me. I really cannot."

He frowned. "Why ever not? I thought you were amenable to this."

"I was, but then your mother insisted…and so I promised her I would not accept your invitation if you offered it to me." She searched his face and noted his irritation. "Just as I would never betray a promise to you, nor would I betray a promise to your mother. Do not look at me that way. And please do not let go of me just yet. I am still in a swoon over this last kiss."

"It cannot be much of a swoon if you are still clearheaded enough to reject my invitation," he grumbled.

"I am not rejecting it, merely explaining why I cannot accept it. Would you think me so honorable if I broke my promise to your mother? And I do not need an answer to that question. I know you would be disappointed if I blithely broke oaths."

He moved away now that she seemed to be on steadier footing, and raked a hand through his hair. "Why did you make her that promise?"

"Because she asked me not to interfere with your chance at happiness. This is what we both want for you."

"But I have made it clear to you that none of those young ladies will do."

"Then speak to your mother about allowing me out of my oath. Even then, I do not think it is a good idea for me to attend."

"Why not?"

"Because it is an insult to those young women. Need I point out it is also an insult to me? They will think I am your… I cannot even say what they will think I am to you. Nothing respectable, I assure you."

"Ailis, I will not take no for an answer."

"*Jonas*, that is too bad, because it is the only answer I can give you." Overset that their beautiful kiss would be forgotten as they bickered, she resorted to helping him as he rolled up his sleeve, fastened the cuff, and donned his jacket. Although she was not really of any help to him at all while her arm was in a sling, so doing things one-handed was proving very difficult. "By the way, I loved kiss number five."

He sighed. "You are now trying to assuage my hurt feelings."

She smiled up at him. "I am doing no such thing. Remain irritated and bad tempered, if you wish. But unless you see a way around my promise to your mother, I shall not be accepting any invitations you send me."

"Gad, you can be stubborn."

"I am merely trying to be honorable. If you cannot accept this, then I thank you for your visit and for sharing your heart with me. I hope you will do so whenever you need a shoulder to lean on."

He tucked a finger under her chin. "Your shoulder is still healing. Never worry that I shall require its gentle support anytime soon. And never think you have won this round."

"What do you mean?"

"You shall be coming to supper at Langford Hall tonight, and it shall be done without your breaking a promise to my mother." He kissed her on the nose. "*That* kiss does not count."

She ignored the remark because she had no intention of counting that sweet peck as worthy of kiss number six. They had set the ground rules days ago. Only a kiss on the lips would count.

But she was more curious about his prior statement.

How was she to dine at Langford Hall without breaking her promise to his mother?

Chapter Twelve

Ailis was stretched out on her bed moping in her bedchamber when her uncle knocked at her open door. "Do come in, Uncle Nigel," she said, forcing a smile.

He studied her with some concern. "How are you feeling, Ailis? Well enough for company?"

"Yours? Or is someone else coming over?" There was nothing on their schedule tonight. She knew this because she was the one in charge of her uncle's appointments and knew none had been made for this evening.

"No one is visiting us, but we are invited to dine at Langford Hall tonight and I have accepted on our behalf."

She inhaled lightly and scampered off her bed to come to his side. "You accepted?"

He nodded. "The duke extended me the invitation on his way out."

"He did? What were his exact words?"

He eyed her quizzically. "What does it matter? He asked me to join him tonight and suggested I could bring you along if I wished, but the choice was mine. Ailis, I said I would bring you with me. I thought you would enjoy attending an elegant dinner party."

"The clever cur." She shook her head and laughed softly, although she was miffed by Jonas's obvious ploy. Since the duke knew she would reject him if he invited her outright, he had asked her uncle instead. If her uncle were the one to invite her, then she was not breaking her promise to his mother by attending, or so he obviously reasoned.

But she would certainly be breaking her promise in spirit. "I cannot go, Uncle Nigel."

"Truly? I thought you enjoyed the duke's company."

"I do…it isn't that."

Her uncle scratched his head. "If you are not up to going, then I shall not go either. I'll send our regrets."

"Oh, but you must attend. The duke will be offended if you refuse him. However, he will understand my reason for begging out. He knows I am still recovering from my dislocated shoulder, since he is the one who fixed it and has been tending to it the last few days. Besides, I am sure there is planning to be done for our Christmas ball that I have neglected. I shall be fine on my own."

"As you wish, dearest." He shrugged and turned to walk out. "I just thought you would enjoy the company of other young ladies. Wouldn't it be a nice change from putting up with an old codger like me?"

"I love spending time with you. As for those elegant ladies…" Ailis knew she was fairly naïve about many things, but her uncle was genuinely hopeless if he believed these *ton* diamonds would ever welcome her presence. "Another time, maybe."

He paused at her doorway and took another moment to study her. "No, Ailis. I think you ought to go. His Grace did not come right out and insist upon your presence, but I got the distinct impression he wants you there. You've just said he took good care of you while you were at Langford Hall. I think his feelings would be hurt if you ignored the invitation."

"You think the duke has feelings?"

He tossed her a cautionary look.

She sighed. "Very well, I'll go. But I shall need Mrs. Curtis's help getting ready."

Her uncle smiled. "I'll run downstairs and catch her before she leaves."

As the eight o'clock hour approached, the duke's carriage rolled around to pick them up. Her uncle was waiting for her by the front door, but he began to cough as she approached, not knowing whether to laugh or cringe. "Ailis, what in heaven's name?"

"I have no idea what you mean," she muttered, almost tripping as she stepped out the door and would have taken a tumble had her uncle not been in front of her to break her fall. It was these wretched spectacles she had borrowed from him, an old pair he had tossed in his bureau and not worn in ages.

"Ailis, why are you wearing my spectacles? And your hair…what have you done to it?"

She smiled brightly. "Do you like it? I thought I would try a new style."

"Oh? It looks like two cats were caught in an alley fight atop your head. And your gown…"

"It is different, don't you think?"

"It is hideous. My dear, what is going on?"

"You needn't fear, Uncle Nigel. The duke will understand completely." She climbed into the waiting carriage with his assistance and told him all about her promise to the duke's mother that Jonas was determined to have her ignore. "He finessed us all by inviting *you*, knowing *you* would in turn invite me. Is this not a despicable thing to do?"

"Well, he wishes to see you. I do not see how that is bad. Or perhaps he means to teach his mother a lesson, for she ought to have known better than to meddle and secure that promise from you. I wonder why she did it?"

"Because she does not want me around while those elegant ladies attempt to gain his attention."

"But how would you distract him? Do you think the duke has developed an interest in you? He did take excellent care of you during the snowstorm. Or is it that he feels sorry for you because your arm is in a sling?"

"Probably the latter. You know what a private person he is. He does not like strangers being foisted on him, even if it is from his well-meaning mother." She glanced out the window as the carriage made its way out of the village and toward Langford Hall. The roadway was a snowy expanse and slow going, since much of it had yet to melt, and the little that had melted left puddles and ruts that would damage a fast-rolling carriage wheel.

"I think he extended the invitation to both of us," Ailis continued, "because we have known him for years and he feels comfortable around us."

"But his mother wants his attention on the young ladies and not on you, is that it?"

"Quite so."

"Is it likely? I understand she has brought along the *ton's* most beautiful debutantes. You are lovely, too. I do not mean to imply you are not. But these are England's loveliest ladies, and…" Her uncle chuckled. "He will choke when he sees you in that hideous outfit and your hair—oh, Ailis—and that abomination you call a hat. What have you done?"

"Nothing that cannot be easily undone," she assured him. "The duke needs to be taught a lesson."

He arched an eyebrow. "I'm not sure what lesson this will teach him."

"The point is, I should not be around him and his marriage prospects. He knows how I feel about this and has chosen to ignore my wishes. So, this is the Ailis he will get," she said, glancing down at her attire and giving her hair a light pat.

It was a short distance to Langford Hall, and they arrived in little time.

Grimes stepped forward to assist her out of the carriage, took one look at her, and emitted a coughing laugh. "Miss Temple, don't you look lovely tonight."

"No, I do not," she said, grinning at the kindly butler. "But thank you for your attempt at politeness."

He cleared his throat. "Let me show you into the drawing room. All the other guests are gathered there."

Grimes led the way as Ailis walked in on her uncle's arm, needing to hold on to him or she would smack into walls, for these spectacles were making her eyes blur and giving her a monumental headache into the bargain.

Perhaps she ought to have left off those spectacles.

A big, dark blotch suddenly appeared before her as she entered the drawing room. She recognized the blotch as the duke by the familiar and delicious scent of him. "Good evening, Your Grace."

It took him a moment to reply while he was struggling to restore his even breaths. Much like Grimes, he was choking back a laugh...or so she assumed, because she really could not see him clearly.

"Blessed saints, Temple." He once again emitted a mix of groans and barely suppressed chuckles. "Is that a chicken sitting atop your head?"

"Very funny, Your Grace. It is a hat."

"A hat? Egads. I am going to rupture my spleen holding back my laughter. What in blazes? Is this your revenge for having to attend this dinner party?"

She tipped her chin up. "I have no idea what you are talking about."

But of course it was.

He was forcing her to renege on the spirit of an oath made to his mother, and she was not going to let him get away with it. Also, this was for her own protection. She did not want his *ton* diamonds thinking she was competition and doing something mean to her.

She was rather proud of the feathers she had stuck in her hat, and thought herself awfully clever for plucking them out of her mattress and fastening them to the stiff material. If this did not put everyone off, then nothing she did ever would.

When the duke's brother joined them, Jonas made a show of introducing him to her—since he was not supposed to know her—and to her uncle. "A pleasure to meet you, Vicar Temple."

"Pleased to meet you, Lord Langford. It is nice to see His Grace surrounded by loving family, especially at this time of the year."

"Ah, yes. Ramsdale was so overjoyed to see me and our mother that he sobbed hysterically," Edward intoned. "And who is this ravishing creature on your arm, Vicar Temple?"

"Creature is right," the duke muttered, for it did look as though she was sporting a chicken on her head. "Come, vicar. Let me introduce you to my mother."

He left Ailis alone with Edward, who immediately broke into laughter. "Dear heaven. You are an utter joy, Miss Temple."

"Why, thank you," Ailis replied, grinning. "I hoped to make just the right fashion statement."

"Indeed, no one is going to forget the way you look tonight. Can you see anything through those spectacles?"

"No," she admitted. "A complete blur."

"Then I shall stay close to you and offer my arm to lead you into the dining room. Oh, gad. Miss Temple, you are brilliant. You should have seen the look on my brother's face when you walked in. His expression was priceless."

"I'm sorry I missed it. I expect he was not pleased."

"You do realize he is not going to let you get away with besting him. He's very competitive, you know. But do not be fooled by his frown. He likes that you are giving him a hard time. He may not like to lose, but he loves a challenge. You are decidedly that. Oh, he keeps glancing this way." Edward chuckled again. "He's smiling. You are a miracle worker. I cannot recall the last time he has done that."

"What, smiled?"

Edward nodded. "Yes. Not to put a damper on the evening, but you have no idea how badly damaged he was when he returned from the war. We were afraid he would never recover, and although his body has healed, his heart hasn't...until now. Uh oh. Stiff upper lip—my mother is approaching."

"Good gracious, Miss Temple...I am left speechless," the duchess said, inspecting Ailis from head to toe. "Your gown...your hat... I have never seen anything quite like it."

And hope never to again, Ailis surmised.

"Bewitching, isn't she?" Edward said, unable to suppress a chortle.

"Edward, do be serious," the duchess intoned, but she did not sound curt or irritated, merely amused. She and her son were now grinning at Ailis. "Truly, my dear. You have outdone yourself."

"I can explain—" Ailis said.

The duchess held up her hand. "No explanations necessary. Your uncle told me all I needed to know. My son can be headstrong." She laughed lightly. "But I think he has met his match in you. Well done, Miss Temple. Shall I introduce you around?"

"It isn't necessary. I cannot see a blessed thing with these spectacles on, and none of the diamonds will be interested in meeting me."

The big, dark blotch appeared in front of her again. "I beg to differ, Miss Temple," the duke said with a touch of lethality to his voice. "They will be most eager to meet the belle of Broadmoor. Come with me."

But first, he plucked the spectacles off her nose and tucked them into his breast pocket. "You will injure your eyes if you keep them on all night. Honestly, Temple. You need to take better care of yourself."

He then took hold of her by the elbow of her uninjured arm and led her toward a stunning blonde he introduced as Lady Viola Carstairs.

The young woman gave a curt nod, then ignored Ailis while engaging the duke in flirtatious conversation. Oh, she was all smiles for him, and—

"Ouch!"

"Miss Temple, are you all right?" the duke asked, looking genuinely concerned.

"Dear me," Viola said with a dismissive giggle, "did I accidentally step on your foot? Perhaps you ought to go sit in a corner and rest it, Miss Semple."

"Miss *Temple*," the duke corrected her. "If you will excuse us, I must introduce her to my other guests."

He moved Ailis away from this first diamond. "Did I not tell you they were not to be trusted? Is this truly what you wish for me? How is your foot?"

"It will recover."

He let out a breath. "I am going to seat you beside me while we dine, and do not dare utter a word of protest. It has all been arranged. Lord Pomeroy will be seated beside Viola, and Lord Whitcomb over there," he said, nodding to a nice-looking young man who appeared to be in his cups, "will attend to Lady Willa Montroy. That's her over there, flirting with my footman."

Ailis looked up at him in dismay. "Are they really as bad as they appear?"

"Yes. And these two are the best of the lot my mother has brought with her. Over there are the Tenney sisters."

"They seem nice enough."

He grunted. "Do not be fooled. They have no scruples whatsoever."

Ailis furrowed her brow. "Your Grace, does this not strike you as most odd?"

"What? That not one of them is suitable for me? I could have told you that before any of them arrived. This is why I dislike London. It is all about social rules that everyone breaks, and yet they are all quick to condemn others who do the same. The sin is not in the doing but in the getting caught."

"This does not feel right." However, Ailis said nothing more as he introduced her to several more guests who also flicked her aside as though she were a flea on their shoulder. But this was as much her fault for purposely dressing as though she had just been chased out of a henhouse.

True to his word, the duke placed her in the seat of honor beside him when they sat down to dine. They did not converse much, however. The duke held court, tossing jests and conversing with the ladies and gentlemen at their end of the table.

Ailis had to admit, he was simply fabulous. He managed to charm everyone, showing none of the tension she knew he had to be feeling, for he was such a private person and parties were not easy for him.

These ladies his mother had brought along were so obviously wrong for him. And yet his mother was no fool. What was her true purpose in bringing these diamonds here? Was it all about that betting book his friends had opened on him?

But his mother had bet he *would* marry. How was her wager helped by bringing along young ladies he would never look at twice? This was most confusing and needed to be puzzled out, something Ailis would do in earnest once the Christmas festivities were over and off her mind.

After supper, the ladies retired to the drawing room for tea and sherry, where she was once again openly snubbed or simply ignored despite the duchess's attempts to include her in their conversations. Perhaps these young ladies and their mothers would have been kinder had she not looked so eccentric.

It was not long before the men joined them. The diamonds flitted around the duke, like moths drawn to a flame, the moment he strode in.

Ailis was relieved when her uncle came to her side. "My dear, you look tired. I think His Grace will understand if we take our leave early."

She nodded. "Yes, let's. I have been stifling yawns for the last half-hour."

The duke must have noticed her fatigue as well. He broke free from the circle of guests surrounding him and strode to her side. "Let's get you home," he agreed, then apologized for dragging her out of the vicarage in the first place. "But I wanted you to see what was going on here and understand why I am so vexed."

She knew he was right. She had watched the four diamonds throughout the supper party. They were obviously no match for him, a man of intelligence and honor, one who was thoughtful and caring, and who preferred a quiet night reading in his library to balls, routs, musicales, and other *ton* affairs.

But this also drew her attention to his mother, an intelligent lady who truly loved him, and had to know the sort of woman he would admire.

It wasn't those peahens.

Once again Ailis wondered what the dowager was doing. Perhaps Edward would know, and she was determined to get the truth out of him if ever she got the chance.

But would he trust her enough to let her in on their scheme?

Chapter Thirteen

Several days had passed since Ailas had seen the duke. She was starting to think of him as Jonas in her mind because they had become closer during her stay at Langford Hall. In truth, she missed him terribly. However, her days would now be filled with preparations for the Christmas ball coming upon them within a couple of days, so she had to concentrate her attention on this important vicarage affair and not on the handsome man who was suddenly filling her daily thoughts and nightly dreams.

"Where shall I put this wreath, Miss Temple?" asked Hanford, the young footman the duke had sent over to help with the Christmas preparations.

The duke had also sent Jane, the friendly girl who had been given the care of Ailis while at his home, to assist with her own personal grooming in addition to lending assistance setting up the tables and stalls, and fashioning the decorative boughs of holly and ivy, bay and laurel, that would go up on Christmas Eve around the vicarage's manse and church. "Set it on the long table for now," she said, pleased with how well things were progressing.

Other villagers had come by to assist, and there was to be a decorating party held after the church service on Christmas Eve for those who had volunteered for the final setting up.

Seeing as things were well under control, Ailis decided to walk over to the village bakery to review the order she had placed with them yesterday. Having them bake all the cakes, pies, and other sweets took an enormous weight off her shoulders, since this was the most time-consuming chore she had taken upon herself in the prior years.

But with her arm still quite sore and immobilized in a sling, even something as simple as kneading dough or stirring batter was not possible for her to accomplish.

The duke rode up on his massive steed, Avalon, just as she walked out of the vicarage on her way to speak to the baker. He dismounted with graceful ease, tethered his mount to a fence post, and strode toward her.

"Dear heaven," she muttered, thinking he looked quite warrior-like and magnificent with his dark cloak swirling around his body in the stiff breeze and his dark eyes trained on her.

"Miss Temple," he said, his voice deep and seductive.

"Good morning, Your Grace." She smiled up at him, squinting slightly as she faced the sun that was shining brightly on this crisp winter's day, its rays glinting through the leafless trees and reflecting off the surrounding snow.

"Going on errands?"

She nodded. "Just to the bakery to make certain they shall have all I ordered ready in time for the Christmas festivities."

"I'll walk with you."

"An excellent idea. Then you shall see what I have charged to your account. I hope it is not too much."

"It won't be," he assured her.

"That is quite generous of you." She tipped her chin up to stare at him, for she had never known him to be quite this loose with his purse strings. Not that she would ever regard him as a skinflint, but he was now opening his purse up to her seemingly without limitation. Of course, she would never take unfair advantage. Perhaps he knew this and felt comfortable placing his trust in her.

"It is something I can easily afford." They ambled along the village's high street side by side. "You'll let me know if you require more."

She glanced up at him, again surprised by his continued generosity. "We'll do nicely with what you have given us, but thank you for offering. May I ask, what has brought about this remarkable change in you?"

"Perhaps it is your kisses that have pried my coffers loose."

She blushed. "But those were for a set sum, and you are now going above and beyond that already generous donation."

He shrugged. "Perhaps I am realizing just how much I have been missing by keeping myself closed off at Langford Hall. How is your arm, Ailis?"

She nudged aside her cloak a moment to show him that her arm was still bound. "Still a little sore, but it is doing much better. I dare not remove the sling until you give me the nod."

"I'll have a better look at it when we return to the vicarage."

They were almost at the bakery now, and the delicious scent of freshly baked bread and cherry pies cooling on the ledges wafted toward them and made her mouth water. She hadn't bothered with breakfast this morning, since she had only managed to fall asleep without pain in the wee hours.

Then, the next thing she knew, Jane was at her bedchamber door informing her the volunteers had arrived to finish building the stalls and make the wreaths and boughs. With Jane's assistance, Ailis had quickly washed and dressed, and then run to the church to get everyone started on their assignments.

Only now had she caught up from her late start.

"How are you faring at Langford Hall?" she asked, curious as to what Jonas had been doing since her appearance at his dinner party. In an act of defiance, which seemed silly to her now, she had made herself look as eccentric as possible. Her intention was to irritate him and make him realize she did not belong at his elegant table rubbing elbows with the elite of Society.

Instead, he had taken her under his protective wing, kept her seated beside him, and seemed most comfortable having her by his side.

"The young lovelies are still chasing me, but I am doing my best to ignore them. Edward and his friends have been invaluable in distracting them. After all, his friends have bet on my *not* marrying, and will do all they can to collect on that wager. If these ladies are the best Society has to offer, then their win is assured. I shall never marry any of them."

Ailis turned silent, for what he really meant was that he would never marry at all.

She knew she was never in contention, so his statement should not have affected her. Yet it did. These past few days, she had ached for his company and could not stop thinking of what life might be like for her if she were to marry him.

It was all fantasy, of course. This dream she had of sharing his days *and* nights would never come true.

Perhaps this ache had grown stronger now that she was back at the vicarage because she had spent so much time in his bed.

And enjoyed his kisses.

Which brought to mind they had not gone beyond kiss number five.

"Ailis, you are nibbling your lip. Is something wrong?"

"No, just thinking. It is nothing." But her mind had now drifted to those charity kisses he had given her.

With only three more days and five kisses left to go, would she get her ten kisses before the Christmas ball? It wasn't about the donations, for she knew the good sort of man he was. He would donate the full one thousand pounds whether they got to ten kisses or not.

He leaned closer to open the bakery door for her, his breath tickling her ear as they were momentarily close. He looked so handsome with the touch of silver salted in his hair, and the lovely breadth of his shoulders that were nicely muscled.

The little bell above the door tinkled to alert the proprietor he had customers.

"Your Grace. Miss Temple. An honor to have you here. What can I do for you?" the portly baker asked, mopping his forehead as he bustled toward them from the back room, where his ovens were going at full blast and filling his shop with the divine scents of apple, cinnamon, cherries, and honey.

"Miss Temple is fretting that she has not ordered enough pies and cakes for the Christmas ball," the duke said. "We have come to add to the order."

Ailis shook her head. "I merely intended to review the list and make certain all would be ready in time."

The duke had other ideas, however. "I think you will need to expand on it," he said, after perusing her order. "I intend to bring all my guests to the festivities and shall be giving most of my staff time off to attend, too. What do you think, Mr. Cardew? Should we double the order? And add a few savory pies along with the sweet?"

The baker's eyes twinkled. "I think it is an excellent idea. It will be done, Your Grace. Never you worry, for Miss Temple shall have a feast worthy of a king."

"Good." Having decided upon this, Jonas turned to Ailis, who was still protesting that it was too much. "Miss Temple," he said with ducal authority, "if anything is left over, then distribute the excess among those in need. Do you have a problem with this suggestion?"

She cast him a generous smile and shook her head. "No problem at all, Your Grace. My uncle and I will attend to it."

They lingered a while longer in the bakery, since the duke had decided to sample some of the fare to be provided for the Christmas ball.

Mr. Cardew set out plates for both of them at a small table in the corner of his shop. There was only the one table with two spindly chairs beside it, for his patrons were merely meant to stop in, pick out their purchases, and be on their way. The village tea shop was just across the street from his bakery, so if anyone wanted to sample his wares, they had only to stop in there and have a proper tea service.

But this little table up against the wall was fine for their purposes, and Ailis spent the most enjoyable fifteen minutes she had experienced in an age.

The duke was delightful and attentive to her. The pie samples were delicious, and she particularly enjoyed the slice of cherry pie that was the best thing she had ever tasted.

Jonas grinned as he watched her. "Shall I have Mr. Cardew bring you another slice?"

She laughed. "Oh, no. I shall burst if I take another bite."

"I gather this one was your favorite."

"Yes, but all the samples were delicious, weren't they?"

He nodded. "I think I must congratulate Mr. Cardew."

Ailis agreed. "He will appreciate your approval."

Of course, he was devastating when he laid on the charm. Mr. Cardew, his wife, and his workers were in the duke's thrall by the time she and Jonas left the shop.

Once back on the high street, he paused a moment to bundle her up more securely in her cloak. "The wind is strong today," he remarked. "Any more errands?"

"No, that was all I needed to do, and I did not really need to do that, either. Mr. Cardew obviously had my order down correctly and my visit to his shop was for no reason other than my needless fretting. Although he will now be pleased that I was fussing, since my order is now doubled, as are his fees."

"Is it so awful that I spread a little Christmas cheer?"

"Not at all. The villagers could do with it." Her expression turned soft as she regarded him. "But I am happiest for you."

He arched an eyebrow. "For me?"

"Am I wrong in believing you are enjoying Christmas this season?"

"Despite my having a house full of irritating guests I would love to ship back to London in a horse cart and never see again?"

"Yes, despite them," she said with a gentle laugh. "But I think having them here has made you appreciate *us*, your local villagers, all the more."

"Perhaps." He placed her arm in his. "Come along, Miss Temple. It is cold out here and the streets are still icy. Let's get you back to the warmth of the vicarage and I shall have a look at your arm."

When they reached the church where preparations were underway for the big day, she asked if he wished to see their progress.

"No, Ailis. I want to look at you."

"All right. Another time, then." They entered the rectory that was the modest home she shared with her uncle. It was a lovely house best described as comfortable and cozy, more than enough to meet their needs but nowhere near as grand as Langford Hall.

He removed his cloak, assisted Ailis with hers, and then settled her on the settee in the drawing room. Instead of taking the chair beside her, he knelt before her.

He merely meant to get close in order to remove her sling and manipulate her arm to test its healing. But Mrs. Curtis, the vicarage's gem of a housekeeper, happened to walk in at that moment and let out a shriek.

Ailis leaped up, believing the woman had just seen a mouse or some other rodent scrambling behind the settee. "What is it, Mrs. Curtis?"

The duke rose, equally concerned.

"But I saw him, Miss Ailis."

She frowned. "Was it a mouse?"

"What?" Her housekeeper now appeared as confused as she was. "No, I am speaking of His Grace. He was on bended knee, proposing to you. Was he not? Oh, I knew he loved you. How could he not love our dear Miss Temple?"

Ailis's mouth gaped open. "You must not spread such a rumor! No, Mrs. Curtis. He was merely about to examine my arm. Dear heaven, what a misunderstanding."

Surprisingly, the duke did not appear put off by this mistake at all.

In fact, he was quite calm about it, and asked the housekeeper if he might have some tea now that the matter had been cleared up.

Ailis groaned. "How rude of me. I should have offered."

"Not at all. You did not think I was going to stay beyond a quick check of your arm."

"But you intend to stay longer?"

He quirked an eyebrow. "Are you going to kick me out?"

She smiled. "Not at all. But shouldn't you get back to your guests?"

"My head will explode if I must be around them a moment longer," he said, wincing. "Will you be so cruel as to force me back there?"

Mrs. Curtis seemed well pleased. "I'll fetch the tea. Miss Temple will be delighted to have your company for as long as you wish."

Once more alone with the duke, Ailis laughed. "That was a close call, Your Grace. What would your diamonds have said if the rumor of your proposing to me had reached their ears?"

"They would have thought I was mad to fall in love with the lady who wore chickens on her head. But we are alone, Ailis. Call me Jonas. After your remarkable appearance at my dinner party the other night, I would say that we are not only equals, but that you are actually my superior, for you bested me that night."

She felt warmth flow through her. "I'm glad you are not angry about my antics."

He chuckled. "You made the entire evening worthwhile for me. But *gad*. Burn that hat. I spent the night waiting for it to come alive and start laying eggs atop your head."

"I thought the hat was a master stroke," she teased.

"I wanted to give you kisses six and seven right there on the spot."

"Even though I looked as though I had been raised in a chicken coop?"

"Yes," he said, his smile now fading. "Ailis, my heart has not felt so light in years. In truth, I'd forgotten how it felt to be happy. So I am going to give you kiss number six right now, before Mrs. Curtis returns and catches you in my arms."

"Indeed, there'll be no stopping the rumors if she catches you kissing me. Perhaps we ought not tempt fate. The kiss can wait."

"No, it needs to be done now."

"Why?"

"Because you deserve a kiss filled with a joy I have not experienced in a decade. This feeling may be fleeting, and may never happen to me again. So would you rather not be kissed by a happy duke? Or do you prefer the surly curmudgeon?"

She closed her eyes and smiled. "Kiss me with happiness, Your Grace."

"Jonas."

"Yes…Jonas."

He placed his hand to the back of her head and gently drew her toward him. When his lips sank down on hers, she felt the full impact of his hope and yearning. The splendid promise of his own healing.

In this moment, Ailis felt true bliss.

She wanted his pain and torment to end, and if her kiss could bring this about, then all the better.

She kissed him back with full ardor and all the happiness she felt in her heart.

He responded by pressing his mouth deeper onto hers, capturing hers in the divine way he had perfected, knowing just how to turn her blood fiery, to melt her and make her legs turn to pillars of ashes, and yet still make her feel safe and protected when in his arms.

If only she could have this beyond ten kisses.

If only he truly loved her.

Groaning, he drew his mouth off hers. "Ailis, I could kiss you forever," he whispered.

"I would not stop you."

She sighed as she heard Mrs. Curtis lumber down the hall toward them. In the next moment, she appeared with a tray in her hands, cutting short any further conversation.

Ailis cast her housekeeper a casual smile, trying to appear at ease and not reveal she had just been given the best kiss of her life, one packed with a sensual heat that still had her body in flames.

But her cheeks were flushed and her breathing unsettled, so perhaps she was not fooling anyone.

The duke—her Jonas—seemed completely unaffected. How did he manage this?

When Mrs. Curtis turned away for a moment to place the tray on a side table, he took the opportunity to give her a devastatingly affectionate smile.

Her cheeks were already hot and now turned hotter. Her breaths were already ragged and remained ridiculously unsteady, so that she had to place a hand over her heart to calm its rapid beating.

Fortunately, her housekeeper mistook the reason for her pink cheeks, and attributed them to her injured shoulder. "Oh, you poor dear. What agony you must be feeling, and never a complaint out of you."

The duke now had her arm out of the sling and was about to test its healing.

"Well, have a cup of tea once His Grace is done. It will comfort you. And make sure to listen to what His Grace tells you. We want that shoulder of yours to heal as quick as possible."

"I shall follow his every instruction."

Mrs. Curtis nodded her approval and marched out.

Ailis let out a breath. "That was close...but worth it. I enjoyed your kiss," she admitted, always wanting to be honest with him.

Well, he knew she had liked it by the ardor of her response.

"I'll bring you the bank draft when I see you next."

Her heart sank. "That wasn't what I meant."

He gave her chin a tweak. "I know, Ailis. Forgive my stupid response."

"There are only four kisses left to go."

"And little time to fit them all in before Christmas Day. Must we rush?"

"No, I suppose not. Jonas…"

"Yes?"

She smiled. "Nothing. I just wanted to say your name aloud while no one but you was around to hear me."

He laughed but did not comment.

However, he appeared pleased as he took gentle hold of her arm and tested her dexterity. But he was very careful not to hurt her, for he kept the movements to a minimum and was quite cautious while gliding his fingers along her shoulder and the length of her arm.

He stopped whenever her breath quickened.

"Right, that's enough," he said, tucking her arm back in the sling. "Let's have our tea and then I must be off."

"How is my shoulder progressing? Is it healing properly?"

"Yes, all is as it should be. The area is still swollen, but that is to be expected. Your recovery will take time, as I warned. I know you are impatient to get back to your normal routine, but it will be months yet before you can manage it."

They did not say much between them after this. Ailis had loved kiss number six, just as she had loved all the ones that came before it. But she dared not mention their arrangement again.

The duke finished his tea and then rose. "I had better be off. I'll try to come see you at least once more before your big day."

He grabbed his cloak and strode out of the house without looking back at her.

She watched him mount Avalon and ride off.

Once he was out of sight, she put her fingers to her lips. She still felt the warmth of his mouth on hers. Her lips had not stopped tingling, nor had her body.

This was an awful situation.

She was falling more deeply in love with him with each kiss.

Was there any hope that he might be falling in love with her? Would he do anything about it if he did?

Chapter Fourteen

Ailis was going about her business on the morning of Christmas Eve and had just finished reviewing the church tithes and balancing the ledgers when Edward barged into her uncle's office, where she had been working. "Miss Temple, you must come straight away!"

She leaped to her feet, her heart plunging into her toes upon her noting his expression. "What's happened?"

"It's my brother," he said, appearing not merely worried but frantic.

Her head began to spin. "Is he hurt?" How could he be? Jonas appeared so strong, seemingly invincible.

"No, but he is in a rage and everyone is frightened. I have never seen him like this before."

"What happened? Never mind, you'll explain it to me along the way." She called for Mrs. Curtis to fetch her cloak and gloves, thanking her when she hastily assisted Ailis in donning them.

The ducal carriage was waiting out front for them, so she hurried to it.

Edward helped her climb in and then took the seat opposite hers as the driver snapped the reins and the team made a hasty return to Langford Hall.

Ailis's heart was still in her throat as they raced closer, every minute seeming to count. "Tell me what happened."

"You know what a private person he is…"

"Yes, and?"

"These diamonds are constantly clamoring for his attention."

"He has complained to me about it," she replied, trying not to sound impatient.

"Lady Viola entered his chamber while he was getting dressed. She saw him without his shirt on. When she shrieked, the other young ladies rushed in, too."

Ailis gasped. "And they all saw his scars?"

Edward regarded her with some surprise. "You know about them? Have you seen him…er… I am not passing judgment…er."

"Nothing of the sort. He rolled up one sleeve and showed me his forearm the other day. He was trying to explain to me why he was so angry with your mother for bringing these unwanted guests to Langford Hall. He honored me by showing me his scars that he has kept hidden all these years, knowing I would never betray his secret agony. Those scars are the reason he will never marry, he explained to me."

"And now everyone knows just how hideous they are," Edward said with a groan. "Of all the people to walk in on him, why did it have to be Lady Viola? Her shrieks brought in those other peahens, their parents, and my friends. The entire household has now seen the body he has kept hidden all these years."

Viola was the worst of this group of diamonds, scheming, manipulative, determined to win at all costs. She must have been lurking in the hallway, waiting for her chance to sneak into his bedchamber in the hope of entrapping him.

Instead, she found herself looking at a man whose body reflected the terrible toll the war had taken on him.

Viola could have run out and said nothing, but she was just the sort to make a dramatic scene and bring everyone rushing in.

Edward groaned again. "She will ridicule and revile him purely out of malice, because he certainly won't choose her as his wife now."

"He was never going to choose her," Ailis remarked, although there was no triumph in her statement, since Viola's loss did not clear the field of play for anyone. If anything, her behavior had reinforced the duke's belief that no one could endure the sight of a man riddled with scars.

Which meant he was more resolved than ever not to marry.

Ailis ached for him, felt awful that he had to endure this humiliating incident.

Edward lolled his head back and groaned. "She will do her best to make him a laughingstock among the *ton*."

"A laughingstock? Because he was injured in combat? Because he was braver than any of his peers who avoided serving in the military and now walk around showing off their smooth hands and peacock silks? Anyone with an ounce of honor will think her the fool and dismiss *her*, never *him*."

"Likely you are right, Miss Temple. But the damage has already been done. No one was ever meant to know his secret torment. Those scars are his pain. Only he ever had the right to disclose them to the world."

"And he had chosen not to."

Edward nodded. "But his privacy is shot to hell now. Soon, all of Society will hear about this."

"Oh, Lord Langford. This is awful. What a betrayal. But why send for me? Did he ask you to do this?"

"No, I took it upon myself. He will not speak to anyone, not even me or our mother. I'm sure he blames us for bringing this nightmare about. I suppose we *are* to blame, but you must believe we only wished to see him happy."

"I know you love him," Ailis said, although she did not agree with the high-handed manner in which they had gone about encouraging his happiness. Perhaps if they had chosen better, selected ladies more suitable for him... Surely there had to be attractive, thoughtful ladies in their mid-twenties who could provide intelligent conversation and see the fine man beyond the superficial damage to his body.

Even she might have been the right match for him, were he not a duke. But his exalted rank put him out of her reach. Why could he not have been a squire or an accomplished commoner?

"Lord Langford, what makes you think I can be of any help?"

"It is obvious he has a soft spot for you. My mother and I hoped you might be able to calm him down."

Ailis shook her head. "He indulges me, and perhaps feels a little protective of me because I was hurt on his property."

"No, Miss Temple. He truly admires you and respects your opinions. You are the only one who can tame his savage anger."

She doubted it. The duke would not want to hear what she had to say. And yet, did she not have to say what was in her heart? Knowing how proud he was, this incident had demeaned him so badly and given that peahen, Lady Viola, control over him.

But the spiteful girl only had control because he was allowing the incident to affect him.

Just how bad *were* his scars? Ailis had only seen his forearm. Yes, the damage had been awful. But why could he not see that it did not change the valiant essence of the man he was?

His mother and Grimes met them at the door as the carriage drew up in front of the house.

"Thank goodness you are here, Miss Temple," the duchess said, guiding Ailis down the hall before she had a moment to remove her cloak and gloves. "He will not speak to any of us."

"I am surprised he did not toss all of you out."

The duchess blushed. "He might have said that as he ranted and raged. But I am his mother and refuse to leave him when he is obviously hurting so badly. Unfortunately, being that tomorrow is Christmas, none of our guests can leave, either. Between the bad weather and so many people closing shop early, we simply could not send anyone packing."

"It will take those peahens a full day to pack, anyway," Edward remarked. "Dressing to trap a duke takes lots of fashionable clothes that cannot simply be stuffed into a travel pouch."

"Has Lady Viola attempted to apologize to him?" Ailis asked.

The duchess shook her head. "No, the girl has spent the past hour cruelly talking about the condition of his body to anyone who will listen."

"The irony of it is," Edward said, "all of them would still marry my brother because they will endure anything to be a duchess."

"They would marry him and yet loathe him?" Ailis let out a breath in disgust.

"Well, there'll be no marriage proposal now. He will never take any of them as his wife. I suppose this will be his fate now, to remain alone and unhappy, renowned throughout the *ton* as the last Silver Duke."

Yet another label he detested, Ailis mused.

But this discovered secret about his scars was far worse. He would retreat behind those fortress walls he'd built up over the years. Was it not better to be alone than wake up each morning to a wife who despised him?

They paused outside the study door. Grimes had caught up to them and took her cloak and gloves. "You would make him happy, Miss Ailis."

She glanced at the duchess. "I am not anyone he would consider marrying. You needn't worry that I'll—"

"Ailis," the duchess said, taking hold of her hand and giving it a gentle squeeze, "you are worthier than a dozen of those diamonds. I was wrong to bring them here."

Ailis could not believe what she was hearing. Was the duchess indicating that she, a vicar's niece, was worthy to be his duchess? Or merely suggesting acceptance because Ailis was useful to have around at the moment? Well, it was the duke's choice alone on whom to marry or whether he even *would* marry. No one else had the right to make this decision for him.

She knocked at the study door.

"I warned you to stay out!" the duke roared, sounding angrier than she had ever heard him. In truth, she had never seen him this furious, and had never once seen him lose control.

Her heart went out to him, for he sounded like an enraged lion, wounded and aggressive.

"Do not bellow at me," she called back with more confidence than she felt. "I am coming in."

She waited to the count of three, just in case he decided to hurl something at the door. When nothing happened, she walked in and closed the door behind her, purposely closing herself in the lair of an angry lion.

"I might have known they would bring Miss Temple of Virtue to calm me down. What made you agree to be their virgin sacrifice?"

"Good morning, Jonas," she responded in the face of his insults and his dangerous glower, glad he was seated behind his desk and making no move to rise. "You are ever a delight."

"Jonas? Are we friends now? Do you feel closer to me because I am a wretched soul and you believe you are my sainted healer?"

She nodded. "I thought it was appropriate to remind you that I am your friend."

"Well, *Ailis*," he said, rising from his chair in a sleek, predatory movement and stalking closer to her, "you are quite mistaken if you believe I consider you a friend."

His words stung, but she refused to flinch. "But I am not your enemy."

Dear heaven.

He looked awfully big now that he was up close.

She took a step back and then another, until she found herself pressed against the door through which she had just entered.

There was no escape because he had put his hands on either side of her body, leaning his palms against the door so that she had no chance of opening it.

Heat radiated off him, no doubt because those flames of anger and frustration burned through his veins.

Yet his scent was divine. Hot and male and dangerous. He must have been caught by Viola just after a shave and bathing, because Ailis also caught the scent of lather and sandalwood on his skin.

He growled softly. "Do you think our kissing bargain has made you somehow special to me?"

"No, I would not presume to be anything more than a casual amusement for you."

His laugh was bitter. "You do amuse me, for you are like no one else. Almost thirty and still untouched. Almost thirty and never been kissed until this week. Almost thirty and still have a body that can bring a man to his knees with longing. Big eyes. Soft lips. Even softer…"

He stopped himself before he spoke of her bosom, but she knew that was what he was going to say because he had glanced down at her breasts, which were heaving, and he had noticed.

He eased off her the slightest bit. "But you do not amuse me just now."

"I see. Then I will not ask for kiss number seven yet. But since I am here, you ought to write out the bank note for kiss number six before you toss me out on my ear."

She had caught him off guard with her impertinent request.

She had done it on purpose, of course.

He wanted to stay angry and intimidate her into leaving. But if he truly wanted her gone, he would not be keeping her trapped between his arms, would he?

"Gad, Ailis," he said finally, letting out a groaning breath. "You are a nuisance. Of all the things to say to me. You shall have your bloody bank draft number six."

She nodded. "I know. You are too honorable ever to renege."

"Then why mention it now? Did you think that catching me off guard would calm me down? But you are ever practical, aren't you? Tame the dragon *and* collect the charity donation."

She looked up at him as he continued to loom over her. "Actually, you remind me more of a lion with your dark mane and deep, angry roar. But you would make a very handsome dragon, too."

"Handsome? Have you not heard? I am disgusting to look at."

"Is that what Lady Viola said? Or is it just *you* hating yourself? And why would you ever care about any stupid thing that girl says? Or what any of those silly geese say?"

"I don't."

"Then why are you so overset? So what if people know you are scarred? How does it change anything of the life you have made for yourself? In truth, you ought to thank Viola for shaking you out of this prison you have built around yourself."

"Thank her? You do not know what you are talking about, Ailis."

"Then explain it to me."

"No. Go away. Our kisses do not give you any special privileges over me."

"Your mother and brother are worried about you."

"Let them be worried. They've brought this on themselves. What did they think I would do? Strip naked for these ladies and show off my body?"

"This isn't about your body. It is about your heart. The girl who deserves to win your heart is the one who will love all of you, and will accept everything about you."

"I did not realize my Miss Temple of Virtue was also an expert on matters of love. Look at you," he said softly. "You are a little bird with a broken wing. How could they send you to me? What if I had been blinded by rage and hurt you?"

"You never would."

"Do not be so sure, Ailis. I am not a nice man."

"I disagree. I think you are honorable, caring, and protective to the very core. Anyone who really knows you would not give a fig about your scars. They would cherish you for the sum of who you are."

She was going to cry if she said anything more, for she could not bear to see the anguish in his eyes, dark eyes that hid years of pain and torment.

"Would *you* love me like that, Ailis?"

She closed her eyes. "I already do. Is it not obvious? I never meant for it to happen. I tried so hard not to fall in love with you. But my heart had other ideas. I am so deeply and desperately in love with you. That is *my* torment."

Her admission must have taken him aback.

"Ailis," he said in a raspy whisper, and caressed her cheek.

"There it is," she said, keeping her eyes closed because she did not have the courage to open them and see the pity in his. "My fate is to love you and know you will never reciprocate. I never intended to tell you. I would have been happy keeping silent and maintaining our friendship. It would have been enough for me, I think. Ten kisses and a lasting bond of friendship."

"We are only up to kiss number seven."

Her eyes flew open. "And now that I have confessed my feelings for you, are you going to end this game?"

"It was never really a game, was it?"

"I don't know." She took a deep breath. "Will you show me what the others saw…when Viola caught you in your bedchamber?"

"No, Ailis. It isn't a pretty sight."

"But that is precisely the point. Now that everyone you *don't* trust has seen you, why hide the truth from me?"

"Is it just morbid curiosity on your part?"

"You know it isn't. I want to prove to you that real friends would not care."

"All right, but do not say you weren't warned."

She watched as he slowly removed his jacket, cravat, and vest, then paused a moment to give her a final chance to stop him before he took off his shirt. His expression oozed pain, so much of it that she almost told him not to take that final step.

But to stop now would be a setback for him.

Despite the turmoil roiling in her heart, she said nothing.

With a soft groan, he removed his shirt in one fluid motion to reveal the damage he had hidden for so long.

Ailis's heart broke.

He stood before her, unflinching and steady as a stone monolith. "There you have it, Miss Temple of Virtue. This is what all the fuss was about."

He had scars all over his arms and partly along his back. He had told her that his legs were just as badly marked, but she was not going to suggest he drop his trousers, since that was obviously a step too far. Merely removing his shirt and giving her a view of his naked upper torso was scandalous enough.

But she was not thinking of scandal, only of the agony he must have endured that left him so scarred.

She threw herself into his arms and hugged him fiercely. "I'm so sorry this happened to you."

"So am I," he said, emitting another soft groan as he wrapped his arms around her.

"This doesn't change any of my feelings for you," she said, resting her head against his chest and not ready to back away. His skin was warm and his body had remained surprisingly firm and muscled. He was quite fine and strong for a man in his forties. In truth, more finely built than most younger men.

"Ailis, open your eyes now."

"They are open. I have been looking at you all the while. Must I care about those scars when there is everything else that is so much more important about you?"

He sighed. "Why do you dismiss them as unimportant?"

"Because this is what they have become with the passage of time." She hugged him again. "The pain they gave you was important, for that injury put your life at risk back then. But now? Why are you letting these scars define you? And why are you allowing the useless opinions of people you would never allow close to you to affect you?"

He cast her a wry smile. "Are you berating me, Temple?"

"I don't mean to. It is just that I am looking at you through clear eyes, and I know what I am seeing. If given the choice of you or another to share my life, there is no one but you I would ever want. And I do not mean in any *ton* way of doing things. No separate lives or separate homes for me."

"Or separate beds?"

She shook her head. "I would hope to share that marital bed every night."

He moved away from her to don his shirt and other attire in order to make himself presentable once again. "Dukes and duchesses commonly have separate quarters, even in love marriages," he said as he slipped the shirt back on.

"That sounds lonely."

"The quarters are usually linked by an adjoining door so husband and wife can go back and forth at their pleasure without having to pass through the hallway."

"That sounds much better. I'm glad you showed me your body," she said as he turned away a moment to tuck his shirt into his trousers. "Thank you."

He grunted and turned back to don his cravat and vest with practiced ease because he always attended to his own grooming.

She sighed as he shrugged into his jacket.

"What is it, Ailis?"

"Will you give me kiss number seven now?"

"Are you serious?"

She nodded.

He stared at her a long moment and then smiled. "Yes, you shall have your kiss number seven."

This surprised her, and she smiled in relief because she was afraid she had overstepped with him and he would no longer want anything to do with her.

"But I have one requirement before I give you that seventh kiss," he said, his voice surprisingly gentle. "I want you to promise me that you will not hold back. If you truly love me, then this kiss needs to be a kiss of love. Will you do this for me?"

She nodded. "I promise."

It was easy to comply, since these were her feelings and she was never good at hiding them, nor would she ever wish to hide them from him now that she had admitted her love for him.

In truth, it felt freeing.

Perhaps he would reciprocate these feelings someday, for he had to trust her already and she knew he enjoyed her company…most of the time.

He would not have taken off his shirt if a strong bond had not been established between them, a bond strong enough to survive his raw, brutal ache.

As his mouth was about to sink onto hers, she whispered, "I love you, Jonas."

"Stop talking, Ailis."

"All right, but I love you."

He responded by delivering a kiss filled with heat and exquisite tenderness, a kiss that devoured her soul.

This kiss went farther than the others before it, as he meant it to do by the intimate press of his muscled body against her soft, yielding curves. She felt his ardor and that purposeful press of his weight against her.

It was a delicious heaviness, just enough to make her feel him.

Not enough to ever hurt her.

Their kiss was deep and bonded by her love. It was also bonded by his desire, for he always made her feel adored whenever he kissed her.

Now, it was her turn to make him feel the abiding love she held for him.

She did it the only way she knew how, by accepting the divine crush of his mouth on hers, the tangle of their tongues and molding of their bodies, the *melting* of their bodies into one. This kiss was about accepting him in every way, about getting to know the feel of him and how her senses wrapped around him.

The kiss was intimate and infinite. It was a declaration of recognition on the deepest levels.

She was memorizing the granite strength of him, and she hoped he was remembering the shape of her curves and the softness of her skin. He tasted of coffee, strong and forceful, while she tasted of gentle mint tea. His scent was spice, woods and earth, while hers was of autumn flavors, of nutmeg, cinnamon, and apples.

This kiss was meant to bind them through time.

And this was how she would love him, eternally and throughout time.

He had not made this same commitment to her, but she did not think he was capable of committing to anyone just yet. It was too much to ask of him.

Still, this kiss was beautiful, and it felt as though he was committing to her, body and soul.

If only it were possible.

She had to remind herself it was an important expression of trust but not a commitment of love.

He had the skill and prowess to make her believe it could be love, to make her feel that he might abandon all rules just for her.

Finally, he let out a ragged breath and drew back slightly to end their kiss. His body was no longer pressed atop hers, and she missed the warmth of his weight on her. "Ailis…"

Reluctantly, she opened her eyes and looked up at him. "Did it feel like a kiss of love to you?"

He smiled. "Yes, it did."

"Does this mean the lion is ready to come out of his lair? Or shall I leave you in peace now? I must get back to the rectory anyway. We are adding all the festive touches today and plan to start decorating shortly after supper. Will you join us?"

"Maybe."

Even after their kiss? She was still a *maybe*?

She hid her disappointment, but what did she expect? It had been her kiss of love, not his. Her feelings were not his. She was the one in love, not him.

But some good had come from their being closed off in his study. She had entered the lion's den and removed the thorn from his paw. He was no longer hurting over Viola's discovering his secret.

As for herself, she had received another scorching kiss from him.

Sadly, she doubted her admission of love would lead to anything more, but that was all right.

He now knew someone in the world loved him truly and forever, scars and all.

Chapter Fifteen

Jonas walked Ailis out of his study, not surprised to find his mother and Edward hovering close by. "Did you think I was going to eat her alive?" he said in response to their sighs of relief when she walked out unharmed.

How could they think he would ever hurt her?

Well, they could not have truly believed he was capable of it, or they would not have sent her into his study while he was on a rampage.

"What are you doing buzzing around me like so many annoying bees?"

"We were worried about you," his mother replied. "Am I not permitted to show concern for my beloved son?"

"If I were so beloved, you would have left me alone from the start," he grumbled. "Is that little viper you brought along with you gone yet?"

He had not outright ordered any of their guests to leave, but why would they stay when he was never going to offer for any of them?

Edward arched an eyebrow. "If you mean Lady Viola, no. She came prepared to dazzle you, and apparently that requires a lot of clothing. It will take her at least another three or four days to properly pack up for her return to London."

"And the others? Have they decided to stay or go?"

"They are staying," Edward said. "As I said, dazzling a duke takes a large wardrobe and a lot of planning. With Lady Viola out of contention, I would not be surprised if the remaining diamonds foolishly believed their chances of marrying you had improved."

"Are they serious?"

"They are determined, I will give them that. By the way, you have arranged a supper party tonight for all our guests at the Marble House Inn in Broadmoor."

"I have?" Jonas shook his head and groaned. "Why in heaven's name did *I* do that?"

"Because everyone was still overset by this morning's incident and needed to calm down. Like it or not, these diamonds and their parents are here until after Christmas. It is unfair to have them travel back to London before the week is out. Besides, Pomeroy needs a few more days because he intends to offer for Viola."

Jonas could not hold back his laughter. "Is he deranged?"

"No, just poor, and she comes with an enormous dowry. As an only child, she also stands to inherit quite a sum once Carstairs passes on. None of his entailed properties, of course. But her father dotes on her and is going to leave her everything he can. Pomeroy's a good man. He won't waste any of it and he won't ever leave Viola without means. She'll maintain her own residence in London and carry on like the princess she believes she is."

Jonas felt sorry for Edward's friend, for he wasn't sure marriage to a girl like Viola was worth it even if she came with a king's ransom.

"Whitcomb intends to propose to Lady Willa for similar reasons," his brother continued. "So, all's well that ends well, isn't it? Their families will believe you are the rudest duke in all of England, but they will be content with the end result of their visit."

"And what about the Tenney sisters?" Ailis asked.

Edward grinned wickedly. "They'll join me in my bed tonight. I'll keep those two satisfied."

Their mother smacked him on the head. "Idiot. Is that any way to speak in front of Miss Temple?"

Ailis blushed, but she was smiling.

Jonas found himself relaxing, too. Ailis was prim and innocent, but she was no sour prune.

"I don't suppose either of you will consider packing up?" Jonas asked his mother and Edward.

"Of course not," she shot back. "We are family and devoted to you, so you cannot kick us out."

"Well, I can," he corrected her. "But you feel entitled to ignore my wishes."

"Family should be together at Christmas," Ailis said quietly.

Jonas heard the wealth of her pain, for he knew she had lost her entire family and still struggled with that loss.

She only had her uncle now, but for how long? The vicar was not a young man. What would she do once he was gone?

She had mentioned having a small inheritance, but this was not possibly enough to nourish Ailis's beautiful soul.

"You are right, Miss Temple." He placed his hand over hers and gave it a light squeeze. "We shall have a Langford family Christmas this year. They are safe from my wrath…for now."

She nodded her approval. "I'm glad it is all settled. I had better return home. Today and tomorrow are my busiest days."

"I'll see you safely back to the vicarage," Jonas said.

"It isn't necessary. However, I would appreciate the use of your carriage rather than walking."

"Walking? In the cold and ice? Perish the thought. The ducal coach it shall be for you. I'll see you later tonight for the decorating."

Her eyes widened. "That would be wonderful. We're starting at seven o'clock. I did not think you would join us."

Because he was a surly arse and had never shown up in all the years before this, Jonas knew. But things had changed and he was going to make the effort for Ailis. "I'll see you then," he confirmed.

Besides, having given her kisses number six and seven, he owed her the bank drafts for each.

He owed her so much more, of course. She had given him all of her heart, and asked for nothing in return.

This was why she was like no other.

Even a scarred duke was a catch, but he knew Ailis would never consider him one in any *ton* sense of the word. She was not looking to check off a list of attributes that included wealth or title, power or its misuse, to further her goals. Her list led with the requirement of love.

Marriage to Ailis would mean sharing one's bed. Sharing one's heart. Holding true to one's vows for all of one's life.

While others might lie to him and claim not to care about his scars in order to gain his favor, Ailis never would.

She had told him that she did not care about them, and he believed her. She would not see them because she looked at him through the eyes of love.

He saw her safely into his carriage and stood at the entryway until the conveyance was out of sight. Edward and his mother were still lingering in the hall when he walked back in, and both were staring at him. "What?"

Despite having held back his temper and making nice with one and all while Ailis was present, he was not in good humor now that she was gone. She had a way of bringing sunshine into his home. He felt the loss of her warming light immediately upon her departure.

"What?" he repeated, when his mother and brother just gaped at him. If either of them dared make a snide comment about Ailis, he would kick them out into the cold.

"That girl is..." his mother said. "That girl is...heaven sent."

"She won my heart when she showed up at your dinner party in that chicken hat," Edward added with a grin.

Jonas eased.

Yes, Ailis was the best thing ever to happen to Broadmoor. She was the best thing for him, as well.

All these years, he had been in too much of a fog to see what was before his very eyes.

"What are you going to do about decorating Langford Hall?" his brother asked.

"Grimes and Mrs. Fitch will take care of it while you'll be hosting the supper party I supposedly reserved at the Marble House Inn, and I will be at the vicarage helping Ailis and her uncle prepare for tomorrow's big event."

"I could join you at the vicarage," Edward offered. "Mother can play host at the inn."

Jonas laughed. "Oh, no. I'm not letting you off that easy. You are to join her and suffer through that meal."

THE HOURS DID not pass quickly enough for Jonas. It felt like an eternity before he finally made his way to the vicarage.

At the same time, the others left for the inn and their supper.

He hoped these unwanted guests would disappear in a snowstorm, save for his mother and brother, of course. Blood was blood, even when said kin were as irritating as nettles.

But it did feel right to have them here with him. Perhaps next year he would invite his sisters and their brood, too. He could not recall a time when the laughter of children rang in these halls.

But as for his other guests, too bad they were only going as far as Broadmoor to dine and would be back under his roof tonight. The sooner they were gone, the better. He did not trust Viola, for the girl thrived on mischief, and not in any adorable, madcap way.

Everyone had left him alone throughout the day, no doubt fearing he would bite their heads off if they dared approach. Even Viola, as vain as she was, understood she had overstepped the bounds.

Of course, it would not stop her from planning something cruel for tomorrow.

Hopefully, Pomeroy, with his fervent devotion to her dowry, would press his courtship suit and occupy her time.

Whitcomb, he knew, had spent most of the day entertaining Lady Willa and her family while Edward and their mother played card games with the Tenneys. He expected Edward played *other* games with Faith and Hope Tenney, but he really did not want to know what his brother was doing with those girls.

Nothing decent, if the smiles on their faces were any indication.

"You may thank me afterward," Edward muttered, climbing into the carriage and taking a seat beside him. "The sacrifices I make for you."

The coachman left Jonas off at the vicarage and then pressed on with the others to the Marble House Inn, which was just down the high street.

The church's meeting room was bustling with volunteers when Jonas walked in at eight o'clock that evening. He was late, for the group had amassed an hour earlier to commence their work, simply staying on after the vicar's Christmas Eve service, ready to roll up their sleeves to prepare for tomorrow's big event.

There was still plenty to do.

Ailis, looking delicious in a plain woolen gown of dove gray that was buttoned to her throat, was on the footstool again.

He strode toward her and put his arms around her waist. "Did I not tell you that you weren't to climb?"

She turned to him with a breathtaking smile once he set her down. "I'm so glad you made it. I knew your timing would be perfect. Or awful. Or awfully perfect."

"Ailis…"

"Or perfectly awful. I had just climbed onto the stool to fix this sagging bough when you walked in and caught me in the act."

"Timing is everything," he teased.

She cast him an impudent grin. "Indeed, it is. And you are just in time to help me put up the mistletoe."

"Does this mean I get to kiss you?"

She blushed. "I hope so."

"That sounds promising. How many are you going to put up?" he asked, thinking he could not have arrived at a better moment.

"I have two balls of mistletoe."

"Good, that will take us to kisses eight and nine," he said, studying her lips with interest. They were just the sort of lips a man would not mind kissing, not thin or pinched, but full and soft.

"Eight and nine," she said in a whisper, and looked up at him with eyes reflecting her regret. "Almost at an end."

"Then I had better make them memorable for you."

"All of yours have been unforgettable," she said so quietly that he had to read her lips in order to make out her words above the festive din of volunteers, who were already exhibiting particularly good cheer.

Many were in their cups, which he found rather surprising, since they were in a church and preparing for charitable festivities. He may have been partly to blame, since he had sent over a goodly supply of ale, wine, and mead along with treacle cakes and other assorted treats to provide them sustenance while they worked.

No wonder the boughs were sagging.

He assisted Ailis in straightening out those that were threatening to fall, but there really was not much left to be done with the decorations other than hang the mistletoe.

Ailis was not the only one stringing them up, but she was the only one he intended to assist and then kiss. Two other young ladies were doing the same, and each had two or three young men eager to aid them.

No one had lined up for Ailis, but this was likely because he was with her now and no one dared approach.

The other young ladies had started on theirs, each playing up their work to the cheers and bawdy comments of those gathered around them. As each ball of mistletoe was put up, a young man of the lady's choosing was invited to kiss her.

Jonas noticed these were not tame kisses.

Good.

His would not be tame, either.

He held Ailis by the waist while she climbed up three steps of a small ladder to reach the height of the first doorway. Since her injured arm was still in a sling, she struggled to hook her mistletoe onto the bough of holly and ivy already strung across the transom. It took her several tries, but she was in no danger of falling while he held her securely about the waist.

He felt a current of attraction flow through him every time he touched her. Even earlier today when he had been in such a rage, the mere sight of her had soothed him. She was soft as a lamb and had magical eyes that always seemed to sparkle, and golden hair that seemed ready to burst from its pins at any moment.

When she was through, he lifted her down from her perch, keeping his arms firmly around her so that she would not fall even when she suddenly lost her footing and accidentally slid down his body.

"Ailis," he said with a groaning laugh. "Are you trying to torture me?"

She clutched his shoulder in desperation, having only the one good arm for support while the other was still bound.

It was a deliciously slow slide.

The crowd enjoyed the show. Everyone moved over to them and began to chant, "Kiss her!"

Jonas winked at Mrs. Curtis, who had been helping out with the church decorations along with her regular housekeeping duties at the vicar's manse and now cheered hardest.

Heaven and earth, he was going to kiss Ailis breathless.

And he did.

A roar sprang up throughout the crowd.

He barely heard the thunderous bellows and whistles, for all had faded into the background the moment he sank his lips onto Ailis's rosebud mouth and felt the soft give of her lips as she responded with shyness, at first, and then gave in to the moment with all her heart.

He did not release her when it ended.

He could not release her, for she looked thoroughly dazed and decidedly out of balance. Nor did he want to let go of her now that she had admitted her feelings. Somehow, she had become a part of him, the missing part he had been longing for during all those years of battle, blood, and captivity.

Other ladies began to offer their assistance, calling out to Ailis to hand over the second mistletoe to them.

He wouldn't allow that to happen.

He took the mistletoe out of her hand and clutched it firmly. "Where do we hang this next one?"

Ailis pointed to another door, one that led out from the nave.

Now all the volunteers followed them to it, cheering as Jonas swept Ailis into his arms and lifted her once again onto the third step of a small ladder. Cries of "kiss her" began before she had finished hooking the mistletoe atop the doorway.

When she was done, he set her down and drew her into his arms.

As he closed his mouth over hers for kiss number nine, he already knew what kiss number ten had to be. For all the depth and heart of their ninth kiss, for all the sweetness of her lips and the possessive claim of his, neither this kiss nor all the others that had come before would match the splendor of kiss number ten.

Still, he held this kiss for as long as he dared. And ended it with greatest reluctance.

But he also realized that as her volunteers sobered, they would begin to wonder if something more was going on between him and Ailis.

Well, that could not be helped.

But he sought to dispel any rumors by staying on after the decorating was done and game stalls had been built, sharing a drink with the men and mildly flirting with the ladies while they cleared the tables and prepared them for the piles of food to be delivered at the start of tomorrow's festivities.

When the night drew to a close, he walked Ailis next door to the manse where she and her uncle resided. The day had been a long one for her, so he did not delay her when she retired to her bedchamber while he spoke to her uncle.

The vicar had not been present during the volunteer work, no doubt hiding in his office while his parishioners drank too much and indulged in a little too much revelry.

Jonas liked Vicar Temple because he was not one of those righteous moralists. He understood that sometimes a little sin was permissible, for the world was too often a bad place and people needed a release from the torments of their daily struggle.

"Vicar Temple, I have something important to ask you."

"Come into my study, Your Grace. It is not nearly as fine as yours, but more than adequate for my needs. Here, let me clear off this pile of books from the chair. Please, do have a seat."

Once they were both comfortably settled, the vicar opened the conversation. "Now, Your Grace, what is it you wish to ask me?"

"Well, vicar…"

THE NIGHT WAS cold and a stiff wind was blowing by the time Jonas left the vicarage and walked to the Marble House Inn to meet his guests, who had only now finished their elegant supper and were ready to return to Langford Hall.

His mother and brother were the first to walk out. The Tenneys and Montroys stumbled into the cold night soon after them, none of them feeling the chill, since they had obviously imbibed too much.

Carstairs and his daughter came out last and did not bother to acknowledge Jonas while they climbed into the last carriage of their small caravan along with Pomeroy.

Only his mother and brother dared to climb into his lead carriage. "How was your supper?" Jonas asked, not really caring but knowing he ought to allow for some conversation.

"Terrible," his mother responded as his pair of matched bays got underway. "The food was excellent, but Viola was insufferable. Her father does no good by indulging her petulance. Of course, Pomeroy fawned over her all night long. He will have Carstairs approving of his match to Viola by tomorrow."

"And Whitcomb? Has he had any success with Willa Montroy?"

Edward shrugged. "Most likely. Neither of those young ladies will get offers from a serious gentleman. Willa's father knows he will get no one better than Whitcomb stepping forward. If his only choice is to pick the best of the fortune hunters lined up in queue at his door, then Whitcomb wins out handily. And how was your night?"

Jonas shrugged. "Good."

Edward laughed. "That's it? Just good? Did you spend the entire evening in Miss Temple's company?"

"It was a madhouse, but all the preparations are now done. The vicar is holding an early morning service tomorrow and then the fun and games begin. I'll have the Langford carriages available for anyone who wishes to attend his service, and for the later festivities as well."

"Pies and games? Sounds dull."

"Edward! Show a little respect," their mother said. "We shall be there, Ramsdale. It is our duty to attend the service and the charity affair. Ignore your brother."

"Yes, ignore me. Everyone else does," Edward muttered.

Jonas caught the undercurrent of hurt in his brother's voice. "Well, take heart," he said, casting him a wicked grin. "I'm sure the Tenney sisters won't mind cheering you up."

"Yes, they are a most enthusiastically bouncy pair."

Their mother sighed. "I have raised heathens."

Jonas winked at his brother. "Join me for a drink in my study before you retire for the evening. There's something I want to talk to you about."

"You are not going to lecture me about my moral decay, are you?"

"No, you clot. Join me, all right?"

Edward nodded. "This wouldn't have anything to do with Miss Temple, would it?"

Chapter Sixteen

Jonas had stayed well up into the night talking to his brother. Both of them could hardly keep awake the following morning while Vicar Temple, an eloquent but soft-spoken orator, delivered the lengthy sermon on the topics of forgiveness, sacrifice, and rebirth. Since Jonas and his family occupied the first pew, he and Edward dared not yawn or close their eyes.

Ailis, looking lovelier than ever in a festive gown of darkest green velvet trimmed with lace and silk, quietly stepped in through a side door as the sermon was well underway and stood partially hidden in one of the small alcoves along the side. She must have kept some extra fabric when sewing her gown, for she had used a remnant of it to fashion a sling for her arm out of the same green velvet material.

She acknowledged him with a generous smile when he glanced at her.

When the sermon finally ended—*praise heaven*—she made her way to him. "Good morning, Your Grace."

"Good morning. Are you ready for your big day, Miss Temple?"

She nodded. "Yes, the pies and cakes have just arrived and are all being set out. Mrs. Curtis is boiling water for the teapots as we speak. The volunteers are about to take their places at the game stalls and food tables. I must run back now to assist."

"Do you need my help?"

"No need—I'll merely be walking around with a teapot offering tea."

"Then you definitely need my help. You should not be lifting anything."

She arched an eyebrow. "So, you are going to do it for me?"

"Yes."

She gave a merry laugh. "The parishioners will adore it. The duke serving them tea on Christmas Day. No one will soon forget that. But no, I would not ask it of you."

Edward cleared his throat. "I think you could ask anything of my brother and he would oblige."

Her eyes brightened. "Truly?"

Jonas nodded. "We are *both* at your beck and call, Miss Temple."

"Make that the three of us," their mother interjected. "I think it is a grand idea. The Duke of Ramsdale and his family serving the parishioners. Now, where shall we begin?"

Ailis looked stunned, but quickly recovered and graced them all with another of her breathtaking smiles. "Very well, follow me," she happily chirped, and meted out the assignments.

Edward was soon flocked by young ladies offering to help him. Their mother was soon chatting up a storm with the elder ladies and gentlemen who looked upon her with sincere admiration.

Jonas was pleased. His family's genuine warmth and dedication made him proud.

He realized something important while he continued to assist Ailis throughout the day. She comported herself with the poise and grace of a duchess, not requiring any training or lessons, for these qualities came naturally to her. In truth, she had more nobility in her than any of those diamonds brought along by his mother.

He watched Ailis as she gave out coins to each child as gifts. She had planned this as a means of providing a little something extra to each family without making it appear as charity, because many of these parishioners were proud and felt ashamed to have fallen upon hard times.

What he realized was that Ailis had a way of making people feel good at the same time she was making things right.

This was how she would always make *him* feel.

She had worked her magic on him just the other day, making him feel worthwhile even when showing her his damaged body. Until that moment, he had been feeling rather *worthless*. Then Ailis came along and saw him with the clarity of her good and gracious heart.

She loved him for everything he was...and was not.

It was his own foolish pride that had held him back all these years. Perhaps not in the beginning, for his injuries were dangerously raw and life threatening. Even the pressure of clothing against his body, something as light as a shirt, caused him agonizing pain.

But he hadn't felt physical pain these past few years. He'd stayed reclusive because of his wounded pride. Having grown up being told he was handsome all his life, having women fawn over him with no effort needed on his part, and having them worship his perfection, had given him a false sense of what was important.

It had also given him a false impression of what *perfection* meant. Until now, he had placed too much importance on appearance. Did this not make him as shallow as these *ton* diamonds he had dismissed as marriage prospects?

For these foolish reasons, he had kept himself imprisoned by his pride. It took Ailis and her persistence to remind him that he was worthy of love.

That she loved him was a final step in his healing. Her love was all he needed and wanted.

As the evening drew to a close, he went in search of her.

He meant to propose to her.

But suddenly, she was nowhere to be found.

He spotted the vicar standing by the doorway, bidding farewell to each parishioner as they left. "Have you seen your niece?"

"Isn't she here?" the vicar replied, frowning. "Perhaps she is seeing to the dismantling of the stalls."

Jonas shook his head. "She told me earlier that it would not be done until tomorrow. Nor is she among the ladies boxing up food for the families in attendance."

"She might have run back to the rectory to fetch something or other," the vicar said, not appearing particularly concerned.

"I'll go look." Jonas strode off to the vicar's residence.

The door was unlocked, so he walked in and called Ailis's name.

When she did not respond, he assumed she was in the kitchen and must not have heard him. But then a light stirring in the parlor caught his eye as he walked by, so he stopped to peer in and noticed a lone candle burning on a small table by the settee, its meager flame casting the room in a dim golden light.

He marched in. She was seated on the settee, turned away from him and crying.

"Ailis? What is the matter? Has something happened to overset you?"

Her response was an emphatic sob.

He knelt beside her and gently turned her to face him. "Why the tears, love?" He withdrew his handkerchief to dry them.

"Why did you come for me?" she asked, her breaths shallow and hitching. "Shouldn't you be with Lady Viola?"

"Why would I be with her?"

She regarded him in confusion. "Aren't you marrying her? You came to my uncle and obtained the license. She told me so herself, and my uncle confirmed it."

Jonas groaned. "What did he confirm? That I obtained a license? Did you bother to ask why I wanted it?"

"I didn't need to. Viola told me you had chosen her."

"Blessed saints, and you believed that lying witch? Do you have so little faith in me, Ailis?"

She stared at him through her beautiful, sad eyes. "I dared not believe it, but then the other ladies confirmed it."

"You mean Lady Willa and the Tenney sisters? And you believed *them*?" he muttered, dabbing more tears off her cheeks.

"I am not that gullible, so I asked your mother and she confirmed it."

"What?" He set aside his handkerchief. "Ailis, that doesn't sound right at all. My mother would not lie to you."

She nodded. "I know, which is why I believed her and finally accepted the painful truth."

"What did she say, exactly?"

"She confirmed that it was still to be kept confidential until the terms were finalized, but Lady Viola was to marry."

He let out a breath. "Yes, but her unfortunate groom will be Lord Pomeroy. Her father has given his consent. I expect poor Pomeroy will obtain the license once they return to London, since that is where they all reside."

She said nothing for a long moment. "She is to marry Pomeroy? Not you? But my uncle said *you* obtained a marriage license."

"I did."

"Whom are you going to marry, then?"

He laughed softly. "Gad, do you really need to ask?"

"No. In fact, I do not want to know. But I wish you every happiness. I just hope you are in your right mind, if your choice is one of those diamonds."

"It isn't one of them. And I am fully in control of my senses. As for your not needing to know, I am afraid I must tell you because you are a necessary party. Ailis, my choice is *you*. If you will have me."

"Me?" She stared at him incredulously. "You are asking *me* to marry you?"

Someone behind him let out a shriek.

"I knew you could not be on bended knee again merely to check her sling," Mrs. Curtis cried out with a joyful laugh.

Jonas turned around to find not only Mrs. Curtis but the vicar, Edward, and his mother standing in the doorway, all of them grinning at him like happy baboons. Behind them were more familiar faces, including those of Grimes and Mrs. Fitch.

Jonas nodded to acknowledge them all before turning back to Ailis. "Well, Miss Temple? Will you do me the honor of becoming my wife?"

"Yes!" the crowd answered for her before she got in a word.

Ailis looked at him in the softest, most loving way. "I did not think dukes were in the habit of marrying beneath their station."

He turned serious, standing up and drawing her up beside him. "Ailis, let us be clear about one thing—I may stand taller in height, but you are above me in every respect. Kinder, wiser, gentler. I readily admit you are far better than I deserve. But I want you by my side for now and always. What's it to be? Are you going to disappoint me and an entire village of your friends?"

She grinned. "I dare not. I would not. Nor can my heart give any answer but yes, I will marry you."

The spectators cheered.

"I expect everyone realizes by now that I have fallen in love with you," she continued as the crowd began to filter in to offer their congratulations.

His brother called for champagne, and bottles of it miraculously appeared along with glasses for everyone. "I knew you would ask her tonight," Edward said, giving Jonas a congratulatory clap on the back after everyone had given their toasts and well wishes. "You did not disappoint. When is the wedding to take place?"

Jonas turned to Ailis. "Is tomorrow too soon?"

She thought he was in jest, but he was not. He ought to have proposed to her years earlier, for he'd felt their attraction from the moment they met. But he was his own worst enemy, was he not? Unable to admit he was not perfect and too busy building prison walls around his heart to ever allow her in.

It had taken her injury during the snowfall to make him realize how wrong he had been to close her out of his life. But having her forced to remain with him for days and days, watching the snowfall and hoping it would never end, had brought home how desperately he needed her and wanted her.

She belonged with him.

They resolved to marry on the eve of the New Year, only five days hence but still an eternity as far as Jonas was concerned. However, it was for practical purposes, since his staff needed to prepare a wedding breakfast and all the villagers were to be invited.

As the crowd dispersed and momentarily left Jonas alone in the parlor with Ailis, she turned to him. "I hope one day you will come to love me as much as I love you. I'll do my best to be a good wife to you. I—"

"Let me stop you right there." He wrapped his arms around her. "That day has already arrived. I knew I was hopelessly in love with you when you mouthed off to me on the day of that heavy snowfall. You put me in my place, and then you were caught in the storm and fell off your horse."

She winced. "I should not have said those things to you. You were entitled to your privacy."

"No, I deserved to be told off," he said with all sincerity. "Once we are married, I hope you will never fear telling me when I am wrong."

She smiled up at him. "Oh, you need never fear that. I was never good about keeping my opinions to myself. Is this really going to happen, Jonas? I've longed for this moment, but never thought it possible."

"Quite real and going to happen, that is my promise to you." He drew her closer into the warmth of his embrace. "Are you ready for kiss number ten? This one comes with a marriage proposal and a promise to love and honor you for all of my days. Is that acceptable to you?"

Ailis lifted up on tiptoes and kissed him on the cheek. "It is perfect. And look." She pointed to the parlor window.

"Snowfall," he muttered with a laugh, watching the delicate flakes fall softly upon the ground against the moon's silver glow.

She sighed. "Isn't it beautiful?"

Ailis was the true thing of beauty on this memorable night, and he told her so as he gave her kiss number ten, which was not an end to their bargain but the beginning of something new and wonderful.

As his mouth captured hers, the last of those walls he had built around himself tumbled and vanished. Gone was the bitterness and private anguish that had chained his heart and held him back from happiness for all these years.

Gone was the need to hide in the shadows.

All these bad feelings vanished like so many snowflakes melting under the radiant sunlight that was Ailis's smile.

He kissed her long and deep, kissed her endlessly as he gave over his heart that she had long ago claimed. "Ten kisses, Ailis, and a thousand more to come," he promised.

CHAPTER SEVENTEEN

EDWARD INSISTED ON serving as valet to Jonas as he readied himself for his wedding, which was to take place an hour from now at the church. "Gad, stop fussing over me," Jonas grumbled. His brother, his *younger* brother, was treating *him* like a child who had yet to learn how to button a shirt or tie a cravat. "I have been managing fine on my own for all my adult life."

"I beg to differ," Edward said, straightening Jonas's cravat, which was already perfect just as he'd fashioned it. "You almost made a royal mess of it. If not for your mother and sibling coming to your rescue, you—"

"Hah! My rescue? You brought that plague of locusts down on me at Christmastide."

"Only you would consider *ton* diamonds a pestilence. Have you opened my letter yet? The one I handed over to you when I first arrived?"

Jonas arched an eyebrow. "No, dare I open it now?"

Edward nodded. "Yes, it is time. Go ahead and read it."

Jonas strode to his bureau and opened the top drawer where he had stuck the letter and forgotten about it. He now opened the missive to find nothing but one name written in it. *Ailis Temple*. "What's this?"

"The name of your blushing bride, of course."

Jonas stared at the parchment, then cast Edward a dubious glance. "How could you know this before ever having met her?"

"Quite simple, actually. I was so certain of your choice that I wrote her into the betting book at White's. I am going to make a killing on my wager. No one else would ever have guessed her name."

"Or that I would ever marry," Jonas replied. "Edward, stop having me on. How could you possibly know about Ailis before you left London? I did not even know my feelings for her until recently."

"Mrs. Fitch and Grimes have been corresponding with our mother."

"And they told her I was going to marry Ailis? That was quite prescient of them, since I only announced my intention to marry a few days ago, and you were already here."

"They did not have to tell our mother anything. She knew it at once. She's quite smart for a duchess."

Jonas laughed. "I know. She has been outsmarting me for years. But seriously, how could either of you possibly know?"

"Several years back, she asked Mrs. Fitch and Grimes to report to her whenever you smiled."

"Me? Smile? When did I ever do that?"

"Never, and isn't that precisely the point? Mother did not mean to be underhanded, but she was truly worried not only for your physical recovery but for your happiness, as well. Imagine her surprise when Ailis Temple's name began appearing in these letters. In fact, hers was the *only* name they ever mentioned. *Miss Temple met with the duke today. The duke smiled.* Quite remarkable, I think."

"Still does not make sense," Jonas muttered. "Why would she descend on me with Viola, Willa, and the Tenney sisters if she knew I liked Ailis? Did she think because I smiled for the vicar's niece that I would smile for these diamonds?"

Edward gave a mock shudder. "You are awfully dense for an intelligent man. Even our sisters caught on immediately to our mother's scheme. Don't you get it? She purposely selected these young doves because she knew they were superficial and awful, and would have you running for cover straight to Ailis. She needed to do something to prod you into action."

Jonas frowned. "She manipulated me."

"Quite cleverly, too, I might add. Although, had we known Ailis was injured and already cozily nestled here with you, we might have scrapped the plan and just come out here by ourselves. By the way, Aggie and Jessie send their love, and regret they could not be here to watch our matchmaking scheme play out. But each had to be with their husband's family this Christmas. Rest assured, we are all going to descend on you next year—unruly nephews and nieces, too."

Jonas ought to have been angry, but he did love his family and it was time to stop putting them all off. "Knowing Ailis, she will probably love having the Langford horde visit us for the holidays, sticky hands, dirty faces, and all. She'll start the holiday planning as soon as we exchange vows, which is happening in less than an hour. Come on, Edward. Stop dawdling and let's get going. Do you think Mother is ready yet?"

Edward laughed. "She has been ready since the day you were born."

They marched downstairs together, met their mother in the entry hall, and then rode to the vicarage in the ducal carriage. "Edward told me what you did," Jonas remarked, tossing her a stern glance.

She tipped her chin up. "How could I pass up the opportunity once your friends opened that betting book? I knew before I had ever met Ailis that she needed to be your wife. But I do apologize if I was a little heavy-handed in the manner in which I went about it."

"A *little* heavy-handed?" Jonas laughed. "You were as subtle as Thor's hammer slamming down upon me."

"Can you blame me?" She gave an indignant huff.

"Yes," he shot back. "But all right. Apology accepted. What are your plans for Edward? Or are those to be kept secret, too?"

She cast him a smug smile. "I am certainly not going to tell you,

Ramsdale. You'll protect your brother as you always do. Just worry about your own wife and do your best to keep her smiling. She has the prettiest smile, don't you think?"

"I have always thought so. Ah, here we are," Jonas said as the carriage drew up in front of the vicarage. "We have drawn a crowd," he muttered as they strode in and he recognized many of the villagers packed in the church. "I don't see Ailis."

"Do you think she ran off?" Edward teased.

"You are such a dolt," Jonas said with a laugh. "I cannot wait for your turn to come around."

He was about to say more, but the breath caught in his throat when Ailis and her uncle walked through a small door behind the altar and took their places.

She looked so pretty.

And she would soon be his.

Her uncle was officiating, which could not have been more perfect and meaningful for Ailis, who was all about sentiment.

Jonas noticed she was not cradling her arm in a sling. This was of concern to him, but he would not remark on it, since this was her day and she wanted to look like a bride, not an injured patient walking out of an infirmary.

Whispers of approval echoed off the stone archways and wood rafters as he strode down the aisle to join her at the altar. He stood beside her and would remain protectively by her side throughout the day to make certain no one accidentally bumped into her sore shoulder.

She was still a wounded dove.

His dove to now love and protect.

She looked strikingly beautiful in a gown of ivory silk, a simple circlet of pearls threaded in her golden hair.

"Ready to marry me, Temple?" he asked with a grin.

"Hmm, still thinking about it, Your Grace," she teased. "But since I am here already, and you seem to be in desperate need of a wife..."

He chuckled. "Desperate, am I?"

"Well, perhaps I am the one who loves you desperately," she remarked.

Once the ceremony began, their jesting came to an end, and everyone in the chapel hushed. Jonas took hold of Ailis's hand and held it throughout, not caring whether it was customary or not. Theirs was a bond of love, and he meant to deliver that message to all who were with them today. Ailis would be his duchess from this day forward, and he would not tolerate any disrespect toward her.

Not that he expected any resistance from the villagers, who adored her and already considered her their angel. It was no leap to now consider her as his duchess, too.

When it came time for the exchange of vows, Jonas did so without hesitation. It felt liberating to commit to this partner he adored and could trust with all his heart. He could tell by Ailis's expression that she was thinking the same, for her voice also rang clear as she said, "I do."

Although it was not the custom to end a wedding ceremony with a kiss, Jonas was never one to conform.

"First kiss as husband and wife," he whispered, and closed his mouth over hers.

Their wedding kiss was the last moment he had alone with Ailis until much later that evening, when the celebrations finally came to an end.

He led her upstairs to his bedchamber, eager to spend the night with his new bride.

She seemed at ease with the arrangement of sharing his bed, no doubt feeling comfortable because she had spent so much time in it already. "Would you prefer a lady's maid to assist you?" he asked.

She shook her head. "I am almost as stubbornly independent as you. We'll manage just fine on our own tonight. Will you help me unlace my gown? Do you need my help in undressing?"

"No, love." He cleared his throat. "Ailis, I do not think you need to see—"

"Let me stop you right there," she said, putting a finger to his lips. "Here's my promise to you. If you undress, then I undress. If you keep your clothes on, even a stitch, then I shall keep mine on, too. It is your choice. Do we keep our bodies hidden? Or are we going to be sensible about this and bare all?"

"Your body is beautiful, but mine is—"

She stopped him again. "I am the one who will be looking at you. If I have a problem with your body, I shall let you know. And you know I will tell you, because I do not have the sense to keep my mouth shut or keep my opinions to myself."

He laughed. "All right, Miss Temple of Virtue. You win—clothes come off. Time to dismantle your prim walls."

And his own prison walls.

"Long past time for every wall to come down," she muttered. "I'll be thirty soon and still a virgin."

"Well, I'll be taking care of that tonight," he said, placing a gentle kiss on her neck as he came up behind her and helped her to undress.

He needed to be gentle, for her shoulder was delicate and not nearly healed. This was another concern he had, the need to be achingly gentle while claiming her.

He meant to give her pleasure, not pain.

The challenge was easily met, for he had spent years engaging in shallow encounters, fulfilling his urges amid shadowed alcoves and behind bushes or up against walls. If he needed contortions to keep from hurting Ailis, he was able and ready.

His worries melted away as they stood before each other completely unclothed. Ailis was not shy about standing naked before him, no doubt because she trusted him and already felt so bonded to him.

She had a beautiful body, full breasts and long, slender legs, a body that brought an ache to his heart because he was gazing upon loveliness while she had to look at him.

And yet she truly did not seem to care that his body was marred.

After giving her the chance to react to his body, which she did with unabashed warmth and interest, he lifted her in his arms and carried her to bed. He settled her atop the mattress and stretched out beside her.

Her body was creamy and soft, her skin silken to the touch. Her breasts were ample and firm, so sweet to the taste. He lingered on them, suckling and teasing, taking his time while Ailis responded to these new sensations of pleasure. Although inexperienced, she was no shy maiden and readily accepted the press of his body on hers, the touch of his mouth upon her flesh, and the intimate way he tasted her and brought her to pleasure for her first time.

She responded with innocent wonder and did not hold back the passion he knew lay hidden within. Her soft moans and the way she arched beneath him, the need with which she clutched him and the breathy whisper of his name, almost sent him over the edge along with her.

But he took his time, caressing and arousing Ailis to ready her for him. She opened to him and bestowed her full trust as he filled her and thrust into her tightness. But this was more than a mere claiming of her body. It was a matter of claiming her heart, binding them to form something powerful and eternal.

He understood it now, this raw, primordial need to mate with her and protect her. To embody her in his soul.

"Jonas," she said in an urgent, breathless moan, "I feel..."

"I know, love. Just let yourself go." His own breaths were hot and ragged as he thrust with greater urgency and neared his own release.

Pleasuring her was the priority, however. It would always be.

He took the time to watch her glorious body respond to his touch, watching the lick of her lips, her heaving breaths, and the way her body moved with his as he aroused her.

She took it all in with typical Ailis enthusiasm and sentiment, took *him* in, and cast him a smile as bright as a moonbeam as she tumbled over the edge of desire once more.

Her eyes were closed and her mouth slightly open, ready to be kissed again.

So, he kissed her and told her that he loved her.

For he did love her and always would.

She circled her arms around his neck and held on as though afraid she might float away.

He joined her in his release, in a sweat and well satisfied as he spilled himself into her. This feeling was powerful and more satisfying than anything he had ever felt in his life. But this was the magic of Ailis, this ability to open his heart, to touch it and caress it, to soothe his pain.

He felt only the pleasure of having her beside him now.

Getting her comfortably settled against him took a little doing, because there was simply no way of avoiding the discomfort to her injured shoulder.

He eased it as best he could, adding a pillow under her arm to lend it support throughout the night. He knew Ailis would never complain, so it was up to him to make certain to take care of her. Was this not part of his wedding vows?

"That was nice, Ailis."

She laughed. "I had no idea my body could feel this way. No wonder you always teased me and called me Miss Temple of Virtue. You knew exactly what I was missing."

He leaned back against the mattress and tucked his hands behind his head, for he was feeling good and completely relaxed. "I admired your resolve. You held out for love because it meant so much to you."

"Had I known what I was missing, I might not have been so dedicated to virtue," she said with a laugh.

He turned to her and caressed her cheek. "Well, it is done. You waited, and I am glad of it. I will admit to being apishly proud to be your first and only. But this moment would not have felt the same were it anyone but you by my side. In truth, there could never have been a moment like this with anyone else."

"Because you trust me?" She leaned over and kissed him on the lips. "This is kiss number… Oh, I've lost count."

"No more need to count, love. We needed those ten kisses to lead us here. But we have moved beyond them now. Just say the word and I'll kiss you as often as you wish." He let out a long breath. "Ailis, did you really not mind?"

"Mind what?"

"My body."

She inhaled lightly. "No, I never gave it a thought until you mentioned it just now. My eyes were mostly closed and I was concentrating on the way you made me feel. Even now, all I am thinking about is the strength of your body and how nice it feels against mine. Promise me there will never be shame between us."

He let out another long breath.

She snuggled against him. "It took a long time for your scars to heal, but they did. Now, it is time for your heart to heal. Also consider this…"

He stroked her hair, those lovely golden curls that slid through his fingers like silk. "Consider what?"

"We are not so young anymore, my *Silver* Duke. I'm sure we will both turn quite lumpy and gray within a few years. You'll yearn for the body you once had," she said with a merry lilt of laughter, "and perhaps yearn for a younger wife."

"Never, Ailis. Your beauty is ageless. It took me bloody long enough to admit I had feelings for you. They run deep as an ocean current and are never going to change."

"Well, ocean currents can change."

"Not this one." He settled over her, careful to balance on his elbows so that his weight was not on her. "We fit together. You are the sunshine to my darkness. The smiles to my grumbles. The gentle snowflake to my storm."

She sighed as he kissed her. "I used to hate the winter."

He arched an eyebrow. "But no more?"

"No, now I love it. The snowfall brought me to you."

He glanced out the window as a sudden gust of wind slammed against the panes. "The wind is beginning to howl again and the sky is covered in clouds. Looks like another snowfall in the making. We might be trapped here for days."

She cast him a sparkling smile. "Oh dear. Whatever shall we do?"

"I'll think of something," he said, and began to kiss his way down her delectable body.

Yes, there was much to be said for a winter's snowfall.

And the right woman who saw him through the eyes of love, who accepted him with the fullness of an open heart.

Epilogue

London, England
April 1818

JONAS STRODE INTO White's on the evening he was to introduce Ailis to his friends and their wives. He was dressed to go about in London Society, impeccably attired in formal black tie and tails, and eager to see those scoundrels, Bromleigh, Lynton, and Camborne, who had opened that infernal betting book on him.

He had not yet decided whether to thank them or punch them for inexcusably meddling in his life. But he had never been more content than these months married to Ailis, so it seemed he ought to forgive them and admit they had done him a good turn.

It hurt his heart to think he might have said nothing to Ailis, never admitted his love, and allowed her to slip away. He might have been that stupid to deny his beautiful wife the happiness she deserved, a happiness they both deserved.

That betting book had set it all in motion, although he did not think anyone could have predicted the snowfall that trapped Ailis in his home after she was injured. Would the outcome have been different if she had not fallen in the snow?

Shaking off the thought, he strode toward his friends and was met with their baboon grins. "Do not say a word," he warned, decidedly loath to receive an "I told you so" from any of them.

"Married life suits you, Ramsdale," Bromleigh said, motioning him to the fourth chair that was empty and awaiting him.

"I was certain you would marry," Lynton added, giving Jonas a pat on the back.

Camborne laughed. "We all bet on yer falling in love and marrying. I knew that if I could reform and become a faithful, satisfied husband, then anyone could. Yer brother claims Ailis is a treasure, and that ye were fated to love her the moment ye set eyes on her…even if it took ye years to acknowledge the obvious truth. She must be something extraordinary to pierce that thick wall around yer heart. We cannot wait to meet her."

But they first settled into the fine leather seats and shared a bottle of scotch.

"Here's to the women who put up with us," Camborne said, "and make us better men."

They all toasted to that.

"Is it true you all wagered I would marry?" Jonas asked, gazing into the amber liquid in his glass as he nursed his scotch.

"Yes," Lynton said. "But only your brother managed to guess the name of the young lady you would choose. He raked in a fortune with that bet. The odds were on Lady Viola Carstairs. But Pomeroy's got her now."

"Poor fellow," Camborne muttered.

"And Whitcomb is betrothed to Lady Willa Montroy," Bromleigh added. "Another poor chap to be mourned, for I don't think the wealth she brings to the marriage is worth giving up one's soul."

Lynton shrugged. "Easy enough for us to opine. We weren't facing ruined estates, and had the luxury of marrying for love."

"Speaking of marriage," Jonas muttered, addressing Bromleigh, "I understand your cousin, Lady Fiona Shoreham, has decided to remarry."

Bromleigh groaned. "Yes, and the gossip rags have splashed the news all over their front pages. This is a disaster in the making."

Jonas took a sip of his scotch. "How so?"

"Now that her best friend has married me," Bromleigh said, referring to his wife, Cherish, "Fiona is determined to find her own happiness."

"Well," Lynton said, clearing his throat, "she is a widow and has duly mourned her husband. No one can fault her for her loyalty and devotion to Shoreham. You do not seem pleased by her decision, Bromleigh."

"I am pleased, but I'm not sure she is going to make the right choice. My nephew and I intend to keep close watch on her, for Fiona can be a keg of gunpowder. There's no telling what might happen now that she has declared herself back on the Marriage Mart. Lord Durham has also assured me he will keep close watch over her."

"Durham?" Jonas arched an eyebrow. "Why is he offering? Is he interested in Lady Shoreham?"

Bromleigh nodded. "But she won't have him. He's too young for her, she claims."

"Fiona needs a younger man to keep up with her," Camborne said with a laugh. "She'll put an older man in his grave. Durham has a steady hand and even temperament. But he isn't one to be pushed around, even though he appears to be an easygoing fellow."

"Are you placing your wagers on Durham, then?" Jonas asked.

Lynton grinned. "We all know that whelp wants Fiona, but will she have him? That's the big question. What do you say, Ramsdale? Are you in?"

"You are bringing me into your schemes?" Jonas asked.

"No schemes, just a wager," Lynton remarked, as though stating the obvious. "I say we open a betting book on Durham. Does he marry or not? More to the point, does he capture the heart of the fair Fiona or will she crush him to sand?"

Jonas sighed. "Is this the same conversation you had when setting up the betting book on me?"

"Any complaints?" Camborne asked.

"I suppose not, but you are having far too much enjoyment playing this game."

Bromleigh grunted. "Well, Durham is no Silver Duke yet. And Fiona is nearing forty, so…"

Camborne burst out laughing. "She is going to kill you if she learns you've given her age away."

"I said *nearing*—that is not the same as giving her actual age," Bromleigh insisted. "Come on, the dinner hour is approaching. Gather your wives and meet me back at my townhouse. Cherish is eager to meet Ailis."

"Will it just be the four couples?" Jonas asked. "Tonight is Ailis's first time stepping out to a *ton* affair."

"She'll do fine. We are all friends. Fiona will be there, too. She and Cherish are inseparable, as close as two sisters. My nephew, Reggie, and his friend, Durham, may stop by. You and Ailis will get to meet them, Ramsdale. Then you can decide whether you want in on the wager."

Jonas laughed. "All right, we'll see."

HE TOLD AILIS about their discussion when picking her up from the Langford townhouse to escort her to the Bromleighs. "What do you think, Ailis? Will Fiona fall for a younger man?"

She pursed her lips. "I don't know. It is quite a sensitive matter, especially for a woman approaching forty. I was turning thirty and believed I had lost all hope of ever marrying. Leap ahead ten years…and it must be a difficult choice for Fiona, even if she does care for Durham. He is entering his prime and she probably feels like a fading star. Still, I like to think true love will always win out. What do you think?"

"I'll reserve judgment. You'll likely meet them all tonight and can make up your mind about them."

She snuggled against him as they rode in the ducal carriage. "I'm just glad I have you."

"Mutual." He placed his hand over hers and gave it a light squeeze. "I love you, Ailis."

"Oh, Jonas, I love you so much."

He spent the rest of the ride kissing his wife in the carriage. They had long ago lost count of the number of kisses each had given the other, but it did not matter. Each kiss he gave Ailis came with a piece of his heart, and it was now big and open, with lots more to give.

They arrived at the Bromleigh townhouse and spent a most enjoyable evening among friends. Seeing his fellow dukes with their wives, Jonas now understood how each in turn had lost his heart. Cherish could not have been a better match for Bromleigh. Nor could Eden have been more perfect for Lynton. Jocelyn had tamed the untamable Camborne, and that was quite an accomplishment.

Bromleigh's cousin, Fiona, was there, as were his nephew, Reggie, and the unsuspecting Durham.

Jonas glanced at Ailis, knowing she was studying them all. "What do you think, love?" he asked in a whisper as the ladies were about to leave the men to their ports.

"Oh, I don't know. Too soon to tell. But if they are meant to be, then I wish them a snowfall…and we shall see what that brings."

Well, Jonas doubted there would be a snowfall in July. This was when they were all to meet again, for Bromleigh and his wife had invited them to a summer house party at Cherish's childhood home, Northam Hall, which was near Brighton and neighbored Fiona's estate.

Ailis, ever the romantic, would not miss it for the world.

As for her wish for a snowfall in July?

Why not?

And add ten kisses.

Miracles could happen.

THE END

Also by Meara Platt

FARTHINGALE SERIES
My Fair Lily
The Duke I'm Going To Marry
Rules For Reforming A Rake
A Midsummer's Kiss
The Viscount's Rose
Earl of Hearts
The Viscount and the Vicar's Daughter
A Duke For Adela
Marigold and the Marquess
The Make-Believe Marriage
A Slight Problem With The Wedding
One Night With Tulip
If You Wished For Me
Never Dare A Duke
Capturing The Heart Of A Cameron

BOOK OF LOVE SERIES
The Look of Love
The Touch of Love
The Taste of Love
The Song of Love
The Scent of Love
The Kiss of Love
The Chance of Love
The Gift of Love
The Heart of Love

The Promise of Love
The Wonder of Love
The Journey of Love
The Treasure of Love
The Dance of Love
The Miracle of Love
The Hope of Love (novella)
The Dream of Love (novella)
The Remembrance of Love (novella)
All I Want For Christmas (novella)

MOONSTONE LANDING SERIES
Moonstone Landing (novella)
Moonstone Angel (novella)
The Moonstone Duke
The Moonstone Marquess
The Moonstone Major
The Moonstone Governess
The Moonstone Hero
The Moonstone Pirate

DARK GARDENS SERIES
Garden of Shadows
Garden of Light
Garden of Dragons
Garden of Destiny
Garden of Angels

SILVER DUKES
Cherish and the Duke
Moonlight and the Duke
Two Nights with the Duke
Snowfall and the Duke

Starlight and the Duke
Crash Landing on the Duke

LYON'S DEN
The Lyon's Surprise
Kiss of the Lyon
Lyon in the Rough

THE BRAYDENS
A Match Made In Duty
Earl of Westcliff
Fortune's Dragon
Earl of Kinross
Earl of Alnwick
Tempting Taffy
Aislin
Genalynn
Pearls of Fire*
*also in Pirates of Britannia series

DeWOLFE PACK ANGELS SERIES
Nobody's Angel
Kiss An Angel
Bhrodi's Angel

About the Author

Meara Platt is a USA Today bestselling author and an award winning, Amazon UK All-star. Her favorite place in all the world is England's Lake District, which may not come as a surprise since many of her stories are set in that idyllic landscape, including her award winning, fantasy romance (romantasy) Dark Gardens series. If you'd like to learn more about the ancient Fae prophecy that is about to unfold in the Dark Gardens series, as well as Meara's lighthearted, international bestselling Regency romances in the Farthingale series, Book of Love series, and Silver Dukes series, or her more emotional Moonstone Landing series and Braydens series, please visit Meara's website at www.mearaplatt.com.

Printed in Dunstable, United Kingdom